Jean Buffong is a Grenadian who has lived in England since 1962. She is a member of the London-based Jenako Writers' Workshop, part of the Jenako Arts' Forum, an arts centre which promotes the art and culture of Africa, Asia and the Caribbean. Jean Buffong is also a committee member of an East London Afro-Caribbean Women's Centre.

Nellie Payne grew up in Grenada and moved to Trinidad when she married. She and her husband returned to Grenada in 1978, when she started working at the School of Continuing Studies at the University of the West Indies. She has three children and six grandchildren.

Nellie Payne and Jean Buffong

Jump-Up-and-Kiss-Me

Two stories from Grenada

The Women's Press

First published by The Women's Press Ltd 1990
A Member of the Namara Group
34 Great Sutton Street, London EC1V 0DX

British Library Cataloguing in Publication Data
Payne, Nellie
    Jump-up-and-kiss-me: two stories from Grenada.
    I. Title   II. Buffong, Jean   II. Collins, Merle
    813. [F]

    ISBN 0-7043-4243-X

Phototypeset in 10pt Bembo
by Input Typesetting Ltd, London
Reproduced, printed and bound in Great Britain
by Cox & Wyman, Reading Berks.

Contents

Introduction

This pair of novellas introduces two voices which tell very different stories focusing on experiences of life on the Caribbean island of Grenada. Part of the fascination of the stories lies in the fact that they are based on different historical periods and on different class experiences. The geographical framework is Grenada; the human experience is international.

A Grenadian Childhood is an autobiographical work, located in Grenada of the nineteen twenties, a period which, in terms of the historical development of the Caribbean, was some thirty years before the beginning of full adult suffrage. It also preceded the escalation of world-wide movements of colonised peoples towards independence struggles and the consequent imperial holding out of 'independence' constitutions. In the nineteen twenties, the British Governor was the powerful political authority in Grenada, there was a severely restricted franchise and the society was noticeably stratified along lines of colour. This explanation is given merely to locate the story historically, for Nellie Payne's story of Grenadian childhood does not concentrate on a more overt political or historical context.

It presents a child's version of her existence, giving a totally credible account of the excitement, dangers, fun and occasional pain of her childhood. Hers is a childhood in which servants feature, telling ghost stories, accompanying their charges to school, supervising playtimes, and doing the general everyday work of the household. The excitement of the child's world includes ghosts who make noises in the night, follow youngsters home, and *sometimes* turn out to be nothing more than the sound of slippers, trailing clothing or waste paper.

But beneath the very real fun and the strange quirks of childhood imagination, there is the hidden pathos of a servant who loses her job because she is accused of stealing a silver fork which really disappeared because her young charges chose to use it to dig a grave for a funeral which they had organised.

Nellie Payne is without doubt a skilful writer, with a fascinating story to tell, and the reader is moved from shouts of laughter to moods of quiet contemplation. This autobiographical work gives us a rare glimpse of one facet of the Grenadian/Caribbean society of the period, recording also stories and practices which progressively disappear as television and other accoutrements of 'modern' society take over.

Jean Buffong's fictional work, *Jump-Up-and-Kiss-Me*, takes its name from the small flower, sometimes red, sometimes white or other colours, which is often grown in tins and flowerpots on Grenadian doorsteps, and which is a particular favourite of Gloria, Jean Buffong's child narrator. *Jump-Up-and-Kiss-Me* is based in nineteen sixties Grenada, although, because of the concerns of this fictional work, the historical period is not as obvious as it is in Nellie Payne's autobiographical story.

Jean Buffong's story has a powerful oral quality, skilfully employed, and the reader is conscious of being also a listener, invited to share the language experience of the Grenadian creole. It is clear, also, that Jean Buffong's I-narrator is of the same social background as the servants who appeared in Nellie Payne's story, a fact which has implications for the language used by various people in both stories, and invites deeper exploration of the historical reasons for language development.

In Jean Buffong's story, too, there is plenty of laughter and enjoyment, and young Gloria's serious, introspective character often leads to quiet philosophical pronouncements:

'When you little, you don't say to your mother or anyone older than you things you like and things you don't like.'

Gloria is opinionated, and the reader definitely gets a very clear view of things she likes, and things she doesn't like, in spite of the restrictions which her mother tries to impose.

Jean Buffong's story is not intended specifically to be an account of Grenadian childhood. It is the story of a woman's search for security in life, told from the perspective of an observant daughter, who is also trying to make sense of her own environment. Inevitably, therefore, it is also indirectly a story of Grenadian childhood.

These two stories make powerful reading and serve as a thought-provoking reminder that literature, whether auto-biographical or fictional, is part of our history, our sociology, and, indeed, of every aspect of our lives.

Merle Collins
London 1990

A Grenadian Childhood

Nellie Payne

Staring at a number of children playing beneath the trees in the Botanic Gardens in St George's, Grenada, my friend remarked, 'I wonder what sort of childhood these West Indians have!'

Something rankled. Had she insinuated that our childhood was different from that of other people?

I turned and said, 'I'll write you an answer – an answer for my generation, true, but it will still apply, I'm sure.'

Blessed with a West Indian father of African descent and an English mother, I dedicate to them my little story with love.

And now I write not chronologically, but as I remember it all.

A Grenadian Childhood

We were having lunch one Friday – Mother, Daddy, Vince, Jessie, Selby, May and, 'course I was there too. My name is Nellie. I must have been about three and a half years old. I can still see Lettie, the maid, with a dish of spinach standing on my left, and Mother with the meat dish half empty in front of her, when the words, magic words, were said by Mother to Daddy, 'I think it's time for Nellie to go off to Miss Slinger's.'

Suddenly my tummy felt funny, a knotting and freeing feeling. When I said 'No thank you,' to the spinach dish *no one said a word*.

Then Daddy looked up and said, 'Isn't she a bit small for that sort of thing?'

Mother said, 'She can read, I don't know who taught her.'

Then my father said to the maid, 'Lettie, bring me the paper.'

In the meantime I heard three other 'no thank you's' to the spinach dish. Still no one said a *word* about this.

I was asked to read a little column in the paper and I did so. It was a poem by John Watson our local poet.

Daddy said, 'Good God.'

Mother said reprovingly, 'Dear!'

Florence Ross was called in to run up a dozen little dresses with matching bloomers, as I was now to discard rompers.

Oh, I was very excited! My tummy kept feeling funny every time I thought of school.

As I said, this was Friday.

On Saturday morning I went off with Mother to Miss Coltart and Miss Kirton, two old ladies who ran a genteel establishment, to get hair ribbons. Mainly, she wanted me out of Florence's dressmaking way.

I told everyone I met, 'I'm going to school on Monday,' and everyone told me, 'My, what a big girl you're getting to be!'

Actually, I was very, very small with a quantity of reddish hair, a terrible temper, feet much too large for my size and suffering from an every-other-day attack of malaria fever which seemed determined to have me buried before I was seven. Even at this age, the servants predicted that I would die young.

Ribbons purchased, Mother strolled over to another darling old lady, Miss Murray, who sold the best homemade sweets in the world. Peppermint pipes with a red boiled-sweet flame in the bowl; chocolate fudge; shaddock; and a brown fudge that made one's salivary glands operate furiously. I have seen sailors come from a ship eating these hungrily with streams of saliva flowing from the sides of their mouths.

Miss Murray was then about eighty years old and had once been a school teacher. She was always dressed in a long, black silk dress with leg-of-mutton sleeves. Various ladies of St George's made the sweets Miss Murray sold. Fresh supplies were received daily and too often after ten or twelve school children came in at the same time, poor Miss Murray was quite a few pence out in her sales.

One day, a few years after this particular visit, I went in for my daily supply of fudge and found the little table empty. I called and a feeble voice said, 'Come child.'

I went into the tiny bedroom behind the shop to find Miss Murray lying on her bed, very small, very pale, and very tired-looking. She held my hand and said, 'I can't manage

4

the school children any more. I've asked the ladies to stop sending the sweets.'

I felt abominably embarrassed seeing the old lady so helpless. Telling her that I would return in a minute, I dashed across the road to Nanny Lomas and told her about Miss Murray's condition. Nanny, not stopping to change her slippers, came over. She sent me home to Mother. That was the last time I saw Miss Murray.

But back to the glorious morning's shopping with Mother. I knew that once we entered Miss Murray's, Nanny Lomas, Miss Allen and perhaps Mrs Ambrose Hughes would be there. This would mean a little chat and the ladies would each give me a peppermint, fudge and shaddock respectively, in order to keep me quiet while they discussed the latest outrage.

Alas, I was not to get a sweet this morning. Only Miss Allen was there. Miss Allen was English. Retired headmistress of her own high school and an absolute dear. She billowed up to me, held my hand and boomed, 'Parlez-vous Français?'

I told her no, but, 'I'm going to school on Monday.'

We had older friends who had been boarders at Miss Allen's School for Young Ladies. These girls made up a little song to the tune of 'There is a Happy Land, far, far away' which went like this:

> There is a happy land
> Far, far away,
> Where you get dumpling and soup
> Three times a day.

So every time I met Miss Allen, the little tune went skipping through my head.

Poor, poor Miss Allen. A lady away from her home in England, too poor to return. She never expressed a wish to do so as I am sure the community would have sent her back. Even at this time, she was too old for that long boat trip.

Miss Allen was forever dressed in a long black skirt, white

shirt with long sleeves and silver links, high collar, white lisle stockings and black sandals. To complete the picture, a white straw hat was perched on her silver bun with a pearl-headed hat-pin keeping it in place.

One day Miss Allen came flying to Mother without her hat, very, very distraught, saying that the woman who looked after her was ill-treating her. Mother gave her tea – it was teatime – soothed her and took her back to her home after about an hour and a half. Actually, Mother stayed with her until she fell asleep, then went to mutual friends to see about other arrangements for the old lady's comfort. When Mother popped in a little later to see Miss Allen, she was still asleep and Mother felt satisfied that all would be well.

In the morning Mother sent the maid over with a tray. The maid returned saying that Miss Allen had died in her sleep.

Mother went to the funeral and cried and cried and cried all night. My mother too was an Englishwoman far from her people, in the island of Grenada, British West Indies.

Sixty years later, Miss Allen's pupils who are still in these parts are women who stand out. They sit beautifully, they walk proudly, they converse logically and wittily and above all, are splendid listeners. Their letters are masterpieces never to be destroyed. I have one friend from Miss Allen's school. Her name is Louise. I'll tell you about her later on.

Saturday afternoon we were sent with Ellen the nursemaid for our usual walk and I met – Eustace Watts! I had to be impressed as he was a goodlooking boy, older than I and he could run faster than anyone. He thought chasing each other was nonsense so he took off his cap and after saying EENIE, MEENEE, MINEE, MOE, etcetera, last man out covered his face with the cap and then chased the others.

About six maids sat on the graves in the churchyard where, I don't know why, we were always taken to play. They were so busy discussing the private lives of their employers that they never saw the beginning of the game.

Now there was, and still is, a wall dividing the churchyard

from the Hughes' home. The top of the wall was level with the churchyard, and about ten feet high, therefore there was a ten-foot drop from churchyard to Mrs Hughes' garden.

This drop fascinated all the children. Often one of us would stand on the edge, leaning over as far as we dared with about eight other children linking hands, each an arm's length apart, forming an anchor.

On this afternoon's first trial of Eustace's exciting game, I had the cap on my face. At the call of 'Coupee', I sped at the sound of feet and voices and – wadam! The wall caught up with me. It seemed very windy and empty and then – BANG! I hit the turf. I screamed and screamed and through it all could hear the nurses jabbering hysterically from the top. Grannie Hughes' maid picked me up while she stood shouting from her window, 'You wretched servants! I'm always telling you to watch the children at play. I'm going to phone Mrs Donovan and tell her of your carelessness, Ellen.'

When Ellen came around the road to the house to meet me, I was so very vexed with her for having let me fall over the wall that I agreed with *everything* Mrs Hughes told her.

Of course, the next afternoon the servants tried to take it out on Eustace, but he was too smart for them. He must have been about seven years old then, and when I think about it now I am amazed that he had already thought of a way to win them over: on the following Saturday he was going to have a sports meeting. It would cost a penny to enter, nurses free. He was going to have a race for the nurses and the winner would get a prize.

Eustace had twelve events carded. He had twenty-four prizes – first and second – I don't remember what was won by us except that he had made a batch of coconut fudge which our nurse Ellen received for coming first in the nurses' race. We were very proud of her and she gave us, her charges, each a piece.

Somehow or other, Eustace was always getting us into trouble. He cut out a lot of pieces of flat wood, oval-shaped, one to two inches long and called them boats. He suggested we have boat races.

'But where are we going to race these boats?'

'Easy,' he replied. 'Down Miss Beddoe's drain.'

Miss Beddoe lived below the wall on the other side of Mrs Hughes.

'How are we going to get there?' we asked.

Eustace had it all worked out. First, the old lady would be out on such and such an afternoon and her daughter would be fixing flowers in the church. Also, the other daughter went for a stroll each afternoon.

'You see that plum tree? Well, we jump on to the branch, climb down, and fill the sink in the yard. Then we say, "Go!" pull the plug and the race will begin, each man putting his boat in the drain.'

This drain was a drain of drains. It ran straight downhill from Miss Beddoe's house to Scott Street, where it wound down this street, tunnelled another road and burst into the sea. It had been built by the French during their occupation in 1650.

The nurses were busy gossiping so one by one we jumped on to the plum tree, got into the yard, filled up the sink, stood at the top of the drain, boats in hand and Eustace said, 'Go!'

We had given the boats names like *Jolly Jim*, *Doctor Vum Vum*, *Greasy Pole*, etcetera, etcetera. Screaming these names, we put the boats in and they dashed headlong down the drain, leaving us staring and feeling we'd been cheated. One minute they were with us and the next they had disappeared.

It was much harder getting back to the churchyard than leaving it. The branch which had been so easy to jump from now seemed yards away from the wall, as it must have been, and not one of us, not even Eustace could leap up to the top of the wall.

We must have been talking pretty loudly as Mrs Hughes could be heard telling the servants off. The youngest maid came running up Miss Beddoe's steps to escort us back to our respective nurses.

Some time after this, Eustace went to England and his foster mother, Miss Killikelly, a very close friend of my mother's, gave us news of him: He's joined the Army, he's married, etcetera, etcetera. Then Miss Killikelly died and all news of Eustace ceased.

Monday, the great day, the day I was off to Miss Slinger's, was here. I awoke very, very early. I knew it was early as no one else was awake and the moon was still shining. I could see Jessie's freckles in the moonlight and I got frightened as the maids always told us that if the moon shone on your face when you were asleep, it would pull your face to the side it was travelling, and, you would always have a twisted face. So I got out of bed and woke her up. I told her about the moon and she got frightened and came into my bed. The next thing we knew was Ellen's arrival and her remark about a big day for Miss Nellie.

The feeling in the tummy came back and I wanted to be sick. I was sick and Ellen said, 'That old fever Miss Nellie, like you go' stay home today.'

She felt my skin but I had no fever as it never came on before eleven o'clock. Ellen would not let me bathe in the bath so she sponged and dressed me and downstairs we went for breakfast. I've never liked porridge from that day. An awful sense of foreboding fills me whenever I see it.

Together with Vince and Jessie we set off for school with our slates and slate pencils. Vince and Jessie also had two books plus a Bible. I had an 'ABC' book. I can still remember that little book with its pictures and titles: 'dog, cat, hen, pig, tub, fly'. I also remember the beginning of Book two: 'Look at me, I am up in the air, see I let go both hands and yet I do not fall'. These books were called Royal Readers.

We arrived at Miss Slinger's.

Miss Slinger was one of a trio of maiden ladies who lived with their mother, a plump, smiling, old lady who was always dressed in grey. I was told that she 'moaned' for her husband. We seldom saw her except when she looked out the window at us playing in the schoolyard. We had Miss Gertie, Miss Dora and Miss Lily. Miss Lily taught us. They all lived in an enormous house, two stories at the front and three at the back, or maybe it was the other way around.

The three of us entered a large wooden gate which Vince had to push open. It had an enormous spring at the back. This gate opened into a cobble-stoned passage way which led to the back of the house, where funnily enough, you found the steps to the front in a walled yard, which was about half an acre big with three very large rocks, a colossal water cistern at the far end and a dreadful, gobbling turkey cock which we kept clear of.

Half way along the cobbled passage way there were two doors, one on either side of the passage. On the left were the kitchen, pantry and a small sitting room where Miss Dora, who wasn't allowed to go up and down stairs too often because of her heart, and Miss Pussy, the outsized cat, sat. Miss Dora reclined in her chair with her glasses on her nose, crocheting, and Miss Pussy lay on a mat purring. Often there would be the smell of guava jelly being made by Cook.

There was a staircase in this room which led up to the dining room, drawing room, long corridors and many bed-rooms.

The other door in the passage way, the one on the right, opened into the schoolroom. To my amazement the school-room had tables and chairs but no people. I turned to ask if this was all, and at that moment children started trooping in. They placed their books on the tables in neat little piles and dashed off to the yard. I followed my brother and sister and was soon in a game of hide-and-seek. I was shown the vast cellar where we could hide. It was very, very dark. I was also told that hundreds of centipedes lived there and that as they were poisonous, if I ever saw one, I was to say, 'By St Peter, by St Paul,' and it would be paralysed and so I could get away without being stung.

It was a horrible place but held great fascination for all of us, particularly since the Devil himself was supposed to inhabit one corner. Again, if one ever heard him calling, one was to quote a passage of the Bible and he'd go away burnt by his own fire. I was rapidly taught the shortest verse in the Bible. I kept murmuring, 'Jesus swept,' and visualised the large broom He used to sweep away the Devil.

The dungeon held a night chair. The wood was a beautiful golden colour and it shone in the dark. We were made to understand that *only in emergencies* was this chair to be used. Such an emergency would occur if the other two lavatories were occupied.

My sister Jessie had a fixation about using the 'golden chair' but somehow no *emergency* had arisen. Unknown to her, I too developed an obsession and planned that after three children had lifted their hands and asked to go to the 'toilet', I would also ask and so a 'state of emergency' would arise.

That day arrived. Four children asked. Jessie was one. I was another. With fear, excitement and, admittedly, hesitation, I gingerly made my way towards the chair. As I entered, a voice said, 'Nellie?' I fled across the courtyard screaming, 'Jesus swept, Jesus swept,' until I arrived in the schoolroom and faced an astonished Miss Slinger.

It turned out that Jessie had got to the golden chair first, recognised me as I was in the light and she in the dark, and had called my name.

There were twenty-four of us in school. How Miss Slinger coped with two dozen healthy kids between the ages of three and a half and seven, I fail to understand. Miss Slinger could not have been more than four feet eleven inches tall. She was goodlooking and had beautiful black, wavy hair, on which she told us she used castor-oil. She wore gold-rimmed spectacles of the pinch-nose type and when she looked *over* these, one was in trouble.

But I must go back a bit, because all this happened a few months after this first day when we were playing hide-and-seek. Our game was getting very exciting and I'd forgotten about being a new pupil and all that, when the bell rang and everyone fled leaving me standing in the yard. I heard them singing 'Gentle Jesus' and promptly burst into tears.

After a while Jessie came and fetched me and I was given some Os to make on my slate, using the O from an old almanac as my guide.

An hour later I began getting ague and tried to control it. A very jolly, fat girl called Talita was sitting near to me and she told Miss Slinger. I was sent home with Ellen who had brought our 'ten o'clock' of orange juice and biscuits.

And so, by eleven o'clock, my first day at school was over.

As soon as you entered the door to the schoolroom there was a wooden screen and I could not understand why every child passed on the right side in order to get to the desks. Sure, there was a table with a basin, ewer and soap on the left side, but room enough for one to get to the desks.

After a few weeks I thought I was on familiar enough ground to consider passing on the left. I first asked Lucille Richards why no one ever washed their hands in the basin. She gave me a withering look and walked off. So, the morning following this attempt at conversation, I took the left turn, stopped, gasped and literally scuttled back to the right turn, put down my books and ran into the bright morning sunshine.

Why was it there? Why? Why? I couldn't ask Lucille. Could I ask my sister Jessie? She was very superior at school, except if anyone tried to take advantage of me, then she'd butt in like a ram! Who could I ask?

'Bangalangalanga,' went the bell. I could ask no one. Perhaps at playtime after our 'ten o'clock'? (I heard Mother once tell another European, 'Oh, stop calling it elevenses, do!') But, by playtime, I was feeling so ill with ague coming on that I asked if I could go home with Ellen, who had brought our orange juice.

About five o'clock in the afternoon, I awoke, was changed into a dry nightie by Mother, given a nice cold drink and made to feel that I was well again. My brothers and sisters came in from their walk at six, and after having their supper and undressing, came in to see me.

'B-boy,' Vince stuttered, 'you m-missed s-something to-d-day. Miss S-slinger took out the s-s-s-strap and n-nearly b-b-beat ffffPhyllis.'

My question of the day could be asked, and ask I did, 'Why does she soak it in the basin?'

Jessie and Vince answered together, 'BECAUSE LEATHER STINGS MUCH MORE WHEN IT IS SOAKED IN WATER!'

I must add that never in my three years with Miss Slinger did I see her strap a child unless the parent requested it. It was used as a very effective threat and I have always associated the strap with torture. The strap was the daily threat but the *beam* was our sword of Damocles.

The beam was literally the wooden beam which stretched over our heads across the schoolroom. There were five beams but one was lower and thicker and lay massive between the other four.

Behind Miss Slinger's desk was a little armchair that could be purchased for one and sixpence in those days. It was, and still is known as a 'potty chair'. It had a hole in the seat. Usually, when children were being house-trained, they would be put to sit in a chair like this with a 'potty' under the hole. They hear the water falling into the potty and one morning it will click that the chair means no wetting of floors. Anyway, this little chair was there and on it were yards and yards of faded blue-flowered cretonne sashes.

If a child got very naughty he was supposed to be tied into this chair, and by some magical contraption the cretonne bands were then flung over the beam and chair and child were swung into the air, remaining suspended until the little sinner repented.

In the middle of term, we had a wonderful surprise. Four new children from America arrived. They were quite different from anyone we had seen to date. Lorna, Alma and Claire were dressed in silk, spoke with a twang and could always produce a bag of sweets, which they called candy. Eugene, their brother, was goodlooking and wore plus fours and plaid stockings. They were tough.

One day Eugene brought a bag of 'turkey eggs' – a large, egg-shaped hard sweet – to school. During class, he could feel the bulge in his pocket. He had spent fourpence and got three lovely eggs from Mr Peters. He felt them, he stroked them, played with them but knew Miss Slinger did not permit eating in class. So he stroked them, felt them and played with them all over again. The Devil himself was tempting him as all he could think of was the delicious almond taste and the complete blocking of his mouth except for gaps at either side which would permit him to suck gulps of saliva until the egg got smaller.

He looked up. Miss Slinger was busy dealing with the babies and their ABC so he popped one in. Miss Slinger looked up and was frightened. There was a child with his cheeks sticking out and spittle falling on the desk.

Eugene too was frightened, for when a turkey egg went in, only melting could get it out.

'Ah!' thought Miss Slinger. 'It's one of those abominable turkey eggs!'

She looked over her glasses and said, 'Eugene!'

Poor Eugene could not speak. He tried very hard but only a rude noise – ffoppp – came out. Up sprang Miss Slinger. She flew across the room and grabbed Eugene's hand.

'*I am going to swing you up to the beam*, you naughty boy!' she cried.

She dashed for the potty chair and sashes. By this time the entire school was petrified and all eyes were bent on their slates.

We heard noises of cloth being drawn through the chair and, I swear, a swinging noise. The class was deathly quiet.

The bell rang. We said, 'Good afternoon, Miss Slinger,' and sped out of the door, up the cobbled path and into the road without once looking up. To this day not one of us knows if Eugene was swung to the beam. He left the school and went to a public primary. His sisters vowed they didn't know if he had been swung or not.

The wonder of Eugene's swinging wore off and we settled down to reading 'Meddlesome Matty', and something which had the lines, 'The shark is killed, Bobby is saved, Hurrah, Hurrah'. I learned that the word C-O-N-T-E-N-T-S which is at the beginning of almost every book meant 'Children Ought Not To Eat Nuts Till Sunday', and, P-R-E-F-A-C-E meant

'Peter Rat Eat Fat Alligator Cat Eat (Nennen Coffee Tea Sweet) – bracketed words added to round off the meaning.

I was taught the Lord's Prayer. This prayer made me suffer for a week or two as each child took a turn in saying it aloud while the others accompanied softly. When my turn came I was thrilled and started in my clear treble: 'Our Father who sat in heaven'. Even Miss Slinger got the giggles. And at Sunday school, I wondered who 'Father Whichart' was in heaven.

About this time I was making some pretty good os and Gs and writing little words like 'at', 'cat', and 'bat'. My interest was tremendous and the oncoming holidays offered little attraction.

I was always the first back after lunch and sometimes I'd pass boldly on the left and stick my tongue out at the strap. I had discovered all by myself, and told no one, that Miss Slinger used only the ruler with which she gave us one or two whacks on the palms of our outstretched hands. I did not know the word 'symbol' but knew the strap was one.

One day, first to arrive as usual, I wandered around, even touched the ruler and found it quite harmless without Miss Slinger's hand. I sat in her chair, opened the attendance book and immediately became the teacher. I took an imaginary roll call and filled the columns for three weeks with violent-looking os and Gs. These were my best letters. Satisfied, I closed the book and went into the yard to have a peep at the golden chair.

A boy came whistling a merry song. It was Alister Hughes. The nicest boy in school but alas, the ugliest. When he saw me, he stopped whistling, picked up a stick and began kicking the turf. After the tips of his shoes were scruffy enough he whistled a few bars again. I was so entranced I asked him to teach me how. We sat on a rock and he said, 'Look.'

He blew a loud, clear blast and told me to do it.

I puckered my lips and blew. Only wind came.

'No, no,' he said, 'do it this way.'

And I tried and tried. I tried everything, sticking my tongue against my bottom teeth, against my top teeth, between the two sets of teeth, but to no avail. I *still* cannot whistle.

Lots of kids joined us and soon the bell rang. Fear gripped me as I remembered my impersonation of Miss Slinger and the fierce-looking letters in her attendance book.

All seated, Miss Slinger opened up for roll call.

'Who's been writing in my roll book?'

No replies.

'Someone did this during the lunch hour.'

Dead silence.

The spectacles were placed a little lower on her nose bridge and over them she gazed at us each in turn.

'I'm going to ask each of you the question, "Did you write in my roll book?" And I want someone to own up.'

Lots of children feel guilty even if they haven't committed a crime. So many children squirmed. Austin Hall, another little American, was squirming so vigorously that he slipped off his chair. He scrambled back on so quickly that Miss Slinger did not see this happen.

Barbara, Lucille, Thelma, Vince, Phyllis, Jessie, Gordon, Percy, Avis, Talita – down the line she came until she was standing in front of me, and I said, 'No Miss Slinger, when I came in I was on the rock with Alister and he was teaching me how to whistle.'

She moved on – Cynthia, Lyris, Caryl, Sybil, Majorie, Leonard, Joyce, Austin. She stopped.

'Austin?'

Poor guilty-feeling Austin. His face showed guilt. His manner showed the same. Yet, I was surprised when he said, 'I did it, Miss Slinger.'

I got sick and was sent home and so missed the wonderful swinging to the beam which everybody swore took place but no one saw.

Austin Hall, I am sorry, but I have paid for this miserably with nightmares in which I was always swinging on the beam where the potty chair turns into the figure eight with the top loop of the eight gaping widely. Once, the nightmare was so bad – the loop widening fantastically in order to swallow me – that my screams and cries awakened the household and I had to go to sleep with Daddy.

The breaking up of school was disappointing in that we were not given things to smash. Despite this, it was exciting and we had an hour-long break during which I learned the lovely game, 'We've come to see Janie', in which one girl who was Janie hid behind someone bigger who was the warder. The other children formed a line about ten yards away, moving up to the warder singing:

> We've come to see Janie, Janie, Janie,
> We've come to see Janie and how is she now?

The warder would answer anything that came to mind and the line would retreat to starting point, singing:

> Farewell lady, lady, lady,
> Farewell lady, and we shall return.

This went on three or four times and then the warder would say on being questioned, '*She's crazy*'.

We would break into wild screams and race in all directions with Janie on our heels. Whoever she caught became Janie and the game continued.

The last bell of the term was rung. We sang a rousing hymn, kissed Miss Slinger goodbye, went over to Miss Dora, kissed her, and patted Miss Pussy. The holidays had begun.

Mother always had marvellous things for us to do during the holidays: picnics; friends for days and days; walks with the Smiths at five o'clock in the morning to the beach (Thelma, Audrey and Mother were slimming); and concerts, the plays of which we wrote, produced and acted. We were allowed to charge our audience a penny each to enter. Mother turned over the drawing room to us. We erected a stage and used two sheets as curtains. We always wrote a drama and could never understand why our parents and their friends and any of the supporting cast's parents and their friends

17

would dissolve into hysterics, some having to leave the room, thus holding up the performance. As we refused to let our audience miss one sentence of the play, we tableaued until they returned.

This stubbornness often made some of the gentlemen get the giggles and they would get up en masse and go into the dining room with Daddy. No doubt they fired a quick round of drinks, composed their faces and came back. All in all, the plays *never* ended before ten p.m. They started punctually at eight p.m. with a rousing singing of 'God Save our Gracious King', with the oldest member of the cast holding a picture of George V and the youngest waving a small Union Jack.

We must have been good to have kept about sixteen adults entertained for two hours.

The following day we always had a party for the actors during which we decided what we should do with the money. We usually collected about five shillings. We never failed to decide on a picnic, giving our parents the money to buy the grub. The five shillings I am sure must just have covered the cost of the cake. It was always a most enjoyable picnic, held in Daddy's little beach cottage, which was called 'Oh, So Cozy'.

We were allowed to have doll's tea parties for which Jessie and I made real cakes and drew real tea. We took it all very seriously and spoke only what we thought was 'grown-up talk' on these occasions.

Even my days in bed with the cursed malaria were not too bad. As soon as the fever broke I'd have a nap and some child, usually Majorie, would come in and show me tricks with pieces of string, and Beryl, Joyce and Caryl would turn up for a game of Ludo, Happy Families or Snakes and Ladders.

On Saturdays, after breakfast, we were allowed with Majorie to go across the road to play with Olive. Olive was the niece of two maiden ladies who lived with their father. He always sat at the window, stick in hand and a captain's cap on his head.

One morning we found Olive convulsed with giggles behind a pillar in the yard. We eventually, after she had wet her bloomers, found out that her grandfather had dozed off and fallen off his chair. His language had so horrified his daughters, good women who went to chapel regularly, one contraltoing and the other harmonium-playing, that the poor dears had not as yet emerged from their rooms.

Olive had about two acres of land in which to play. Fruit trees to climb, rocks to hide behind, and a very crabby old lady who lived on the right, reputedly not all there in the head, who would stone us with the ball if it went over her wall.

But this was not all.

In the middle of this glorious playground was a little, tiny house with a half-moon cut in the door. This was the servant's lavatory. It had a rather rickety appearance but it looked so clean and doll-like that we opened the door and peeped in. There was a long seat stretching across the whole building and in this seat were two round holes. These holes were covered with the wood cut from them with a cotton reel fixed in the middle of each for easy lifting. The cesspit was below.

We were caught peeping in and were told NEVER to visit it as only the servants used to go there and it was full of *germs*.

The rest of the morning was spent discussing germs and we made up our minds to investigate these creatures on Saturday coming. Olive added, 'Please God' to ward off the evil eye.

Our entire week was filled with excitement and Saturday could not come fast enough. It now seems to me that only on Saturdays were we allowed to run across to play with Olive.

At last, Saturday was here, and Majorie was at home as early as eight a.m. She had breakfast with us and we hung around until ten o'clock when Mother told Ellen to take us over and keep an eye on us in case one of the twelve cars on the island should be using the street.

19

We held a 'confab' in whispers. The elder of Olive's aunts called and gave us a dish of plums and French cashews with which to play shop. We quickly gobbled them and knowing the old lady would be baking her Sunday cakes, bun and bread, prepared to visit the little house.

Jessie and I had both been given a dose of senna that morning and we had tummy aches. We thought we should use the little house instead of returning home. Wide-eyed, Olive watched us enter while Majorie nonchalantly told us to hurry up as she wanted to go too and there were only two holes. Jessie finished before me and as she was coming out, Majorie, jumping up and down outside the door said, 'Hurry, hurry, hurry.'

Jessie leapt out of the building and there was a terrific crack, groan and crumble as the entire seating accommodation caved in, carrying with it poor little Nellie.

I remember keeping my mouth shut and looking around with my eyes wide in horror. The next conscious thing was of being under a tap with the two old aunts washing me down and quarrelling, quarrelling with Olive, who stood there weeping.

Wrapped in a clean blanket I was sent home where the servants advised Mother to give me some special bush tea to clean me out and Mother again bathed me in a tub with, I think, lots of Lysol in it.

The servants predicted a very early death for me. About ten years old. I believed them.

Holidays were fast coming to an end. Jessie and I had terrific excitement one night. From one of the windows in our bedroom we could look down into the home of some Americans, about five of them. Our parents were horrified at their loudness. Today, they would simply be called very happy people. They laughed all the time and horror of horrors, their gramophone could be heard at least a half-mile away. Their favourite records were 'The Black Bottom' and 'Tiptoe through the Tulips'. Needless to say, they fascinated us children and often were the times we would accept pieces of candy casually offered across the back fence.

One day, after we were put to bed, we could see lots of coming and going. We could smell a turkey roasting; a lorry pulled up with ice and cases and cases of drinks. One of the younger women looked up as she was passing with a tray of glasses and said, 'We're having a party tonight. Want to come?' We ducked inside and discussed how we could peep for the entire night.

The party began at about eight-thirty – half an hour after we were put to bed. The gramophone was going hell for leather and crowds of people came. Mother came into our room to see if the noise was too much for us, but fortunately we heard her coming and jumped into bed, Jessie making sure to snore and keep her mouth open. Convinced, Mother went away and we heard her say, 'They must have been exhausted. How wonderful to be a child!'

Out we sprang from bed and gazed in wonder at the dresses. Somebody called Gladys was the belle of the ball in a silk, peak-skirted dress with a sash round her bottom and there was a soft feather floating about. Everytime the gramophone said, 'The black, black bottom' she wriggled her bottom and everyone screamed with laughter. More and more people came, more and more men with *bottles and bottles* of booze came to the party.

We heard a terrific cracking sound and amidst loud shouts and laughter out came a dozen men bearing a very large partition which they threw in the yard. They swigged from a bottle and returned to 'wiggle' with Gladys or some other female.

Jessie and I were enthralled. Fancy ripping out a partition because it got in one's way!

Mother came in to check again and we were both more or less asleep at the window. She and Daddy lifted us into bed and into the Land of Nod.

The first thing we did on awakening on Sunday morning was to rush to the window. The Americans' yard was a shambles. The partition looked terrible with flapping strips of wallpaper. Bottles of all sizes and shapes littered the grass. Paper streamers and a full-blown balloon, so bright and gay amongst the rubbish, made us feel sad without knowing why.

We went for our afternoon walk. On our return, the house at the back was in darkness, the gramophone silent. Our nurse, Ellen, while undressing us glanced through the window and with a sniff said, 'Thank God they gone by the boat, back to where they belong.'

Even though we hadn't known them, we missed them. An old lady and her granddaughter moved in. The district was on its way down and Mother said, 'As soon as this baby is born, we move.'

Baby! I dashed to Jessie and asked her what baby was being born. She did not know so we asked Vince who was older and he didn't know either. Mystified, we asked Ellen. She told us very primly that respectable children didn't ask such questions.

One day Vince told Mummy that she was eating too much as her tummy was getting very fat. Daddy stared at us with interest and said, 'Mother is looking nice and fat because she is happy. Do you know why she is happy? Because in a couple of months' time, she is going to give you a lovely little baby.'

Jessie got very jealous and wanted the baby for herself. Mother then said, 'Well, if you do have it for yourself, you will have to feed her, dress her, and look after her, with Ellen's help, of course. Do any of you children want her for yourself with all this to do?' Mother asked.

Only Jessie wanted her. Daisy was born on the twenty-ninth of May and was claimed by Jessie who adored her and believed her to be her very own.

Now there were six of us. And it was time for Selby to go to school. So along came Florence to run up little pants and blouses with a string at the waist. Mother also knitted many pairs of socks.

On the Saturday prior to school-opening-Monday, Caryl, Cynthia and Majorie came to spend the day. We spent the morning marching in orderly rows with stiff backs and sticks

on our shoulders saying: 'Free paper burn, free paper burn.'
Oh, it seemed grim having to go back to school.

After lunch, when we were all supposed to be resting (but Ellen told us that as we had visitors we could play Snakes and Ladders or Happy Families *quietly*), we tiptoed out of the house and up to Majorie's home where there was a laden mango tree.

Majorie's older sister, Ernestine, who was about fourteen, got very tired of our voices and called us in to have fudge as she'd just made a batch. 'Free paper burn, free paper burn,' she teased, and we begged her to let us help her cut out little squares of paper in which to wrap the fudge. I got bored and ran back home where I fell asleep to be awakened by, 'Oh me Gawd Master Vince, *Oh me Gawd Master Selby!*'

I dashed out of bed and there on the landing were two strange boys. Ellen was spinning them around and around and they were beginning to look frightened.

'Oh me Lawd, what madam go' say! Who do dis to you Master Vince?'

By this time, Mummy had joined us with a 'Good gracious me!'

It turned out that Ernestine had got bored with wrapping fudge and had cut Majorie's, Vince's and Selby's hair, all in most uneven patches and some parts right down to the scalp. She had also cut off their eyebrows. Ellen took Vince and Selby to Mr Gomez the barber to see if he could make anything of their heads and Majorie went about looking like a ferocious boy for the next four weeks.

We started school on Monday, taking Selby with us. All the girls made a fuss of him as he was chubby and cute, and in games had such cunning that he was great fun.

Besides Selby, there were four new pupils. André Salhoum, 'Poo' Richards, his sister Lyris and John Copland. André wore his hair long in beautiful golden curls, 'Poo' was a born little gentleman and was always correct in appearance and ways, but John was our interest that term. He had a cataract and was completely blind in one eye. Miss Slinger told us about it and explained why one eye was white and the other brown.

We must pray each morning and afternoon to God to get John's eye better. Thirty pure little hearts begged God twice a day to make John's eye good. Each day John was inspected by thirty interested kids to see if God was giving him a new eye.

One morning a brown patch appeared in the white eye and Miss Slinger, her eyes wet with tears, told us God was answering our prayers and we prayed harder and harder.

John's mother came to school to see Miss Slinger and told her that she was taking John to Canada to see about his eye. Miss Slinger was most upset and showed Mrs Copland the great improvement in his eye. But John was taken away, and off to Canada he went.

We still prayed for him. One day, he appeared again in school with two brown eyes and he told us that one was made of glass.

Miss Slinger left the room and went over to Miss Dora. I heard her telling Mother afterwards, that, 'The day John came to school with his false eye I had to run across to Dora and have a good cry.'

Selby seemed to be getting along fine because he never once came to Vince, Jessie or me to ask for help. He was very independent. Even when it came to choosing sweets with our pennies, he knew exactly what he wanted and no persuasion could make him change his mind. He made his own friends and once or twice we saw him standing on his chair for making the children laugh.

Miss Slinger began to pay special attention to him as he was always up to mischief, bringing spiders, lizards, and so on, to class and making the little girls scream and wax hysterical with his 'monkey faces'. It reached the stage where Miss Slinger threatened to make him sit alone. This quietened him for a while until the day Miss Lottie Wells dropped in to see Miss Dora and popped her head in to say goodbye to Miss Lily (our Miss Slinger) when she was leaving.

Miss Lottie Wells was a delight. Droll, oh, she would have

us in peals of laughter when relating her tale of the centipede that she attacked, cut in half and was satisfied that it was dead. The following week she saw something running across the floor, and there if you please, was the very centipede; it had joined itself together, but crookedly, and was waddling across her room. So, she cut it in two again and to make sure it would not join itself another time, put it in a little box and threw it on the fire.

Miss Lottie Wells had a fearful squint.

As Selby saw Miss Wells, he began nudging the girls and squinting horribly. Giggles filled the classroom. The bell rang for lunch hour. On our way out, Miss Slinger glared at Selby and we all told him that he'd be going to the beam on our return.

As we entered the classroom at one o'clock we saw the little chair and sashes set out. Nothing was said. Roll was called, work was set and we must have been hard at it for half an hour when Miss Slinger asked, 'Where is Selby?'

No one knew.

Miss Slinger got very pink as it dawned on her that Selby had dared to run home.

On our return from lunch Miss Slinger had looked at Selby *over* her glasses. At that moment, Selby made up his mind that as soon as Miss Slinger's head was bent, he was leaving. Miss Slinger bent her head and Selby simply walked out of school.

The policeman stationed at the top of the hill whom we all loved and whose name was Joseph (a huge mountain of a man) sized up the situation immediately he saw Selby emerge from the school-gate at one-thirty. He gave him a tiny salute. Seeing encouragement, Selby walked into Green Street with chest out, head high and wearing a ferocious expression.

Harold Smith, Caryl and Cynthia's brother, was looking out of his window. He too sized up the situation and said, 'Atta boy Selby, you're running away. Chuts man, come up and have some sweets.'

Selby slipped through the gateway and upstairs where

Harold fed him on sweets and congratulated him on his bravery for running away.

With all this approval, Selby marched proudly home where he was promptly taken back to school and Miss Slinger was told to give him the strap.

Stoically, Selby received his correction by ruler and settled down to lessons.

Miss Claudine Lomas, retired matron of the Colony Hospital, played a most important part in our young lives. We affectionately called her Nanny and were disgusted when our little friends, behind her back of course, named her Nanny-Goat.

She was a tiny, dark-haired, blue-eyed Irish woman with the hottest temper and kindest heart. She had delivered all of Mother's babies except me.

Nanny spent every Christmas with the Wilson family and every Boxing Day through New Year with us. When the Wilsons moved to another island she spent Christmas through to the third of January with us.

At this terrible age, Nanny amused us no end by the fact that she *never* wore drawers and, whenever she crossed and uncrossed her legs, we would see grey hairs. Later in our rooms we would have laughter fits.

One afternoon, Jessie dared me to go for a walk without panties. If I won the dare she would give me a shilling. I went for my walk minus this protective garment and the wind blew my dress up and scandalised nurses, children and passers-by. I received my shilling and bought from Mrs Patterson's sweetie shop twenty-four chocolate sticks and got sick.

Nanny suffered from a stomach cough and a weak heart. She lived by herself in a little flat and spent most of the day in her easy chair crocheting and embroidering slipper tops.

After we moved house and lived a few miles away from school, we lunched daily with her and some nights when she felt a little afraid of old age, Mother, Jessie or I would take it in turns to sleep with her.

Nanny's dressing-table was a delight. There were little silver and cut glass scent and smelling-salts bottles, powder bowls, vases, picture frames and candlesticks. We loved playing with these beautiful things. On the left side of her dressing-table, in a silver frame, stood the words, 'Trust in God and keep your powder dry.'

Jessie and I naturally thought this was a charm to prevent the body-powder from getting damp.

During one lunch hour, the rain began falling bucket-a-drop so I said, 'Nanny, God can't keep your powder dry if I don't shut the windows.'

She gave me a strange look as we pulled the shutters in. 'Sit down,' she said. 'Those words have nothing to do with the powder on my dressing-table. They were spoken by Oliver Cromwell . . .' and I received a long lecture at the end of which we both laughed at me and my interpretation.

Mother visited Nanny one evening each week and either Jessie or I would accompany her, taking our homework along. She told me I must go to the library and read *Mrs Wiggs of the Cabbage Patch*.

The following afternoon I trotted off to the library, asked for *Mrs Wiggs*, selected a little rocking-chair and began to read. I roared with laughter and Elizabeth the old caretaker came and asked me to keep quiet. I tried but got the giggles, fast developing into hysterics. Miss Webster, the Librarian came across and said gently, 'If you can't read without disturbing others, you must leave.' This sobered me and with an embarrassed, 'I'm sorry Miss Webster,' I continued reading. In ten minutes I collapsed with shouts of laughter and had to crawl out of the library holding my stomach.

This book is the funniest I have ever read. Years later, when I had children of my own, I tried to get a copy for them, even writing to two large booksellers in England, but failed. *Mrs Wiggs* no longer existed.

At Nanny's we met two adorable little old ladies, Miss Musgrave and Miss Cole. We chatted, and to our surprise they asked Jessie and me to tea on Saturday afternoon. We accepted with pleasure and they said they would send the girl (servants, no matter their age, were called girls) to the foot of the hill to show us the way.

Miss Fanny Musgrave's home was in Mardigras, at the top of the hill. There was no road to it, only a rocky path, and we wondered how these old ladies managed to get to and fro.

We saw the girl standing barefooted with a white cap and apron and a wide smile. She led the way skipping over the rocks nimbly.

We reached the top and found a fairytale house with fairytale furniture. I have to mention the strawberries as this was the tropics and strawberries were a most unusual sight. Actually, this was the first time we had seen fresh strawberries. We ate these with very beautiful silver teaspoons.

We were shown family albums and rare little bits of china and beautiful silk fans with programmes of dances held in bygone years. On every other page in the album was a picture of an angelic-looking child and we asked who she was. It was Miss Musgrave's sister.

'Did she die?' we asked.

'Oh no, she is alive and lives here with us, but she is not well.'

We begged to meet her. For exactly two minutes we were allowed to visit, Miss Cole standing by looking at her watch.

Yes, the other Miss Musgrave was an invalid. Bright as a bird she lay on her very white sheets surrounded by books and pictures of birds. At her window live birds visited, tame as could be. Two minutes were up and we begged very hard to be allowed a little more time but were told that we were so young and Sister's illness was catching. We promised we would not catch anything but Miss Cole took us from the room. Sister was consumptive.

Six o'clock came all too soon and the girl took us to the bottom of the hill where Daddy was waiting to drive us home.

One day Jessie and I went to Nanny's to spend the day and learn how to make little woollen pompoms.

'Nanny,' said Jessie, 'you are so pretty, why didn't you get married?'

'Oh, my child, I had opportunities. I was engaged once,' she replied.

'Do tell us about it,' we pleaded.

Nanny sat quietly snipping lengths of wool then said: 'It was in 1886. He was the Captain of a ship. A fine looking chap with the bluest of eyes and how I loved him. His boat called regularly every two months at Kingstown. I met him at a ball and my guardians asked him to the house. So each time his boat docked and he had completed his business with the ship's agents, he would visit us. Now and again he brought another officer who was younger and very sensitively handsome. The Captain asked for my hand in marriage and we became engaged.'

'What was his name, Nanny?' we asked.

'We'll call him "He",' she said.

'I began getting my bottom drawer in order,' she continued, 'living for each visit. I was very busy too as I was almost a qualified nurse with one more midwifery test to take. The wedding was set for June. It was now January, then February, March, April . . . his boat was in and never was I so happy. The two days he spent on our island were filled with morning, afternoon and evening parties. I now claimed St Vincent as my home as I had no parents and lived with my aunt and her husband.

'We were left alone to say goodnight before he sailed. He held me close, speaking in my hair, "Claudine, no matter what, promise you'll marry me and be mine for ever." Of course I promised. Nothing could come between us.

'During the next two months all preparations were completed as the wedding was to be on June the tenth. The boat came on the ninth. I was upstairs when a carriage pulled up at the door and I ran downstairs, disappointed and a little apprehensive to find, not my affianced, but his friend there.

' "Do come in," I said.

' "Thank you, Miss Claudine," he replied and stood twisting his cap. There was a mistiness in his eyes as though he were about to shed tears and I felt quite sorry for him.

' "Claudine, you can't marry him. I told him if he tried to go through with it I'd be forced to tell you."

' "Why? What?" I asked, frightened.

' "He is married to my sister." He left and I went upstairs, the world a dark place indeed.

'Another carriage came and "He" had arrived. I came to the top of the stairs and we looked at each other. He stretched his arms wide and sobbed, "Oh Claudine, my Claudine." I turned, entered my room and locked the door so as not to be disturbed.'

Jessie and I sobbed to break our hearts and in order to divert our minds from our first tragic love story we were hustled into laying the table for tea.

Nanny lived until the early forties. We all wept bitterly at her passing. We knew how old she was even though she always told us with an impish smile when asked her age, 'sixty-five.' At the funeral I broke down completely when I read on the hymnal sheets, 'Claudine Lomas, Aged 65'.

May had now reached the stage – about two and a half years old – where at the slightest provocation she would strip off all her garments. Ellen was forever saying, 'Little ladies are never seen without their clothes.' She also began crying each morning as we set off for school. She set up quite a hullabulloo with, 'I-wanna-go-too-I-wanna-go-too,' so that she would be allowed to go with Ellen for the walk.

One day, seated in class, we heard a voice by the gate saying, 'All right little girl, don't strain yourself, I'll push it open for you,' and May appeared in the classroom dressed only in a chemise. Vince, Jessie, Selby and I felt most ashamed and Miss Slinger got up and asked, 'How did you come May? Who brought you?'

May lisped, 'I thum,' and bent down to pick up some child's pencil that had fallen, showing, to her brothers' and sisters' complete mortification, a pink bottom.

Ellen came bustling in, explaining that the child had run

away and, 'How she find dis place by sheself ah just do' know, ma'am.'

Everything seemed to be happening at once. Vince got the ruler because on the top of the steps he took out his Mr Muffet and tried to wet the bottom of the steps. Vince was sent to a boys' school.

Lucille could not subtract two from two. Miss Slinger put it on the blackboard ⅔ and Lucille guessed all answers ranging from one to nine and Miss Slinger was beside herself with frustration. She stuck two fingers in the air, showing two objects, she hid the two fingers, showing no objects and Lucille answered eight. Lucille went to another school and I really don't know if this was because Miss Slinger gave Lucille two across the legs with the ruler.

Then there was a terrible explosion in the Salhoum's garage and Miss Slinger kept us away from the window. A mechanic was fixing a car, leaning over the gas tank while smoking, and he was blown into the air. André Salhoum, whose father owned the garage, didn't come back to school.

Soon it was December and we kept looking at the almanac to see the date December the twenty-fifth in red. Each day Miss Slinger made a big x over the day which had passed. I asked her what would happen when she crossed off the thirty-first.

'We'd just go on to the first of January, 1925.'

'But where would December the thirty-first go to?' I asked.

'Nowhere at all, it simply would be the end of 1924.'

'But it must go *somewhere*,' I insisted. 'It couldn't just float about.'

I could not be made to understand and went home that afternoon sad and thoughtful. How could a year which had held so much and been so wonderful be forgotten by simply turning the almanac over?

The following morning we found huge, black ribbon bows on the doors of the schoolroom and kitchen/sitting room. Not knowing why, we tiptoed into the classroom and did not dare to run into the yard to play. If anyone talked it was in whispers directly into the ear for which it was meant.

Miss Slinger came in red-eyed and told us that a very sad thing had taken place last night. Chokingly, she said that Miss Pussy had died and we must all go in to see her before the boatman came to give her a burial at sea. After we had done this, we were to take our books and go home as there would be no school that day.

We formed a long line, tallest leading, and entered the kitchen.

Miss Pussy lay in a huge white cardboard box lined with satin. Miss Pussy looked colossal and asleep. Miss Pussy had an enormous new ribbon tied around her neck. Miss Dora and Cook were standing by red-eyed, listening to our exclamations. Lyris Richards stumbled in and out of the room with her eyes shut and was quite hysterical. Miss Dora thought it was because she had such a tender heart and gave her a peppermint drop.

School broke up the following week and we sang 'God Save the King' lustily. After this, we were saddened. Miss Slinger took off her glasses and delicately blew her nose.

'Children, next term, you will all be going to larger schools, most of you either to the Grammar School or the Church of England High School for Girls. I have done as much for you as I could, in making you acquainted with your letters and figures, and in getting you ready for the give and take of a larger school. Come and see me. . .' Here, Miss Slinger wept openly.

Many of the boys began cuffing each other, trying to cover the embarrassment of tears and one or two of the very sensitive girls were bawling.

Miss Dora saved the day with a bag of peppermints and we kissed both Misses Slinger wet, minty, loving kisses as we left this little school for good.

Moving house was most exciting. We now lived in a lovely old house called 'The Raven' on Richmond Hill, next door to the prisons. Oddly enough, my great grandfather, after there were no more slaves for him to supervise, became Superintendent of Prisons and had lived in this very house. It possessed one of the finest views of the town and we also looked straight downhill into the botanic gardens. The gardens had been laid out to look like a spider's web.

There is so much to explore in a new house. Vince found his bearings almost immediately, but it took me ages to find the bathroom, and before we were settled in, I was spanked for sitting on a stone and 'spouting'.

I went sulking into the garden and discovered a snail. It had a beautiful pink shell and it was moving along the wall, its antennae signalling leisurely. Flying inside, I called Vince, Jessie and Selby to witness this marvel.

We stood staring at it and the slow silver trail it left as it crept along. We asked each other questions to which we had no answer, and Vince at last thought that we ought to put it in a box until Daddy came home. We found Ellen unpacking the servants' cups, plates, and so on from a whisky crate and we begged for this.

Vince was the bravest so he lifted the snail – we all screamed – and he put it into the box which was about eighteen inches tall. As far as we were concerned, this was absolutely safe as in the entire hour we had looked at the snail, it had moved only three inches.

Ellen called us to tea and she disgusted us by saying that if you were very hungry you could eat a snail as it was not poisonous.

By the time we were bathed and dressed to go for our walk, Daddy came in and we all earnestly explained to him about the snail, its capture, etcetera. He went into the yard with us and we all looked into the whisky box, but there was no snail. We looked under and around the box, but there was still no snail. We were called to start our walk during which we spent a long time discussing the snail's escape but could come to no decision as to its fate. Vince turned to us and said seriously, 'I think Ellen ate it.'

We were so shocked that we hated him and Ellen for the rest of the afternoon.

My father's work often took him into the country and we spent delightful days during the holidays with many of the country families. 'Mount Rodney', 'Bagatelle', 'Nyangfoix', 'Grand Bacolet', 'Springfield', 'La Sagesse', 'Providence' are some of the delightful memories. Mount Rodney, as far as we were concerned, was the nicest, as the lady there was a dreamer who let us ride the donkey without warning and let us run wild without feeling sure that we would all kill ourselves. Her table literally groaned with food, just what children loved on a day out.

One day I saw my father with tears in his eyes and we were told that a good country friend, Mr Copland – the Mount Rodney Mr Copland – had died. Ellen wouldn't let us play as Mother was upset because Daddy was upset, so she confined us to our rooms with books.

Daddy went to the funeral alone as Mother was not too well. Jessie and I, locked in our bedroom with books that had been read and reread, dolls that had been dressed and undressed, became very bored. Jessie suggested we play 'Mr Otway'.

Now Mr Otway was an enormous, handsome old gentleman who owned, among other things, a funeral agency, a mart, a delightful home and a huge bell which he used to have rung prior to holding a sale in the mart. He fascinated us, particularly as he was so very big and his wife so very small.

He had a sister who looked just like him and her name was Mrs Pittman. She had two sons – they were my first love, but that is another story.

Mr Otway dressed in tails, striped pants and top hat for his funerals. The hearse was drawn by two or four horses which were in fine condition and so it was by no means an easy thing to play 'Mr Otway'.

Jessie squeezed the door open, looked up and down and crept into Daddy's room. She returned laden and made three more trips.

The first thing we did was to find a doll we did not want,

as we were having a real funeral and were going to bury her. We found a Kewpie doll but no coffin.

Jessie made another trip and came back with a shoe box. (Mother had ordered some shoes 'on sight' for Daddy and those she wasn't keeping were in their boxes waiting to be sent back to the Supply Stores. Jessie had emptied one of these boxes.)

We laid the little doll in the box and I was informed that I was to be the hearse, horses, mourner and grave digger. Jessie was to be Mr Otway, the Reverend McFarlane and the doll's mother and father. We were both to be the choir.

We knew so much about funerals. Perhaps it was that every afternoon walk we took with the maids. All, except the Sunday walks, ended in the churchyard. Our benches were graves and the tombstones were ships, horses and trains. Our usual informant on graveside scenes was Jimbo the bellringer. Jimbo would sit there in his clean white pants and shirt, chipping coconuts for Mrs Martin's chickens, and, fascinated by the four or five plum-sized bumps on his head, we would listen to the mournful, 'Dust to dust, ashes to ashes,' from Jimbo's lips. Edward Martin would slip away whenever these tales started and Jimbo would slip us pieces of coconut with a sly wink.

Well, Jessie began changing into Mr Otway. Daddy's evening suit was put on over her dress. She placed her feet in a pair of new gent's shoes; a top hat graced her head. I sat on my bed gazing at the transformation.

Jessie, living her part, got more and more serious, her freckles standing out in excited patches. Her hands disappeared and slowly the hat slipped down, covering her face. I began to giggle and could not stop. I lay across my bed and laughed and laughed, my stomach aching so much that I thought I must be dying. Tears ran down my cheeks. Jessie, thank God, got highly indignant and smacked me properly, telling me to 'come on.'

Weakly, I followed her. In her right hand she held a Bible and was reading aloud. Out of the room, down the passage, down the steps, into the yard we went.

Striding back and forth as she supposed Mr Otway would have, Jessie ordered me to begin digging. The dinner fork kept bending and after a few attempts had been made at straightening it, it snapped in two, so I used a piece of stick instead. The hole was taking very long to dig and 'Mr Otway' got most impatient. So impatient did he become that he threw the coffin aside and buried Miss Mary-Edna naked as she was.

We mournfully sang one verse, tune only, of 'Nearer my God to Thee', and it was all over.

Jessie was not satisfied. She stamped and jumped on the shoebox, and dragged herself and costume across the yard, up the steps and back to our room. Here she took off her suit and hat, pushed them into their cupboard and neatly placed the muddy shoes on them. She closed the cupboard door.

The damage was discovered the next day. The maid was fired for stealing a silver fork. We were spanked and not allowed to go to 'Woodlands' the next day with Daddy.

The following week, however, we did go to Woodlands with Daddy. Mr and Mrs Georgie Steele lived there, and what a wonderful time we had. Doris and Eric played with Vince and Jessie, and Beryl and I were left to occupy ourselves as best we could. We took a walk and Pop Tibbets appeared suddenly out of the bushes with a popgun and shot us. We fled and went under a plum tree, and were quite happy running to the cow pond and back with water cupped in our hands. Soon we had a gorgeous mudcake made. Beryl's father passed and asked, 'What you girls doing? Dirtying your clothes, eh?'

We looked at ourselves and we were filthy. Beryl thought her mother would be furious so we went back to the house and used a whole block of whitening on our frocks and went happily in to tea.

Shortly before departure time I heard Mrs Steele (Auntie Marie) telling Daddy with laughter in her voice, 'Had I taken any notice of their condition I would have had to wash their hair, bathe them, dress them – my God, they seemed so proud of themselves – I could see at a glance that they had used the entire block of whitening.'

Daddy seemed equally happy and we were bundled into the car for home.

Doris had shown Vince and Jessie something marvellous. You soaped under your arm, put your palm on the soapy area, flapped hard and golly, you made a wonderful noise – plocka, plocka, plocka. I tried very hard but I think my armpit must have been too small. I could get no sound at all.

We never talked of sweating – we 'perspired'. We never farted, we merely 'passed air'. The private part of a male was called 'Mr Buster Brown' and the female counterpart was 'Miss Muffet' – sometimes we forgot and called the male part 'Mr Muffet'. Excreta? Solids were called 'noo-noo' and liquids, 'wee-wee'. But these words were hardly ever spoken.

Nobody but Glynn Evans would think of nicknaming Jessie and me 'Big Noo-noo' and 'Little Noo-noo'. We in turn called him 'Loupgaroux' and his brother Willie 'La Diablesse'. They always succeeded in getting us annoyed and they always laughed at our names for them. Poor Mrs Rose, with whom they lived, used to put her head through the window and say very gently to us, 'They're naughty boys, don't mind them.'

Mrs Rose died and the Evans boys, Glynn, Willie and Terry went to live with our best friends the Jimmy Commissiongs. Terry, being our age, became a friend. (Mother and Mrs C. always thought that there would have been at least one marriage uniting the Donovan and Commissiong families. *We* knew each other much too well for this to have happened.)

In the meantime, the wife of Daddy's friend Mr Copland moved into town so her children could go to school. Mrs Copland was supposed to be 'moaning' dreadfully for her dead husband. Mother had received a message from Mrs Copland that for God's sake she was not to call, she was to come on in and have a cup of tea. In the face of such recent bereavement, the visit started in very sober vein. Hardly a smile, not a laugh. Mrs Copland dropped a spoon and Mother bent hastily to pick this up. She nearly died. Audibly, she had passed air. Both ladies, very conscious of what had happened, pretended that nothing had happened and Mrs Copland said, 'Sugar, Mrs Donovan?' Their eyes met. Mrs Copland, an utterly irrepressible character said, 'Well, that should have broken the ice.' The afternoon was a great success.

We no longer saw Olive on Saturdays as we lived a long way from her but Majorie was always around and so were Beryl, Caryl and Joyce. Now, on Saturdays either Majorie would spend the day with us or one of us would spend the day with her at the Douglas Hotel which was owned by her aunts, Tanna and Aunt Connie. The main excitement here was sliding down the bannisters and trying to frighten Mr McGilchrist, a boarder of a decade or two, by saying 'Boo!' unexpectedly when he was reading the papers. He would be good for about a dozen boos then he'd send us packing.

One morning we heard that the Governor's ADC had shot himself in the bathroom of the Douglas Hotel and Majorie, full of importance, promised us a tour. We did not go the usual way, walking down Church Street and entering the Hotel. We crawled through a huge drain which led into Mrs Ella Smith's bathroom, moved into Mrs Ella Smith's garden and jumped over Mrs Ella Smith's garden wall into the yard of the Douglas Hotel. We crossed this yard and entered the bathroom. Majorie was at her most dramatic. Pointing to the ceiling she said, 'His brains.' To the left wall; 'More brains!'

Actually, there was nothing to see as the entire room was as clean as clean could be and Majorie, sensing our disappointment, told us that Inspector Lloyd had begged her to look for pieces of brain, etcetera, and she would let us help her. We began the search but Aunt Connie spied us and told us to play in the yard; it was much healthier for children.

Vince was at this time spending almost every weekend

with Alec Hughes and on the whole thought himself much too big to play with girls. He also began keeping rabbits which we were not allowed to feed or anything. We could only look at them.

Selby's best friend was Cynthia Smith and they seldom failed to have a daily fight.

A Spanish boy came to live in the area and he called Vince 'Bimps'. They played a lot of cricket together. After about a year this boy returned to his homeland. Thirty years later he returned to Grenada; he had become an Army General and wanted to find Bimps, the one boy who had been kind to him when he was so lonely. He wanted to see how Bimps had fared in life and to take him back to his homeland for a visit. Vince was unfortunately in Peru at that time.

Anyway, to go back to the story, Christmas was fast approaching. In early December Vince and Jessie went to Carriacou, an island dependency of Grenada, with Daddy who was on one of his inspection trips. They had a marvellous time on this islet and the trip provided inspiration for our theatricals.

It seems that they had attended parties at many homes. They had listened to chirruping little songs and tinkling little tunes on ancient pianos and they had been completely captivated by Mrs Otway's rendition of 'Take back the heart that thou gavest.' Her dramatic warbling had taken possession of Jessie's mind and she was now in the process of producing A Grand Opera.

Caryl and Cynthia Smith, Joyce and Lester Paterson, all the Donovans, Majorie, Clive and Gordon Commissiong, Terry Evans and Beryl Steele were roped into the practising at every convenient moment. We practised in our dining room, in Miss Ivy Smith's garden, in Mrs Commissiong's gallery, in Caryl and Cynthia's seaside-grape tree, on our walks, in our baths, and we never tired. The more we practised, the more we improvised and the more interesting A Grand Opera became.

At about this time Miss Douglas, who opened the first cinema in Grenada, was showing the first talkie, Hit the Deck.

We all went to see it. From this we drew further ideas for our opera. We began secreting away old tubes of lipstick, used pots of rouge and pieces of charcoal.

We saw our first Tarzan film. We learned the Tarzan call. We inserted the historic lines, 'Me Tarzan, you Jane,' into our opera. The boys, Vince, Selby, Clive, Gordon and Terry began practising the Tarzan swing on a tree which grew at the junction of Upper Lucas Street and Observatory Road. We girls were green with envy as we were not allowed to grab at the rope vines that dangled, to swing ourselves clear across into Mr Noble Smith's yard where his dog Nero chased all and sundry intruders with such vigour that people were always scattering and scaling hibiscus hedges at terrific speeds.

The boys were at it again, and just when we should be practising the final chorus. We looked out of the window at them and Jessie, envious that she wasn't a boy, said, 'I hope they break their bloody necks.' Very bad language, but we all agreed heartily.

Terry was swinging through the air when Jessie said these words. He could not have heard, we were sure, as we were hundreds of yards away, but we heard a cracking sound, and Terry and a piece of the rope went sailing through the air while the other part of the rope stayed behind dangling from the tree.

Terry landed in a forlorn little heap and all the boys ran to Mrs Commissiong's home to call her and Glynn to the scene. Mother was first there and fast on the telephone for a car to take Terry to the hospital.

All the hanging vines on the tree were chopped down by the Agricultural Department and Terry, in great pain, went around with tears in his lovely dark eyes.

The whole of *A Grand Opera* was changed to accommodate a Romeo with a broken arm.

On Saturday afternoon the curtains opened to a full house comprising Evans, Donovans, Commissiongs, Smiths, Patersons, Holmes, Steeles, Killikellys and Nanny. We charged all adults an entrance fee of fourpence which covered the cost of a sweet drink and cakes in the interval, and all children one penny.

We made eleven shillings and sixpence profit. The play was a complete success and even when it was over the adults kept sitting in their seats laughing their heads off. When I sang to Terry the beautiful ballad, 'Take back the Arm that thou gavest', the roars of adult laughter lasted a full five minutes.

Mother took us to the library one afternoon when Ellen was off and Miss Webster allowed us, against the rules, to look out of the window which faced the Almond Yard. A circus, a Spanish circus, had come to Grenada and the animals were put in this enclosure until they could be sent to the circus site.

We saw our first llama. We also smelt it. How the animals stank! But we stayed, hanging out of the window, looking at the caged and uncaged animals.

The circus people were hustling back and forth and though they were filthy from their sea voyage, gave off such promises of excitement that Jessie and I could barely contain ourselves.

We were literally dragged home and when we talked about our experiences, Vince and Selby were annoyed that they had missed so much.

The first circus matinée was attended by us all. The clowns were wonderful. Oh, how ferocious were the lions, and how magnificent was the Lady with the Steel Hair!

On one side of the tent a huge cannon stood. This cannon had a human cannon ball called Manuel, but alas, he was only fired at night and we were permitted matinées only. Manuel had a brother called Vincenti who was invariably dressed in yellow pantaloons; he did a trapeze act. Jessie fell desperately in love with Vincenti and everything she said or did was self-consciously performed, as she believed that so great a love as hers would naturally be surrounded by mirrors all visible to Vincenti.

I must admit that Vincenti was glamorous but his hair looked very greasy. I caught sight of a lad dressed in brown corduroy in the band and, to me, he was perfection. Every now and again he brought his cymbals together with a resounding clash and chased the music sheet with his eye until he banged again. I was changing my teeth and felt great kinship with this cymbal clasher as, when he smiled, he showed a gap where two teeth should have been.

Jessie took all her pocket change, which was one shilling and sixpence, and bought three of the finest Irish linen handkerchiefs for Vincenti. At this period a cotton hanky cost only a penny ha'penny. A problem arose. How were we to get these to him? We certainly couldn't get near while he was performing and Ellen would have nothing at all to do with this as her firm opinion was that Spaniards were nasty and they always spat on the floors.

Majorie thought it quite an easy thing to do. Why not go to their home before the show and give it to him? Caryl, who was now in the know, thought it more practical to make curtains for our doll's house with the hankies.

Ellen told Mother and Mother solved the problem. Ellen would take us to the house Vincenti lived in. We would knock on the door and leave the parcel for him.

When we arrived at the door, who should open it but the boy in brown corduroy, blushing, and smiling without two teeth. He spoke no English. Jessie, gripping Ellen with one hand, clutching the parcel with the other, spoke no Spanish and, apparently believing the boy to be quite deaf, shouted, 'Vincenti!' The boy, apparently also believing Jessie to be quite deaf, shouted back, still smiling, something we did not understand and pointed a dirty finger in the direction of the circus.

Jessie handed over the package on which was written in red, 'VINCENTI'. In handing the package, all her love seemed to have disappeared, as she said to us later on, 'I don't like Vincenti anymore.'

We concentrated now on the Lady with the Steel Hair and we trained our hair into long plaits heavenwards. My plait was longer than Jessie's so it was bound securely with fine wire which ended in a reinforced loop, similar to the loop at the end of a hammock. Over a doorway a nail was driven through a rope on which dangled a hook, and the hook fitted the loop in my hair. The boys had erected the contraption and had promised to supply the music for the performance. Malarial Nellie would be the first performer.

I had greatly frightened myself by looking in the mirror. My hair had been combed skywards and my eyebrows, and eyes, seemed drawn in the same direction. My entire face was most uncomfortable.

I stood on a box; Vince put the hook into my hair and the box was pushed away. Blood-curdling yells filled the air and Mother and servants came running. Mother held me so as to take the strain off my scalp and Ellen unhooked me. My hair was very gently unbound and unplaited. We were forbidden to play such dangerous games and the hook and rope were taken away.

A few days later we heard Ellen shouting, 'Madam, madam, O me Gawd madam, come quick, come quick.' Everyone who was at home rushed to find Ellen whimpering. And, swinging by her hair, dressed in a silk Chinese kimono, was May. Her rouge was startling; her lipstick stretched from ear to ear; her smile disappeared behind her neck, thus accentuating the smudges on her nose and teeth. To create momentum she was paddling her little feet and never had we seen anything so ghastly.

How she had managed to become the Miss Steel Hair of the family we did not know and could only think that she must have been a 'natural' for this sort of thing.

Our plans on building a cannon from which one of us would be shot were scotched almost immediately and we had to satisfy ourselves by expressing bitter thoughts on the unimaginatively unappreciative adult world.

Our hair was very, very long, daily giving Mother more and more trouble and taking up too much of her time.

A barber had arrived in Grenada. He was from St Lucia and could hardly speak a word of English. Mother said she was going to send us to him to have our hair cut off.

43

Jessie informed me that we have seven million, nine hundred and ninety-nine hairs on our heads and that each strand of hair that was cut, ached and pained one so much that it was almost unbearable. Seeing how affected I was she also told me that the *first* time one cut one's hair, it bled profusely.

I could neither sleep nor eat. I was getting quite ill and Ellen informed Mother that she thought it would be a good idea indeed to have my hair cut as it was 'sucking' the strength from my body.

One Saturday afternoon, at two o'clock in the year of our Lord nineteen hundred and twenty-six, Jessie and I marched off to Mr Mauricette the French barber to have our hair cut off.

Mr Mauricette's shop was situated at the bottom story of Miss Dawes' home. Jessie and I walked in and Mr Mauricette, all smiles, bid us a delightful 'Bonjour,' and many 'asseyez-vous s'il vous plaît'. Talk about butterflies! Jessie kept saying, 'You go first.' I kept saying, 'No, you go first,' and Mr Mauricette kept smiling and saying, 'Ah, ah, ah.'

Jessie went first and was now very proudly sitting on a chair waiting for me to climb into the barber's chair. I had not looked at her once while the scissors were snipping as, in my mind, I knew exactly what was happening. She was dripping with blood, her shoulders were bright red and the floor around her was a fast-forming crimson pool. I got into the chair and as Mr Mauricette took the first chop I noo-nooed my pants. It seemed a great quantity and by the fourth or fifth snip I could hear Mr Mauricette sniffing. Very wisely he asked, 'Ah! Vous tata vous-même?' and continued cutting my hair very, very quickly. I slid out of the chair and Jessie paid him one shilling and eight pence for both heads.

We left him gazing at us, shaking his head. By the time Jessie and I had reached Chapel Alley I was most uncomfortable and decided that the only thing to do was to get very quickly out of my drawers. I told Jessie I was going to slip down Chapel Alley, hide behind one of the buttresses of the chapel and take off my drawers. She agreed wholeheartedly as I was smelling worse and worse as the minutes dragged.

44

I took off my underwear but, realising that it was a very good pair, full of Ellen's crochet edging, I folded it so that the dirty part was hidden and the crochet edging, more or less clean, surrounded the little ball I held in the palm of my hand.

Proud that everything had been so efficiently handled, I continued my journey home. I was almost there when a little ragamuffin began following me, singing, 'You number-two your pants, you number-two your pants.' I ignored him.

The tune kept on for another fifty yards or so. I'll stop this, I thought and also remembered the constant advice from adults to 'always be a lady'. So I turned to him with what I thought great dignity and said in my best voice, 'What is the matter with you, little boy? This happens to be my mother's tea cloth I'm taking home.'

And the little devil minced after me saying, 'What is the matter with you, little boy? This happens to be my mother's tea cloth I'm taking home.'

Church and God began to be very important. We visualised Jacob and his ladder and Moses hidden in the rushes so vividly that we began getting pious little faces. Daddy was upset. He expressed his thoughts to Mother. 'Are they turning into little hypocrites?' Actually, Mother was quite happy that we were going through this phase as we spent most of our time drawing pictures of Jesus and trying to think 'holy thoughts'.

At night in our beds we could hear in the distance a triumphant singing of hymns and we thought it was the angels. When we told Eva, the cook, about this heavenly choir she informed us that it was no angels at all (she was Roman Catholic), it was the Seventh Day Adventists trying to take God's people away from their churches.

We had to make inquiries. Who were these Seventh Day Adventists? We found out where they lived and Jessie and I called on them. They were an American couple by the name of Mr and Mrs Coon and they had one little daughter, Juanita. They were delighted to see us and gave us peanut butter sandwiches. They asked where we lived and soon they called at our home and we were all invited to pay a visit to the tent where the Gospel was being spread.

We went, we 'saw the light', we signed covenants, but Daddy refused to let us be baptised. We ran away quite often and joined in the lusty singing of 'Throw out the Lifeline' and at night had nightmares of going to hell and being baked by Satan.

No amount of persuasion could alter our parents' minds about our being baptised. We wanted so desperately to be 'washed in the blood of the Lamb'. Jessie and I saw ourselves as lost souls and were seriously thinking of a painless way we could die and end our sinful life on earth.

We searched the heavens for a sign that the world was coming to an end, a sign the size and shape of a man's hand. Should we see this, we knew that we had, had, had to be baptised or heaven would be denied us. In this event, we kept the baby's unused bathpan full of water so I could quickly baptise Jessie, and she me.

One afternoon while we were at our post at the window, looking for the sign, we grabbed hold of each other. There in the sky was a dark cloud, the shape of a man's hand, forefinger upright. The finger seemed to be bending and pointing to two little girls looking through a window. We forgot all about baptising ourselves and thought only of saving Mother and Daddy who *must* go to heaven with us. The idea of our floating upwards and they sinking downwards brought sobs to our throats.

Mother and Daddy were out. Frantic, we grabbed at the telephone and asked the operator if they could get Mrs Donovan for us. Oh, what a wonder telephone system that was. You grabbed, asked, and the operator always knew where anybody was. In a minute we heard Mother's voice, quiet yet anxious, asking what was the matter. Jessie and I were sobbing hysterically by this time, telling her that she must be saved as the end of the world was at hand. Assured that she was coming home immediately, we followed Mother's instructions and waited as best we could for her arrival.

Daddy listened patiently to our jabbering, took us outside and, believe it or not, there was not a cloud in the sky.

We eventually returned to the kirk where Jessie was asked by Miss Brathwaite to hold a Sunday school class as one of the teachers had not turned up. Very proudly, Jessie, at the tender age of ten, held her first Sunday school class. Actually, all she did was read a passage from the Bible – very nasally – to a group of little boys.

Whenever Jessie was emotional, her freckles stood out in dark patches. She was very, very proud of reading the Bible to a dozen little boys and could not help but look up from her reading every now and again to see what impression she was making. One little boy was staring at her in a hypnotised manner and each time Jessie glanced up the stare was still on her face.

'What are you looking at, little boy?' she asked.

The little boy answered promptly, 'Your face, it look like a quashie mango.'

That was the first and last Sunday school class Jessie held.

Damsons were now in season. The nurses changed the direction of our walk. We were to forsake the churchyard for a couple of afternoons and head towards the botanic gardens, where, enroute, damson trees were laden with their acid little yellow fruit.

We filled our pockets and went along to the gardens to eat our fill. On our return, we again picked some more and the greedy ones like Vince ate them on the sly. When we were almost home, Vince began groaning and moaning. His tummy was aching. We could see it getting fat like a balloon so Ellen unbuttoned his pants and we all raced home.

Mother took Vince to the dressing room and put him on the day bed. Ellen brought a kettle of hot water and a cake of blue soap. Mother put us out and shut herself in the room with Vince. Ellen went downstairs to lay our supper table.

Jessie thought we should peep, but as there was only one keyhole I was roughly pushed aside while she had a pretty good view of what was taking place. We went to supper when called, but Jessie would say nothing of what she saw.

In the morning, we went to the market with Eva, the cook, and helped her select green vegetables and fruit. While she went off to the butcher's we waited at our grandparents' home. Here we fed the hundreds of pigeons and watched Claude, the houseboy, scrub the roof, which was almost white with dung. We washed our hands and had a glass of coconut water and a slice of something nice which Grandma had made.

Grandma had two pianos with lace fronts, and elaborate candelabra. Both pianos were out of tune. Jessie and I each banged on a piano, expressing all our childish hopes and fears in discordant duets; we could not understand why on leaving we received a very-glad-to-see-you-go farewell.

Home again, we made mudcakes. After lunch the clatter from the kitchen ceased and the entire house settled for its afternoon siesta.

Jessie's freckles stood out darkly as she put a finger to her lips and beckoned with the other hand. I tiptoed to her and she told me that she was going to give me an enema. '*That is what Vince was given last night after eating dirty damsons.*'

She got a basin, water, castor oil and a cake of blue soap, a syringe and a waterproof sheet. She laid the waterproof on my bed, mixed a basin of suds with a dollop of castor oil and put me to lie down.

Thank God the handle of the door turned and Mother entered.

Do you remember Mr Otway of the doll's funeral? Well, the real Mr Otway's sister, Mrs Pittman, arrived from Chile, and Mother and Daddy called. Mrs Pittman had two sons, Eric and Hubert, and we thought them marvellous-looking. Unfortunately, they were years older than we were, so we hadn't a hope of seeing much of them.

To our surprise, while we were having a game of cricket, they appeared in our yard, dressed in long flannel pants, and looked at the game. After this first visit, they would appear at any time, sometimes batting, bowling, fielding or merely sitting on the grass looking on.

The first time they came I got terribly shy and the game stopped. Vince asked them if they'd like to play. Coming from British parents, they had heard of the game, but this was their first go at it. Soon, they became enthusiastic and while Jessie was allowed to field, I was told by Vince to 'Stay away!'

Shy, insulted and more hurt than imaginable as this had happened in front of strangers, I hung my head in shame and the tears spilled over.

Suddenly, I was lifted into the air and hugged gently. A voice said caressingly, 'I'll play with you in a little while.' I buried my face in his neck and knew that I'd love Hubert Pittman until I died.

We were working very hard one Saturday morning preparing for the doll's wedding. Majorie, Caryl, Cynthia, Joyce and Myrtle were helping with decorations, dress and food.

Caryl had discovered some little silver balls and had decorated the cake which Jessie had made. The cakes had been baked in a herring and a sardine tin and the two-tiered result was grand. Majorie and I laid the table, placing clumps of begonias down the middle.

We found pennies and dashed off to Mrs Paterson's for chocolate sticks, and Mrs Paterson laughingly gave Joyce two more at no cost – a gift – for the bride. She asked who the lucky groom was to be. We clapped our hands to our mouths in horror! We had completely forgotten about a groom so Cynthia pelted homewards for her chew-eared teddy bear, and we dressed him hastily in a dress which Daisy had outgrown.

Jessie was the parson, I the choir, Majorie sang the chimes of the Anglican bells as the Presbyterian bell only tolled, and lots and lots of rice was thrown on the happy pair. We minced to the reception eagerly looking forward to the 'gazoos' (bottled sweet drinks which had a glass marble stopper), 'graza' (small cheap sweets), chocolate sticks and cake.

The cake had disappeared. Unknown to us Myrtle had eaten the silver balls and decided that now the cake looked so terrible, she hid it under the table. Rover had then found this treat and polished it off.

Majorie called Myrtle a *damn-blasted*. Myrtle with great dignity picked up her hanky and went home. Joyce wanted the two chocolate sticks her mother had given the bride and Jessie called her a greedy pig. Joyce pouted, picked up two chocolate sticks and went home. Cynthia grabbed a chocolate stick before everything disappeared and ran like blazes homewards. Majorie, Jessie, Caryl and I sat down and drank the gazoos, shared the remaining chocolate stick and ate the graza sweets.

The bride had fallen forward on her face and the groom stood staring, no doubt thinking of the terrible night in store for the Smith family when Cynthia realised that her teddy was away on his honeymoon.

In addition to cricket matches and doll's parties, we continued to plan concerts and write dramas. Money was now very low so we decided to produce something that would add to our finances. We all got together and wrote a play. Majorie thought we should scrap the usual lullaby as this was too childish, and have a love song instead. The boys thought a love song sissy. Mr Terry Commissiong solved our problem by giving us the music about a naughty, sporty college boy who threw all his books away. Majorie was to dress in Vince's clothes, wear Selby's cap and sing this song.

During practice, Majorie threw all her books away so vigorously that they hit Cynthia on her nose, and before you could say Jack Robinson rehearsal had descended into a free for all, worthy of Saltfish Hall.

We pulled each other's hair and scratched each others' faces and no one was on speaking terms for at least two days. In that time, something happened.

Franklyn arrived in our midst.

For months now, John, David, Dolly and Cynthia Copland had been telling us that their grandparents and

Uncle Franklyn were coming to Grenada from Canada. They had told us this so often that we no longer believed it.

We got messages through the servant grapevine on Saturday morning that we were to gather at Mrs Copland's home to see Uncle Franklyn.

By ten o'clock the playroom in Church Street was filled with Copland, Munro, Smith, Richards and Donovan children, all pretending to be very busy tidying the doll's house but waiting impatiently to see this Uncle Franklyn.

Dolly told us to keep calm and hold on as Grandpa and Granny were coming to lunch so Uncle Franklyn would definitely be coming too.

A strange, blond boy passed outside our door, scowled fearfully and shook a clenched fist at us. He passed again, his wizened face scowling ferociously as he dashed up the steps.

Dolly announced through stiff lips, 'That is Uncle Franklyn.'

We all spoke at once. 'Impossible!'

'He's only a boy!'

'How could he be your uncle?'

'How old is he?'

At last there was silence and Dolly and Cynthia said sadly, 'We are older than he is and he says we *have* to call him "Uncle".'

After Franklyn got over his hatred of his age he was good fun except that he used to eat the toothpaste in all our homes, much to our mothers' annoyance.

One day, Franklyn introduced a strange expression which could mean 'Shut up, I don't believe you', 'Tell that to the Marines', 'Go fly a kite', or, just plain, simple 'Blah'. I think he made it up and it certainly rolled off one's tongue smoothly. The expression brought to my mind green lawns, croquet sticks and glasses of lemonade.

So when at table a remark was made that demanded I put the speaker in his place, I used it. I opened my mouth and proudly said, 'The crabs are playing cricket with my father's balls.'

Daddy choked. Mother whisked me out of my chair, into

the bathroom where she soaped my mouth, and I was put to bed with only a glass of milk.

Then there was carnival.

Every year on the two days before Ash Wednesday the island held a carnival, and Vince and Selby were allowed to play in the streets with the other Grammar School boys. They were now making a long-mouthed mask. They had built a mould of mud which was baked in the sun and they were slapping on layer after layer of newspaper until it was about quarter of an inch thick. When this dried it was lifted off the mould and painted in black with red eyelids. The paint dried quickly and they were now sawing a mouth with huge teeth, and punching eyes and nostrils. By moving their jaws, the mouth with huge teeth opened and shut with the aid of pieces of elastic. They took about a week to complete the job and we girls were not permitted to be near them as each boy's mask was a secret.

Majorie, Jessie and I hated all males violently and were not happy that we would only be allowed to disguise for the parade at York House. But, dressed for the occasion, we were quite pleased, and I do feel that Jessie's costume was the most authentic and prettiest. She was a perfect Japanese maiden with her black hair. Unfortunately, she spoilt the whole effect by scowling fiercely and persistently whilst parading and did not get a prize. This made her sulk for another week.

The big day, when the conch shell would blow at five a.m. and the Pissannies in their long, white sheets, wire masks and pôt chambres would chip-chip along the roads chanting 'Pissannies in strength, hol' him Jo', was here. The Pissannies would open the celebrations. The schoolboys would have their bands of horrific masks and they would play all Monday as their headmaster, Mr Ambrose Hughes, knew that boys just had to be boys.

We girls went to school in groups as the masked boys always waited in Church Street to scare and pinch us. We did get frightened because they were some seventy strong and thoroughly enjoyed our falsely brave pleas of, 'Let me pass *please*.'

On Monday afternoon our nurses took us to homes that overlooked the popular mas' routes. After we were installed at one of the homes – the Francos, for example – we had a marvellous time looking at all the riotous behaviour, listening to the guitars, bamboo sticks and drums, and seeing the maypole danced; the Moko Jumbie and Lady Katy on fourteen-foot stilts; the donkey mas' doing its little dance; the cha-cha-o, which was dangerous, as two sticks of bamboo slammed and parted while the dancer performed in and out of the slamming bamboo. Should he miss a step, he would break an ankle. At the end of this dance, the dancer would mount the parallel sticks and cha-cha above ground until a new crowd of spectators wanted to be pleased.

We munched nuts until we were sick and swore we would eat no more for years to come.

On Tuesday, armed with our bags of nuts and confetti, we again went into town to see the 'pretty mas' '. Throbbing with excitement, we were allowed after an early supper and attended by our brothers, to meet the other girls with their brothers. We visited two or three homes where some member of the Munro family played gay tunes on the piano and we danced to our heart's content until ten p.m., when we went home to bed exhausted.

We made a new friend. His name was Buddy. He was very old and he came every Saturday morning to Mother for help. He was always well-treated but felt he had to do something in return, so he sang and performed for us. He sang very romantic songs in a tuneful but wavering voice: about gold in Californee; a picture set in a beautiful frame; and the 'Prisoner's Love Song'. Sometimes he brought a little drum and would thumpingly accompany himself.

Buddy kept on visiting for many years and if we had to go out on the day of his visit we would not leave home until he had sung his song.

One Saturday he did not turn up and Mother heard through the servants that he had slept his way to heaven.

Not far from us lived an eccentric hermit. He emerged about once a month and as he was always heard before seen, we would fly to the windows to get an excellent view.

We never knew his name but he must have been a very clever person, born at the wrong period, as no appreciation, only ridicule was shown him.

He was a one-man orchestra. He had drums, cymbals and a mouth organ fixed together with wire and solder, and he played the fiddle while setting time by the drum, blowing his mouth organ and clashing the cymbals. It was pretty good music, chiefly marches and hymns of the Salvation Army tempo, and we enjoyed it all. He would stay at the bottom of our drive, no doubt feeling our kinship with his performance and would give us a concert of about half an hour. He disappeared after a couple of years and we never knew what had happened to him.

Then once, spending the night with Monica Franco, we heard the most beautiful singing about eleven o'clock. We dashed out of bed and to the window, and there in the street, leaning on the railing was a girl, a street-walker, and her soul was soaring. I have never heard a voice as pure or as sad. When her song was finished I called, 'Pst! Pst!' She looked up and I whispered, '*Sing again*,' hoping she could lip read. She sang 'I'll be loving you, always' and walked away still singing the end of the song.

Neither Monica nor I fell asleep for a long time and Monica said, 'God must have put that voice in her throat.'

The girl must have recognised me, as two nights later she wandered into our vicinity and sang 'Always'. For me, I was sure.

Then there was that character, Mr Gun-Munro, a musical genius, and, an impossible person. He was Franklyn's father. He was also adorable.

My first big shock in life came from him. I did *not* want to go to school as I had a cut on my forefinger and it throbbed and throbbed. Mother had dipped it in hot water but oh, how it still ached. I was sent to school despite this and left the house very sad. By the time I reached the top of Church Street I was in tears and really sorry for myself.

Church Street is divided from Gore Street by wide concrete steps, some forty in number, and a cobbled passage. These steps are called Church Steps. I was just about at the top of these stairs when Mr Gun-Munro completed his climb from Gore Street and stopped for a blow. Seeing me he said, 'Hello Nelly Bly, why so many tears?'

'Oh, Mr Munro,' I said, 'I have a bad finger and it's hurting me.'

'Hrump,' he replied and glanced across at the Bishop's turkeys that were gobbling loudly in the rectory yard. 'Child,' he drawled nasally, 'you see the Bishop's turkeys?'

'Yes, Mr Munro.'

'Well, if you want to get your finger better, just stick it up a turkey's bambam!'

I flew to school and forgot all about pain and throbs in the profound shock I had received.

On Friday night Jessie and I had to go to a Christian Endeavour meeting at the kirk and so pleased were we to be out after six o'clock that we arrived half an hour early. Mr Gun-Munro was the organist and he too arrived early. He said good evening and went to the organ. His fingers ran up and down the manuals improvising and then suddenly the 'Lost Chord' rose and swelled and filled the church with magnificent thunder and my heart just about burst.

I have heard world-famous musicians – singers, orchestras, violinists and piano players – but the musicians that have given me most were Buddy the beggar; the one-man orchestra; the street-girl with her 'Always' and, Mr Gun-Munro, who, despite his unorthodox prescription for cuts on little girls' fingers, stands head and shoulders above them all.

One day, Lucille was looking as smug as a bullfrog. So were Godfrey, Lyris and Poo. We all wanted to know why, but we met with excited silence. Almost the entire school guessed and guessed but could find out nothing.

As the afternoon classes ended, Lucille turned to the Donovans, Coplands, Munros, Smiths and said, 'I have a beautiful something. Come after tea.' And with that, in case more was said, she dashed through the gate, up the hill.

We fled to our homes for tea, bath and a change of clothes. It was four-thirty on the dot when we entered Mrs Richards' home. Mrs Richards was a delightful lady who often gave us chunks of icing from large cakes, and read us *Winnie the Pooh* and *Wee Wisdom*.

'I suppose you've come to see the dancers?'

'Dancers?' we chorused.

We envisioned rhumbas, ballet, waltzes, etcetera, performed by circus people or visiting guests.

'We'll wait for Lucille to come downstairs. She was the last to have her bath.'

In what seemed hours but was really four minutes by Vince's fob watch, Lucille entered the room. She wound up the 'His Master's Voice' gramophone, put on a record and asked us to shut our eyes. We did.

'When the music starts, open your eyes and look at the record!' she said.

The music started. We opened our eyes to see two little figures dressed in full evening wear, dancing on the record. In time to the music, they waltzed and waltzed, around and around, creating a magic spell that lasted until the music stopped.

We begged for more, and more, and more. Then Lucille set the gramophone to a slow speed and the record growled slowly with the waltzers moving in tired whirls but still keeping time.

'Enough, enough,' Mrs Richards cried. 'All of you should be playing out of doors; now run out into the sunshine.'

But we never tired of watching the dancers and whenever we could we went to Lucille's to see them. One day, they were bent and danced leaning backwards. Some of us laughed, others were saddened without quite knowing why. Poo, trying to fix them, had broken something and no longer could they enchant us with their fascinating dance. A period of fantasy had ended but we had all learned a lesson in which grace and beauty had played a part.

Jessie and I were now taking music lessons from Miss Killikelly and as we now lived at Richmond Hill, a mile and a half uphill from school, we changed our lesson time from the mornings to the afternoons after school. Thus, three times a week we remained in town until Daddy passed to pick us up at about five or six o'clock.

Miss Killikelly's home was a three storeyed house with door-length windows on the second floor. In the top level, Miss Killikelly and her mother lived and gave music lessons. One half of the second story was occupied by her brother Mr Brian Killikelly, artist, who had his studio and bedroom there. The other half was occupied by the Cochrane girls. The bottom, at street level, was rented by a firm of lawyers.

After our music lessons were over we dashed downstairs to the Cochrane girls, Bernice, Louise, Mona and Alethea, and sat in their cosy sitting room. We enjoyed looking out of the windows at a ship coming into harbour, at Eustace Watts racing his bicycle up and down the street, or chatting across the street to the McLeish girls.

The Cochranes were products of Miss Allen's School for Gentlewomen and we were not permitted to hang out of the windows. We sat by them and could see and converse just as well.

These marvellous people put up with us three times a week, regaling us with aerated drinks and biscuits and very often chocolates, paradise plums and Turkish delight.

Bernice and her mother left for America and we still visited, not really feeling the gap, as we were always given news and read bits of exciting letters. We were also always allowed to see the contents of splendid packages sent from the United States.

Then Mona left, but I cannot remember when, as life continued in a steady stream of laughter and preparation for parties and Jessie and I would admire the gorgeous dresses and high-heeled shoes to our hearts' content.

As time went on we learnt from these delightful people that there were different shades of rouge and lipstick and that sisters could share, weep with each other and differences could be settled without bashing each other's heads in. Fingernails were things of beauty, not to be used for scratching opponents' faces.

One afternoon, Louise came in, changed her clothes, put on slippers and went to the bookcase. Armed with a formidable looking leather-bound book, she threw herself on her bed and began reading.

There was nothing for us to see in the street. We had finished our homework and Eustace had gone to England. I peeped around the corner at Louise lost in her book. Jessie and I crept into her room and sat on the edge of the bed.

'What are you reading? Is it exciting?'

Louise lay quiet for a long while then she said, 'Come, Jessie, you on the right, Nellie, you on the left.'

We three lay on the bed, our eyes on the book and Louise said, 'We'll read this one.'

She turned to *The Merchant of Venice*. She read and our eyes followed silently.

When Daddy arrived we wanted to remain but could not, so Louise promised to continue reading next time we came.

For days we read and my heart thumped and thumped when I realised that the pound of flesh demanded would be from Antonio's heart and of course he would die.

Louise was wonderful. She opened up a whole new world for us. From one play we moved on to another, shocked by crudities, sympathetic with lovers, moved by great loyalties, excited by intrigue and always eager to read on. Then we moved house again, further into the country, to the Great House at Morne Jaloux. Our afternoon visits continued and Jessie and I wished Louise could have been our sister and live with us forever.

Louise was about fifteen years our senior and we never realised it. We would tell her our little troubles and get good advice. We would tell her our little jokes and she would laugh with us. She was marvellous.

Through the years we remained friends. We got married and she came to our showers and receptions. Her other sisters married and she stayed single. We could not understand this. She was goodlooking, kind, clever and had a superb figure. We told her so.

One day she told us, 'I'm going to surprise all of you and get married so don't keep nagging me.'

She did get married and bought from my father a piece of land a minute's walk from our home. She is now our closest neighbour and we share the same driveway. Who better could we have chosen to have living so near to us than Louise?

A few years ago, when my mother was gravely ill, I left my husband in Trinidad to be with her. Except for two visits which I made to Trinidad and one which he made to Grenada, we did not see each other for one and a half years. If it were not for Louise, I would have gone stark, staring mad. Mother suffered from anarthria and the only person who could understand her needs was me. She had great crying spells which tore at my heart. Poor darling.

When she was asleep in the afternoons I would trot downhill to Louise for the odd half-hour and she would let me pour out my distress for Mother and loneliness for my husband. She would soothe me with her silence and distract me with tit-bits of witty gossip and I would run uphill to Mother a new person, ready for the evening and broken night's rest. Ready for everything except my mother's death.

But back to the Great House at Morne Jaloux.

Mother was having a housewarming party. The house overflowed with visitors of whom I can recall Mr and Mrs Neal Smith, the Smith girls, Thelma, Audrey, Heather, the Campbells, Rupert and Ivan, Gittens Knight, Nanny, Ulric Lawrence and his wife, and Gladys Johnson. But there were at least fifty other people there.

After a colossal lunch, during which I kept feeling that I wanted to 'poopse' (pass air) but could not, Jessie decided to fill the Roman bath which was six and a half feet deep and had a number of steps leading to the bottom. The taps were running, the water level rising. When the bath was about half full we decided to bathe.

Jessie, May, Daisy and I went to the bathroom and undressed. Still very uncomfortable that I could not 'poopse', the thought struck me that something must be stuck (perhaps a piece of toilet paper) in my bottom. I told this to Jessie and she thought she had better look.

Adjoining our boundary was an acre or two of land owned by a strong, ugly man called Allen. We nicknamed him 'Monkey Allen', calling him this behind his back. We were, however, most civil when face to face with him as we were secretly a little afraid of his strength.

Allen was working his canepiece and we could hear his cutlass chopping away and his voice singing Sankies.

Jessie told me to bend over, looked and bawled, 'A *worm*.' She fled through the door to the nearest person for help. She fled towards the canefield screaming, 'Monkey Allen, give me two sticks, there's a worm in Nellie's bottom.' She was naked.

May, also naked, ran upstairs, into the drawing room, directly to Gittens Knight, lisping excitedly, 'Mitter Nat, Mitter Nat, tumtin up in Neyyie intide.'

Daisy, also naked, was simply running. She ran and ran from that worm and had to be looked for.

I stood in the bathroom, naked, fixed with terror to the spot, still in a bent position.

Mother came, covered me up and took me to the dressing room. There, with the aid of toilet paper, she extracted the worm, which I refused to look at.

All the children came and examined it in the slop pail and from descriptions I am sure it must have been six feet long, vivid pink with grey blotches and evil looking.

I was given worm powders and was later told that I had passed another worm of similar size and colour.

Miss Killikelly moved into a smaller house; Alethea Cochrane got married; Louise lived with her married sister; so we waited for Daddy after our music lessons at the Walter Knight's home in Church Street.

This family had a mother who didn't say much but every deed to us was one of kindness. If we fell and cut ourselves, there was no fuss. She would bathe the wound, plaster it and would tell us to play a less boisterous game.

We were allowed to bring out the ice-cream freezer, mix custards and churn buckets of delicious ice-cream. She seldom ate any of it but would sit at the window looking at us enjoy ourselves, sometimes laughing when we ate ourselves cold and asked for a blanket.

The only thing I ever saw her get annoyed about was when some child had dirty teeth. To that child she would say, 'Reindeer could feed on your teeth, clean them.' Or, 'You're raising a pasture for the cows on your incisors, clean them.'

The Knights had a pianola and we would insert roll after roll and pedal away, pushing levers wildly and making the music go slow, then fast, then so very fast that the music sounded high and crazy.

One of the Knight boys got hold of a roll of wallpaper and decided to make music. With razor blades he cut the notes in the paper and after a half hour's work we tried this out. To everyone's amazement, the pianola pumped out a tune. The roll was taken out and more and more cuts made. When the paper was completely covered with little cuts the roll was reinserted and the result positively weird. While we, pedalling, thought, 'What a long pause, it must be finished,' a bass note would startle us and a weak treble would ping in the air.

Mrs Knight discovered what use had been made of her wallpaper. She said between clenched teeth, 'My God, couldn't you have used something else – newspapers for one?' And she let it go at that.

The sea, blue, clean, vast, played an important part in our childhood. I recall being thrown off a sail boat when I was not quite four years old, and told to swim for shore. Jessie was also thrown overboard. We obeyed. So it seems as though we were always able to swim, but we were taught to respect the sea and learned the well-known West Indian proverb: 'The sea 'en ha' no branch.' Now that we were a little older we were given permission to picnic on Saturdays. Sometimes, these were Brownie or Guide picnics in which we passed cooking, fire-lighting and swimming tests, but more often we were just a bunch of girls going to the beach or country with tins of bully beef, bread, fruit, cakes and very often split peas, salt beef and flour for making a grand cook-up of split pea soup and dumplings. We always ate enormously and came home exhausted as we walked many miles to the beach or country.

By the time I was nine and Jessie eleven, walking became our hobby. Any holiday or Saturday, Jessie and I would take off and cover a minimum of sixteen miles in the scorching sun without batting an eyelid.

Three walks stand out in memory.

One Good Friday, after a breakfast of fruit, cocoa, boiled eggs, hot-cross buns and marmalade, we thought we should go to the botanic gardens and smoke the two cigarettes Jessie had pinched from Daddy's tin of Capstans. We couldn't light them, as we had forgotten to bring matches, so after catching a couple of crayfish in the ponds we thought a walk would be in order.

We were soon at the sugar factory in Westerhall, some four miles away, hungry and tired. Mr 'Diable Negre' (pronounced Jabneg) Renwick saw us and told us, 'Great seeing you girls walking, nobody walks these days,' and to our dismay he jumped in his car and drove off. We *did* want a ride, oh, how hungry we were!

Well, the only thing to do was to continue walking. Jessie had an idea. 'Let's go to the Alexis' house at Providence'. Providence was some ten miles further on. We passed La Sagesse and went deeper into the country. It was now half past one, the pitch was so hot that it burnt our soles through the leather of our shoes and we began walking on the verge, which was all sunburnt by the dry weather and equally hot. We were thirsty and came to a house.

62

On this house was written: 'Enoch de Gale, licenced to buy cocoa'. Jessie said, 'They're East Indians and bound to be Presbyterians,' and we knocked with the little lion knocker on the front door.

A lady came to the door and said, 'Good afternoon.' We bade her the same and asked if she could give us a glass of water please. She asked us inside and oh, how cool it was. Before we had finished our drink we were questioned as to why two little girls should be wandering in St David's and we told our story.

'You must be hungry,' she said and brought us a tray with tea, hot-cross buns, cheese and guava jelly, oh yes, and some delightful little toasted cassava cakes. We tried our best to eat slowly and after a while asked, 'How far is it to Providence?'

Seeing a telephone, we asked permission to use it and rang the Alexis' and spoke to Lionel, their elder son, who had just returned from England. He said, 'I'll be with you in a jiffy.'

Lionel dashed over in his sports car and was thrilled at our pluck in walking that distance. 'Where do you plan to go now?' he inquired.

'Oh,' we showed off, 'around the island, via Hermitage.'

'Holy Mackerel!' he drawled, 'that'll take you through the night, a pity I have to work tomorrow or I'd come with you.'

We decided to let Lionel drop us at Hermitage where his cousins lived and agreed that we would walk on through Sauteurs and back to St George's later on.

Lionel whisked us off in his car. His cousins at Hermitage were thrilled with our escapade and marvelled gently that we had walked so far. Mrs Alexis asked, 'Do your parents know where you are?' Finding out that they did not, she made us telephone immediately. It was now five p.m. and Daddy asked, 'From where are you speaking?'

'Hermitage,' Jessie replied.

'*Hermitage?*' he shouted. '*Let me speak to Mrs Alexis!*'

Mrs Alexis was told to prevent us from walking any further and that Daddy was on his way to meet us and take us home.

Nibbling a nut from a little silver dish Mrs Alexis murmured, 'Your father is angry, my dears.' This we found to be an understatement and we were given reason to remember that such marathon walks without parental permission must never never be made again.

Another walk took us to the Grand Etang – all uphill – some 1,980 feet above sea level. This was a planned walk, approved of by our parents.

We took haversacks with juice, sandwiches, water, bread and cheese. At five a.m. Vince, Jessie, Selby, Majorie, Caryl, Cynthia and I set off. After three miles Cynthia turned back.

We stopped off at the Ogilvie's at Mount Gay to say good morning and Bonnie gave us coconuts and mangoes; we paddled in the stream and took off again, not stopping until we reached the Grand Etang, which filled the crater of an extinct volcano. This lake was reputed to be the home of mermaids and to be bottomless. This was our destination.

We breakfasted on bread, cheese and fruit and began looking for monkeys in the trees. After half an hour, we were again hungry so we emptied the haversacks and consumed everything in sight, even picking crumbs from the wax paper which had wrapped the sandwiches.

It was not yet noon and we began talking about mermaids and saracas (shango dances) held by the villagers to appease the mermaids, and the colossal amount of food that was brought to the lakeside to feed these maidens of the lake. *Food!* My, we were hungry and Jessie remembered that in the grub Mother had given, she had seen two tins of sardines. Vince looked guilty and said he had put *one* tin in his pocket. He gave this to us and after bursting it open on jagged bits of iron that protruded from the little jetty, we swallowed this, running our fingers around the tin to get the last drop of oil.

Still frightfully hungry, we decided to go home and have a good meal. Vince spotted a monkey and running excitedly, pointing to it, he tripped and fell. Out of his pocket tumbled another tin of sardines. Food, we thought and with one mind ran towards the tin. The tin shifted towards the edge of the jetty. Our pounding feet raced to catch it and within an inch it tipped over and sank to the bottom of the lake.

Vince had already begun his record-making sprint homewards and by the time we all met again our anger had dissolved into laughter.

The third walk which I will never forget was Vince's idea. It was again to be the uphill climb to Grand Etang.

The people of Beaulieu (pronounced Bo-lee-o, *not* Bewlee) were holding a saraca for rain, and the mermaids of Grand Etang would be left many cooked chickens, roast sheep and pig, also freshly baked bread and cakes and an assortment of fruit. The saraca would be held on the night of the new moon so we must go to the Grand Etang the following morning.

We left home at five a.m. on the appointed day – Clive and Gordon Commissiong, Terry Evans, Jessie, Vince, Selby and I. Our only provisions were empty bottles which we would fill with water at the standpipe nearest our goal.

We arrived at the lake famished and tired. The food laid out for the mermaids far exceeded our expectations but our minds, filled with fear of obeah and mal yeux, made our stomachs contract and our mouths dry. We drank water and lay still on the grass, dying from exhaustion and hunger.

A bird hopped among the cooked dishes picking and eating and Vince said that the bird had not died, so why should we? Two monkeys hopped by and daintily took two bananas; they loped off chatting excitedly with their prize.

Vince picked up a chicken and buried his teeth in it. He did not die. Soon the seven of us sat up to a Lucullean feast and were so filled that we could barely crawl the sixteen miles home.

We kept this feast a secret.

Clive and Gordon Commissiong had an older brother called Vivian. He was so shy that he never came to play. He and Vince became friendly and maybe because Mother dressed us in little khaki pants and shirts he got friendly with Jessie and me, and I think he considered us 'boys'.

Vince asked Vivian home for a weekend and on the Saturday afternoon, on the front lawn, we played 'Who sees the Robbers passing by', 'Sally Sally Water', 'Jane and Louise' and 'There's a Brown Girl in the Ring'. I was the girl in the ring and the singers requested that I hug and kiss my partner. I flew to Vivian, threw my skinny arms around his neck and kissed him.

Daddy was looking at the game and told me to come inside immediately. The lecture I received about developing into a hussy scared me off kissing until I was nineteen and even now I can count on one hand the men who have been kissed by me.

I feel I have missed a lot of fun.

In my mind, Vivian became my boyfriend and the heroics I performed in imagination would put Batman to shame. I saved Vivian from drowning; I discovered lost treasure and presented this to him; I became a missionary and saved his soul from damnation; I nursed him through crippling illness; I married him on his deathbed and on his death, stabbed myself through the heart and we were buried in the same coffin.

The daydreams always reduced me to tears and I was always being asked, 'Why are you crying again?'

Vivian grew up and became a parson. Sitting with my fiancé during his induction service, I thought of my childish dreams and was sad.

During the holidays at Morne Jaloux Great House, we had a superb time: taking visitors to the tomb of La Grenade, a French general, who was supposed to have given Grenada his name, changing it from Conception Isle; making and setting traps for doves; picnicking and revelling in tales of the supernatural.

We made friends with two impoverished ladies who lived in the next village and who, because of their terribly reduced circumstances, always wept when Mother asked them to sit in her drawing-room. They were then in their sixties and God alone knows why they were left to drag out their lives until in their late eighties. We visited them for years and years after we left this area and were always welcomed with open arms.

Vince had got a super cricket bat at Christmas, complete with stumps, bails and ball. We formed an eleven and would play anyone, anywhere. Mother was captain and a formidable batsman.

As our home was built in an old fort we found wonderful coins, buttons and cannon balls. We did not bother to inform our parents of these finds, and so bits of history got lost behind doll's shop counters and as payment at games of marbles; cannon balls were shot into ponds and canefields in mock battles and buttons were sewn to replace lost eyes from various teddy bears.

We now had a new batch of servants as Eva's husband was lost at sea while fishing and she decided to work in town. Ellen, with no more babies to tend, and a too long walk to and from work, went to another home with babies and Lettie went to Trinidad.

We now had Freda, a delightful person and years younger than Eva (we called her Perweeda), Francis the maid, Pitt the chauffeur and, although I can see the yardman's face, I cannot recall his name. But he once roasted a centipede and ate it.

Perweeda and Francis (this was her surname) were the most superstitious women imaginable. They believed in everything from obeah to jumbies.

We were fed on gruesome tales of obeah, frightening sagas of ghosts, loupgaroux – the human vampires; la diablesse – the female devil who lured males to their death and had a cloven foot; and hair-raising episodes of jumbies.

This reputedly haunted Great House with its large rooms where one was forever skipping across courtyard or pantry to get to the other side of the house was the ideal setting for ghost stories convincingly told by servants to wide-eyed believing children.

Whenever Mother and Daddy were out in the evenings, Perweeda and Francis remained with us as neither would leave the Great House on their own and walk into the village after dark.

We loved both these women and on our afternoon walks would visit their homes, climb their fruit trees, admire their pictures and love their spotlessly clean sitting rooms. We became acquainted with their families and thought Perweeda's family such clever people as one and all were wonderful cooks who all had fabulous calves from much walking. We were all slender-legged.

One night, when we had been left with these two women in this haunted old house, Perweeda went into the kitchen and turned the mortar so that its open mouth was resting on the table. She hid the pestle in a cupboard.

'Why are you doing that?' we asked.

'Chile,' she replied, 'this thing they call loupgaroux (pronounced ligaroo) comes in the night and before it sucks your blood it puts its skin in the mortar. If you quick, quick, and they sucking someone else, you could put salt and black pepper on the skin and they cyant put it on and so die.'

Loupgaroux also had the capacity of turning themselves into balls of fire and could fly from victim to victim, visible to anyone who was crazy enough to be still awake.

Perweeda looked through the kitchen door, pointing to the plateau-like pasture a mile away. 'I see them rolling on the pasture,' she said, 'a huge ball of fire and downhill they'd tumble, not catching a single blade of grass afire.'

We all crept close to her, Francis closest of all.

We stared in the direction of the pasture, and sure enough a huge ball of fire began hovering and dancing, bright enough to illuminate the grass. Spellbound with terror, we watched. It floated to the edge of the hill and with terrific speed it pitched downhill, rolling and tumbling, increasing in size until it disappeared. Not a blade of grass on the hillside had caught fire.

We had seen a loupgaroux. And, tightly packed in a solid little group, we made our way to Jessie's bedroom. Very frightened, we moved to my bedroom, which seemed safer, and sat on the floor where Perweeda told us of other things she had seen, making herself, Francis and us shiver with fear.

The cat came into the room. It was a black cat called

Minnie. This started Perweeda off on black cats and the jumbies that entered them.

God alone knows what happened but Minnie arched her back, her tail stuck out straight and every hair stood up in stiff bristles. She raised a paw, claws out, scooted across the room and straight up the bedroom wall, where, with nothing to cling to, she fell on the bed and ran shrieking into the yard.

Francis had taken out her chaplet and was muttering what sounded like, 'Hailymarymmmmmmmmmmm.'

The wind began blowing and howling round the house, the lamps went out and we piled one on top of the other in a stranglehold of a heap. When breathing seemed impossible, Perweeda pushed us off and suggested we go to the kitchen for matches to relight the lamps.

At the door, we stuck, as all pushed to get through at the same time. Somehow or other, we reached the kitchen. Lamps lit, Francis armed herself with black pepper and suggested we go to Madam's room as this was nearer the front door. Here we kept glancing through the windows to see if Daddy's car lights were approaching. On his arrival, he explained to us the phenomenon of the ball of fire – cow dung, phosphorus, gases. The cat he was sure had had a fit. Jessie was allowed to bring her bed into my room to have the company of May and me.

Although we were genuinely frightened of 'lost creatures', we persistently implored Perweeda to tell us more and more tales. Her supply as inexhaustible and daily we dreaded the approach of night when the supernatural roamed and got up to mischief.

In that house we, including Mother and Daddy, heard the sound of carriages rolling up to the front door, silver being rattled in drawers, faint music and pounding footsteps. Daddy tried but could give no logical explanation of these noises and Vince, Jessie, Selby, May and I lived on a diet of the ghostly damned.

Selby, because of a bruised toe, and I with fever, stayed from school one day. I really had no fever at all but as Selby was not going to school I thought it would be more fun at home, so pretended.

We played with Vince's train all morning and after lunch, with Mother having her rest, decided to go and ask Monkey Allen for some sugarcane. He was very nice to us, choosing two thick, long ones which he peeled with his cutlass.

We took these with many thanks and went to the cow pond, which was a sunken pit filled with brown water. It had a little downhill track and was overhung with cedar trees, so quite dark and cool, and, without a great stretch of imagination, eerie.

We sucked our canes, washed our fingers in the dirty water and got on to our favourite topic: jumbies! Discussing the cat Minnie, which we firmly believed had been taken possession of by a devil, Selby uttered a horrible thought: 'Suppose something entered me and something entered you and we didn't know who we were!'

We pondered this a while and got alarmed. I said, 'I do feel different.'

Selby felt different too. We gazed at each other in dread and knew without a doubt that we had been 'entered'.

We began to cry and Selby asked me the question which shattered my wits, 'Are you Nellie?'

Having some doubts of this myself, I was in a terrible state and asked him tremblingly if he was he and what we should do.

Holding hands, we scrambled up the path. Selby gave me a leaf to hold and said, 'The one with the leaf is Nellie,' and he grabbed a stick muttering, 'The one with the stick is Selby.'

It took us ten minutes to get to the house, where we burst in on a sleeping Mother, jabbering, 'Who am I? Is she, she?', the questions dissolving into hysterics.

Poor Mother had a time sorting us out into individuals called Nellie and Selby, two tots, who finally decided that school was much better than being 'entered.'

An hour later, Francis was cleaning shoes in the courtyard and Selby and I joined her. Each time she buffed she sang a note of music and between the flop of cloth on the leather and her notes, a lively tune grew. Selby bowed and asked me to dance.

Soon we were doing a lively jig and Perweeda came out to watch. The music continued and Perweeda caught hold of a corn broom and sashayed round and round the yard. Laughing, we threw ourselves on the step and Perweeda hugged us saying what wonderful dancers we were and we became again very pleased with life.

Mr David Lang who also worked in the Department of Agriculture with Daddy, but in the country, had come into town for meetings and was asked to stay with us.

Vince and Selby were moved into Jessie's room, May went into the dressing-room and Jessie moved in with me. Mr Lang would have the boys' room. We were banished from the dining room quite early that evening and consoled ourselves cutting out pictures from magazines and sticking them in our scrap books. We got sleepy so got into bed without tidying up our mess.

It was a lovely, cool night and Jessie and I snuggled under our blankets and fell fast asleep.

I awoke and could feel Jessie gripping me with fear. Alert, I could hear slippered feet dragging themselves towards our bed.

Now if anything bothered me, I would keep quiet and seek the best way out. Jessie was entirely different; she would let it be heard by all and sundry that things did not suit or please her and someone *must* come to her aid.

The footsteps approached the bed and Jessie yelled, 'Oh Gawd, help, *help!*'

Vince in the adjoining room did not wait for anything more and shot out of bed making for the safety of his own room, where he was grabbed by Mr Lang and sent back to his bed.

The footsteps started again, sweeping towards us, nearer, nearer and Jessie yelled, '*Oh, Gawd, Oh Gawd, O Gawd!*'

We both knew it was an evil ghost. I begged her to keep

quiet as Mother and Daddy would be ashamed of us, what with a guest in the house and all that! Jessie cuffed me and bawled, '*I don't care!*' And the footsteps scraping the floor came yet nearer.

'*Murder, police, help!*' shouted Jessie, and Vince again took off to Mr Lang, who was thoroughly annoyed and literally chased him back.

So far, Selby had slept through everything.

'Hush Jessie, no one can hear us. Let's pretend we're asleep,' I whispered.

'*Pretend!*' bellowed Jessie, '*this is no time to pretend!*' and, as the steps swished across the floor, the scream she emitted sent Vince *and* Selby scuttling. Selby made a beeline for Mother's bed where the jump he made awoke both parents.

'Jumbies,' he said, 'jumbies all about.'

Jessie's bellows were like angry waves. They pounded relentlessly one after the other and Mother and Daddy arrived bearing lamps. Sitting on the side of our bed, we hugged them, trying to tell our tale of the slippered ghost; just then, the feet began approaching again. We buried our heads in their laps, utterly terrified.

Daddy made us sit up and very sternly told us that our fright had been caused by ourselves. Pointing to the many pieces of paper we had cut from magazines and had left on the floor, he told us, 'Keep looking.'

We did. The breeze blew, scraping the crumpled paper along the floor. We felt awfully silly and were tucked into bed with a reassuring, 'Good night.'

In the morning at breakfast, Mr Lang, on hearing our side of the story, gave his, saying how he'd nearly taken a pot shot at Vince, mistaking him for a burglar.

We laughed so much in the beautiful daylight that Selby was made to leave the table. He had popped a piece of toast into his mouth. Then, because he was overcome with laughter, the food had shot out, sprayed across the table and landed in the butter dish.

Another evening, Mother and Daddy had to go to a cocktail party and Perweeda told us she had a surprise for us . . . after supper we were going to have a corn roast in the yard as she had brought a present of sixteen ears of corn – two each.

Naturally, we wanted an early supper so we could get cracking at the corn, but Perweeda said, 'No, we are going to have it in the moonlight and ask riddles.'

As soon as the moon came up, huge and wise-looking it shone, Perweeda, with a lighted coalpot and Francis with a basket of green ears of corn, led the way to the front lawn. We stripped the green protective layers from the corn and the marvellous smell of roast-corn soon filled the air.

Perweeda asked in general, 'Water stand up, water lay down?'

We answered triumphantly, 'Cane!'

She fired another riddle, 'Round as a biscuit, busy as a bee?'

'A clock!' we shouted.

'A lady in a boat with a red petticoat and two stones down her throat?'

'A cherry!' we screamed.

'A pretty lady in a green dress, yellow chemise and brown hair?' she asked.

'Corn!' we shouted.

'Oh, you know all the answers,' Perweeda lamented. 'We'll have nancy stories instead.'

We went through the formal opening of telling nancy stories. The narrator said, 'Tim, Tim,' and the listeners replied, 'Brashus.'

'Once upon a time,' said Perweeda, handing each of us a hot, roasted corn, 'there was a city where only rats lived. There were big rats and little rats, good rats and bad rats, pretty rats and ugly rats, and one day a large grey cat wandered into this city and began eating all the rats. He ate good rats and bad rats, big rats and little rats, pretty rats and ugly rats. So the head rat called a meeting to see what they could do to get rid of Monsieur Chat. After they talked and talked late into the night without finding a solution and were preparing to go home, one old, wizened rat stood up and squeaked,

"Let us make a drum so we can beat it when we see Monsieur Chat approaching."

' "Bon, bon," they chorused. "C'est idée fine, mais avec quoi nous fait cette drum?"

'Up sprang the little old rat again, who said, "We each must donate a piece of our skin and Monsieur le Tailor will make us a grand drum."

'They all agreed to give a piece of skin, all except the ugliest rat, Monsieur Laid. "Oh no," he said, "no one is going to get a piece of my skin."

'Each rat, little, big, ugly, pretty, good and bad, except the one who said "No, no," cut off a piece of his skin and the tailor worked for days and nights and at last the drum was made.

'The rats were very proud of the drum and only those who worked hard towards improving the colony were appointed to beat it, and soon, Monsieur Chat, unable to have rat dinners, departed and left them in peace.

'One day, a strange rat limped, gasping, into the city. Everyone gathered around staring curiously.

' "I am Monsieur Petit Rat from La Sagesse," he panted. "We need the help of every honest rat to get rid of a huge cat that is in our parish killing us all." He tottered and fell, so exhausted was he from his long journey.

'The town rats lifted him into the cool, bathed him with water from the well, and gave him a cheese sandwich and some ginger beer.

'The drum was beaten and all rats gathered. They decided that they would go to La Sagesse to give what help they could.

'Monsieur Laid, who had contributed no skin, refused to go.

'As soon as the party left, Monsieur Laid rubbed his feet together in delight and squeaked, "Ils ça allez, ils ça allez, maintenant mon rappe le drum."

'He mounted the platform and stood with his mangy paws on the drum. "Thump, thump," he beat, singing:

Tee dee boom, tee dee boom,
Dey gon' dey done gon'
Dey gon' to goat heaven
Dey wan' me cut out
Piete a me kin kin! Oh!
Tee dee boom, tee dee boom!

'Mais, mes enfants,' Perweeda continued, 'this drum music was so sweet that Monsieur Laid charmed himself and he played the drum from morning till night and could not stop. He played for days and days, the beat getting weaker and weaker and at last, with a faint thud, he dropped dead. And, the wire ben' and the story end.'

'Oh, Perweeda,' we cried, taking another corn from Francis, 'tell us more, tell us more.' And Perweeda, shelling a few grains of corn, shook them in her closed fist saying, 'Ships sail, sail fast, how many men I have on deck?' We guessed and soon were in a delightful game, winning and losing grains of corn at a rapid rate.

'Tim, Tim,' said Francis.

'Brashus,' we replied.

Francis related, 'Compère Tigre and Compère Ziah were very good friends. Compère Tigre was a big tiger and Compère Ziah was a little spider. So one morning Compère Ziah in his tree saw Compère Tigre passing underneath and called out, "Bon matin Compère Tigre, est ou ça allez?"

'Compère Tigre looked up and said, "Bonjour Compère Ziah, mon ça allez nambouk."

' "Today only Tuesday, Compère Tigre, why you going to town?"

' "Me daughter getting married, Compère, and I have to buy thing little bit, little bit till ah get everything."

' "Oh, ho," said Compère Ziah, his brain doing a double flip. "What you buying today?"

' "Ah going for la beurre for the gateau, mon cher."

' "C'est bon," said Ziah. "When you passing back, give me a shout."

'Compère Tigre bought and paid for his goods and on his

way back with the pail of butter called out: "Ay, Compère Ziah!"

'Compère Ziah spun a long thread and dropped in front of Compère Tigre. "Compère Tigre," he said, "ah been thinking and ah feel in me bones you mussen go hom wid all dat butter. You have too much chile and afore de wedding dey go eat all and you cyant make no cake for de guesses."

'Compère Tigre thought a while and said: "You have a point, ami, wha' fa do?"

' "Hang it in me tree," suggested Ziah, "and ah go guard it fo you."

'The butter was hung in the tree and Compère Ziah decided that he would have a taste. All week he kept dipping into the butter and when Compère Tigre passed on another journey to the shop he called out, "How tings going, Compère Ziah?"

'Compère Ziah replied, "Quarter, quarter!" Ziah had eaten a quarter of the butter.

'On other trips when Tigre asked Ziah how things were he answered, "Half, half!" and "Three quarters, three quarters!"

'Compère Tigre was a bit slow of mind so he thought that clever Ziah was just being funny with his answers and so, the following week when he passed, and in answer to his question Ziah told him "All," he merely shook his head and said, "Ziah boy, next week is de wedding. Ah passing Wednesday for de butter and we go catch up at the wedding, eh?"

'Ziah said: "Fine, man, fine, man."

'Compère Ziah was in a dilemma. He had eaten all the butter and the pail hung empty, swinging in the breeze. What was he to do?

'*He took a dose of salts* and soon the butter pail was full of the results.

'On Wednesday morning, Compère Tigre came under the tree and called out, "Bonjour, Compère Ziah, moca venir pour le beurre."

' "Look up," cried Compère Ziah, and when Tigre did so

he emptied the contents of the pail in his face, and de wire ben' and de story end.'

'Now,' said Perweeda, 'it is time for all good children to go to sleep.'

We hugged and kissed these delightful women, thanking them for a lovely party and went off to sleep.

We had been told that the gru-gru patch was haunted by people who 'deal with the Devil.'

We simply loved gru-grus – after cracking the hard skin we would suck the slimy, yellow, fibrous coating until we got to the shell, then we would bash the little nuts open and eat the hard jelly. Gru-grus were found under gru-gru palms, so how were we going to get them without meeting the Devil?

Another little friend, Malcolm Banfield, told us that he did not believe all that nonsense, and he would come with us. Armed with a large basket, we set off for the gru-gru patch.

There, before picking up the fruit, we examined the under-growth to see if any serpents were coiled in the branches. We saw beautiful red and white ones and a black and white one. Knowing them to be harmless, we began collecting the little round balls.

The earth began shaking and at first too stunned, we stood staring at each other, then in a couple of strides we rolled forward and gripped each other. A serpent dropped with a thud, uncoiled itself and slithered further into the bush.

The earth again shook violently and a voice as loud as thunder that echoed round and around us asked, '*Who you down in there?*'

We catapulted up the hill, scrambled home frantically and flopped on the garden bench. In amazement, looking at Vince, Jessie asked, 'Vince, in all that commotion, you remembered the basket of gru-grus?'

Yes, in that horrible scramble for home, Vince had had one thought, 'Devil or no, I came for gru-grus and I'm going with gru-grus.'

Selby, however, was in deep trouble. He had that day been

given a new pair of shoes and had been told that on our afternoon walk, he could wear them. Unknown to Francis, he had put them on and was determined to even sleep in them that night. In his mad flight from the Devil's voice he had lost a shoe and we were as worried as he.

We told the servants and Pitt, the chauffeur, told us that he had been born 'upside down' and was left-handed so the Devil could not trouble him. He would go and look for the shoe. He found it, and very grateful, we offered him the basket of nuts which he kindly refused.

Even now, I cannot understand the vibrating depth of that voice. We must have had an earth tremor or two and somebody must have been in the gru-gru patch besides us. Perhaps a prisoner from the nearby gaol? Whatever it was, it was a hair-raising experience and we avoided that area ever after.

It was said that one or two people in the village were 'dealing with the Devil' and nearly all the houses were marked with the sign of the cross. This sign was also effective against loupgaroux and les diablesses.

In order to 'deal with the Devil', one was supposed to read the Sixth and Seventh Book of Moses. It was also said that at one part of the books you were warned to stop and consider before turning the page, as, from here on, you now entertained the Prince of Darkness. Before turning the page, the page with the warning, you had to get a preparation of silk cotton seeds, ashes of a white cock, petals of a white rose and white sand from the seashore. From the four cardinal points of the island you scattered this concoction repeating the Lord's Prayer backwards. The Devil then appeared in gruesome form and you pledged your soul to him.

Riches, glory and fame attended you, but according to the servants, you paid the price yearly of one soul.

The servants also told us that at horse-racing time, a young child was always murdered and its heart given to a special horse in his feed, so that it could win the main event. Also, the meeting place of the Devil was under a silk cotton tree.

The walk from our home to town, some three miles, had

at least twenty silk cotton trees, so daily we lived in fear. Jessie and I hold, I am sure, a record for repeating the Lord's Prayer and the twenty-third Psalm.

Of obeah, we heard lots. Mixing pineapple and lime and throwing the liquid on someone's doorstep would result in a life sore for the person who stepped in it. This is done if one bears a spite against anyone.

Jessie and I looked at everything we stepped on.

If one had a bad disease – we could not imagine what this could be except consumption – one could bathe in a mixture of spring water, ratchet leaves and copper coins and, at midnight, the bath contents thrown in the crossroads, then whoever picked up the coppers would get the disease and the bather would be cured.

Jessie and I changed all our money into three-penny pieces.

At school we were told, and every girl believed, that the Head, Miss Garraway, could read our minds but you had to look her in the eye. I often had to look Miss G. in the eye and I always thought of St Peter with long, white-feathered wings flying over the church steeple with the communion chalice in his hands. If Miss Garraway could read minds, she must have thought me crazy.

With hundreds of such tales, the ghosts, jumbies, la diablesse, loupgaroux and 'entering', it is amazing that we lived and grew up as other children did.

Jessie had now decided that as Daisy was no longer a baby, she was going to have one. I asked her how and she said you got a catalogue and ordered it. I thought that would need lots of money and told Mother that Jessie wanted to have a baby, and she told us we would have to wait until we grew up and got married.

Jessie was determined and began making enquiries. She came flying to me after school one afternoon and told me she had found out how to have a baby, but not now, after supper tonight she'd let me in the know.

After supper, we went to our rooms and Jessie told me to go and borrow the potty from my room.

'Now,' she said, 'sit on it and *force*.'

We both sat on our potties and forced and forced. Red in the face and grunting for all we were worth, we forced.

Mother came in and said, 'What on earth are you doing?'

We replied together, 'We're having a baby.'

Another little lecture about growing up and getting married and we were no nearer the truth than before.

Not long after this, Jessie informed me that she did not want me in the bath when she was bathing. I couldn't understand this and complained. Mother said that everyone wanted a little privacy now and then and that Jessie was growing up.

I badgered Jessie mercilessly to let me bathe at the same time as we always did and she stunned me by saying, 'I can't. I have *four* hairs on my body.'

In this Great House Jessie and I held our last doll's tea party. We baked pastry shells and filled them with guava jelly, iced a small cake and made minute sandwiches filled with cheese and begonia flowers. We invited Mother, May and Daisy to this and we sat around the little table chatting in prim voices about the weather and May's imaginary Mrs Adee. We nibbled daintily on our super tough pastry and were complimented by Mother on the delightful spread.

When it was all over, the tea cloth folded, Jessie said, 'Well, that's that.' I knew that this was our farewell doll's tea party and wanted to cry.

Selby now became my closest friend, as Jessie thought herself too big to play silly games when she could be knitting or making Christmas presents. Selby was only sixteen months younger than me, whereas Jessie was three years older.

One morning, when Pitt had slipped to the back of the house for a bucket of water for the car and Daddy was still inside, Selby told me to 'Hop in,' and he got behind the wheel. He let down the brake and we took off for a drive. This was the most exhilarating experience in my seven years. Selby turned to tell me excitedly, 'I can drive, I can drive!' when there was a terrific thud and the front of the car went into a deep drain. Daddy, Pitt, and everyone within earshot came flying. We were lifted shaken from our seats and Daddy called some men who were laying a charcoal pit to come and help. Between them, they lifted the car on to the roadway. All Daddy said was, 'Headlight broken boy, don't do it again.'

The very next day Mummy decided that she did not like the strange noises of the house and the weird happenings of the previous night – the chimney of the lamp cut neatly, on a level with the globe, and the jalousies flapped and flapped, seemingly on their own. An armless hand was seen waving sadly.

Daddy, who knew that Mother would not make up such a story, was worried. Grandpa, William Galway Donovan, patriot and journalist, died the following day and everyone said that the 'happenings' were his farewell.

Selby and I were not allowed to go to the funeral. We understood that Grandpa was going to be put in a hole and hymns would be sung.

We sat on the front steps mending a kite and talked for a while about dying.

'He used to call me Jim,' said Selby. 'He said too that he was a son of the soil, "I must love my country, die for it, if I must." '

'He told me,' I said, ' "Nellie, you are a West Indian. In your lifetime the islands will be one large state. You must love this state. It will be yours." '

'We won't see him again, you know,' Selby added.

We both began to cry, and sobbed and sobbed to break our hearts.

Perweeda told us that it was better to cry at such a time and didn't we think it a good idea for us to make some fudge?

Shortly after this we moved and although I loved this house, I have no recollection at all of leaving it or saying, 'Goodbye House.'

May had a friend called Mrs Adee; an imaginary friend who called to see her every evening. Mrs Adee wore a hat. May, who did not yet know colours, told us that Mrs Adee wore a mauve hat.

Mrs Adee would sit with May at the doll's tea table and they would chat and laugh and May again surprised us by saying that Mrs Adee was Chinese. There were no Chinese that we knew of in Grenada. Sometimes May would hold hands with Mrs Adee after she was in bed, her little hand curved as though lying in another hand; it gave us the creeps.

Mother said that some children have little friends or guardian angels that no one else could see.

We didn't hear of Mrs Adee for a long, long while, until one afternoon there was a knock on the front door. May and Daisy, dressed in Mother's clothes, hats, shoes and handbags, waited on the steps. Mother glanced through the jalousies, saw them, and came to the door.

Very seriously she said, 'Good afternoon, do come in.'

May and Daisy minced in and sat, their lipstick set in prim little lines that stretched to the cheeks.

Mother said, 'I'm Ethel Donovan,' and turning to Daisy asked her name. Daisy was Mrs Blum.

'And you?' asked Mother, turning to May.

'I'm Mrs Adee,' May replied.

Mrs Blum offered, 'It's very hot weather, Mrs Donovan.'

Mother agreed, expressing the hope that the rains would break soon.

Mrs Adee inquired after Mrs Donovan's children and thought they were growing fast.

Mrs Donovan asked Mrs Adee about her children and Mrs Adee replied sadly that all three had been drowned.

Mrs Donovan offered lemonade and cake and the little ladies accepted and for the first time glanced – a triumphant glance – at each other.

They sipped and nibbled, Mother keeping a straight face. With the last crumb of cake downed, they rose saying that they must get home before the Night Brigade began.

That was the last mention of Mrs Adee. May and Daisy, happily undressing, thought that they had completely fooled

Mother and were more than happy about the lemonade and cake.

How well I remember the Night Brigade! You see, we were then still literally in the dark. No electricity, no sewerage system, very little ice.

For lights we used kerosene lamps, candles and Coleman gas lamps and lanterns.

Ice was made by an engineer called Mr Eric Smith and amusing tales circulated in St George's of people buying a pennyworth of ice and sending it by schooner to their families in the eastern town of Grenville who felt cheated on receiving a soggy piece of newspaper; of others packing a few pounds in their suitcases to take as a treat to their less fortunate friends in Sauteurs, another town twenty-five miles away in the north of the island: on arrival they found their clothes mildewed and ruined!

I still find the nicest drink of water is from an earthenware goblet. There were two shapes and most families had goblets placed in a jalousied recess called a 'cooler' – ferns grew in profusion in these coolers and my father grew lovely little strawberry vines which multiplied through holes and bore fruit for many a year.

No sewerage meant pôt chambres under the beds. There were enamelled ones and china ones. The china ones were beautifully decorated by the artist in the family and I recall bending forward to examine a spray of forget-me-nots, over-balancing and making a horrible mess on the floor.

Then there was also the Frenchman's hat, a beautiful piece of pottery in terracotta and brown, about three feet tall with a handle. The lip served as a seat. These were heavy pieces and often a maid would grumble at their weight.

There was always a night chair in the dressing room.

Pôt chambres, Frenchman's hats and pails from the night chair were emptied in the 'closet'.

The closet was a room in which there was a throne-like chair with a hole in the seat. Under the hole a giant pail stood, waiting to receive the contents of pôt chambres and hats.

The women who toted the pails were the simple, fearless type with ribald humour.

They made a weird procession, all jacketed and with large, floppy headgear. With pails, buckets and kerosene tins balanced on their heads, they performed their duties with incessant chatter.

Most people tried to be off the streets when the Night Brigade passed. If one happened to encounter them, the scented handkerchief, ever in readiness, was put to one's nose and one could expect a comment from one of the carriers.

Mother, on leaving the library at closing time – nine p.m. – put her hanky to her face as she saw the procession approaching. A voice from the bottom of a pan cackled, 'No stap yo' nose, is you own mess ah hauling.'

We never knew who these women were, but I do know we changed our woman once as Cook told Mummy, 'She dead, ah get anoder one for you ma'am.'

One night, our woman tripped on the steps in the yard and the smell was unbearable. Before shutting all the windows, Daddy poked his head through the window, hanky to face and asked, 'Would you like some Jeyes Fluid?'

'No, sah, dat would raise de smell,' the woman shouted and began scooping the mess back into the pail with the aid of a flat piece of wood.

Sometimes the bottom of a bucket would cave in and the woman to whom this happened (and after her head was clear) would say, 'Blarst! Is only boiled corn and split peas dey eat dis week, oui!'

A story circulated about old Mrs V., an elderly French lady in terribly reduced circumstances.

It really was very hard finding the two-pence weekly, so when her carrier called out one night, 'Madame V. oo pou bah moi lautre kappa,' Mrs V. was greatly upset. A whole penny more, how could she meet this?

She stood behind her jalousies and said with great dignity,

'My good woman, vat you carry is ver' good kind, ve eat ver' good reech food in thees 'ouse.'

Nonplussed, the carrier grunted and walked away with her burden. Unfortunately, the tin sprang a leak. Spluttering and wiping her face, the woman bawled to Madame V., 'Eat good food me eye! De same split peas and rice as meself, who yo' tink you fooling!'

Mrs V. thought it best for her to die, what with the insolence and drastic cost of living!

Many, many were the leaks. Mother was quite ill one night after a game of whist and for days Daddy shouted with uncontrolled laughter, much to Mother's disgust.

On their way home after the game, they had smelt the Brigade and hurried round the corner only to come on a woman struggling with a tin which had caved in and buried her head. Daddy said, 'Gent or no, on I go.'

Another story which tickled Daddy was the one of the woman who constantly spoke to herself in a loud voice, calling the contents of the pan by the four-letter word we read in the dictionary. Mother couldn't bear it so she called through the window to correct her.

'What fo' ah mus' cawl it den, ma'am?' the woman demanded.

Madam primly said, 'Number two.'

Convulsions from the woman! She, pan on head, minced out of the yard saying, 'Woy oh yoh! Me mus cawl it "Number two", why ah yih!'

I now had a pen-pal in Canada. Her name was Laverne Horde and we wrote each other jealous letters concerning who had first heard the latest tune and whose country was nicer.

Why we bothered to write I cannot imagine – our handwriting was appallingly bad, our spelling worse, and subject matter worst of all.

Laverne had the audacity to write and tell me that her country was bigger than mine, better than mine. 'What!' I jealously replied, '*No place in the world is bigger than Grenada, no place in the world is better!*'

My younger sister May was so outraged with Laverne and the fact that Canada was bigger than Grenada that she wrote a postscript on my reply. It read:

> Dear Laverne:
>   It good your mother has no breadfruit tree.

Then I got a letter from Canada which started, 'Dear pen-pal Nellie' and went on to say that she was in isolation with chicken-pox and that the letter had to be fumigated before it could be mailed.

I dropped the letter to the floor feeling I was covered in germs and no amount of telling could make me believe that I would not get chicken-pox.

About nine days later I went down with the sniffles, which fast developed into chicken-pox. Soon Mother had five of us with it and she kept begging Selby to roll in bed with us and become contaminated. Selby remained unfevered and unspotted.

We all got better and were taken to the sea to wash the scabs off. Majorie, Joyce and Franklyn went down with it; then Cynthia Smith succumbed and Selby decided he would get it too as he was fed up of all the fussing over all the spotty, ugly children.

He got into bed and began groaning and carrying on and we took no notice of him. At teatime he said he didn't want anything to eat, his throat was hurting. Mother felt his head and cheeks and told him to stay in bed. He didn't even want ice-cream.

Selby had measles. Mother said, 'Oh my God, don't tell me that all the kids are going down again with this!'

All of us within a few days of each other were down with the measles and Mother had a time. She moved all our beds into the largest room and kept all windows open night and day for sunlight and fresh air.

We played games and ate huge custards and soon were running about the yard and up to mischief again with our constant companions Majorie, Terry, Clive and Gordon.

In this hot weather, ice-cream carts were pushed up and down the streets daily. Each vendor had his special call. One man shouted, 'ICE CREAM CONES' in a lovely bass voice. Another rang a bell singing,

> One cent for a cone
> And you can buy it
> From Mis' Moe.

Towards the end of the month, as it now was, no one had any pocket change and the vendors shouted up and down the streets in vain. Little heads leaned against window panes regretting the rash spending of that last penny.

A vendor's voice could be heard shouting from the bottom of the street, 'Ice-cream cones, hard as iron.'

Rattle, rattle, rattle went the cart.

'Ice-cream cones, HARD AS IRON.'

Rattle, rattle, rattle.

'ICE-CREAM CONES, HARD AS I-ron.'

Rattle, rattle, rattle, rattle.

'ICE-CREAM CONES, SOFT AS – – – –' And here the man used an obscene word that the Night Brigade loved.

Windows were pushed up. Servants called shame on the man. Telephones rang and rang in an effort to get through to the owner of the cart. Children whispered in horror or giggled at the agitation and confusion caused by the man.

Terry giggled and giggled and could not stop. His face was slapped. Vince stood on his head in the corner and said he knew just how that man felt – up and down, up and down and nobody buying any ice-cream.

Gordon Commissiong jumped into the clothes basket to hide from it all and he got the giggles and wet all his clothes. The more he thought of it, the more he giggled and his tummy hurt so much from laughing that he doubled up and got stuck. Jessie, Clive and I pulled and pulled but could not get Gordon out. Vince would not get off his head to help. Terry was giggling in gasps.

Jessie thought perhaps we should pull the basket instead of Gordon, which we did, and somehow he was released.

The man who had caused all this panic was fired from the job and a woman who merely tinkled a bell took his place.

A lot of my childhood was spent reading. I hid only when the book was on the shelf for 'over fourteen'. This meant that there was a kiss of two in it, or some heroine had consumption and whenever she was kissed, two drops of blood appeared on her lips.

The only friend who would read as much as I was Terry. Terry was a bookworm and almost any day or Friday and Saturday evening you could find him and me stretched out on rugs in front of a bookcase reading.

Daddy had a formidable amount of books on all subjects, for all ages and standards; excellent reference books; encyclopaedia and volumes of Thiers' *French Revolution* in beautiful, gold binding with splendid illustrations; books on animals, particularly horses, cows and goats; actually, anything we wanted to do and didn't know how, we could find out from one of these books.

Daddy's room was one holy mess but no one could clean or dust and disturb his pattern. Many a day Terry and I would go in and sit with Daddy and read. He never spoke to us and I must have been very, very young when I read of diseases of horses and knew that they got the staggers, while sheep got the gid and humans, vertigo.

I picked up any amount of information which has been invaluable in the solving of crossword puzzles and answering quizzes, but otherwise useless. I learnt the words 'quey' and 'stirk', I knew what 'galyak' was. Oh, I knew so much but so little, and the fact for example, that five poles, three feet apart could have four spaces in between seemed extraordinary.

Only once did any of the material I was consuming come in handy. I was asked to write an essay on an insect and I chose the louse. It was a good essay with delightful illustrations of two lice having a race. My teacher undermarked me and said, 'I'm sure you do not understand half of this.'

Oh yes, there was another time too. At RK class that is, Religious Knowledge, which was held in church and conducted by the Reverend McFarlane, he told us a story and asked if anyone in the class could name it. There were many senior boys from the Grammar School and girls from our school and no one put up a hand but me.

'What is the name?' asked Reverend McFarlane.

'*Silas Marner*,' I said.

He afterwards told Mummy that he was sure I had been prompted and Mummy told him she was positive that I had not been. The good Reverend looked doubtful.

All our friends liked reading but Terry and I could not be satisfied. We read and read, our eyes getting bloodshot, trying to squeeze in the last words before it was time for him to go home.

Sometimes we would talk about what we read and invariably I would discuss the emotional side and he the practical. I always got annoyed that he could not see the depth of feeling, and he superior that I could not see that everything lumped together made a complete unit.

Daddy used to pick up books and books and give them to inmates of various health institutions. When they were returned he'd be so upset that he would drop them in the incinerator and make us have baths in Lysol.

'Why did you return the books?' he'd ask.

'But they're such good books, Mr Donovan,' he'd hear. He hated burning the books but between the germs, his children and his wife, the incinerator always won.

Allowing a child to read without supervision can be disastrous for the structural atmosphere of school. I could not buckle down to organised study and hated competitive work. I loathed Shakespeare when it became a battle of learn-by-heart passages and the only thing I learned by heart was the 'Lays of Ancient Rome'. This happened by accident. The words refused to be erased and I could see verse after verse unfolding in glorious pictures; of dear old Lars sending his messengers back and forth; Horatius; bridge; and Romans – the whole caboodle keeping me awake at night with blood, shields and spears flowing down the Tiber. It was uncanny.

If you wanted to find me, look in some little corner, some little bed, or up some little tree and there I was with a book. One day I sneaked off to the mango tree, which was laden. Lovely, tiny mangoes called table mangoes which grew like bunches of grapes. I planned to read and eat, eat and read.

It was a lovely still day and I could hear the doves cooing in the botanic gardens. I climbed my tree, found a comfortable seat and got lost in my book. Some while later, I could feel that I was not alone. Scared to look, I kept my eyes on the page pretending. When I could no longer stand the strain of pretending, I lifted my eyes and dropped from my ten foot perch to the ground in a neat plop. I raced home without stopping and found Mother in the kitchen making cakes.

Mother picked me up and put me to lie on the kitchen dresser. In my leg, protruding from the side of my knee was a long piece of iron. I had not felt it, so frightened was I. Mother extracted the rod, and squeezed it until it bled freely. She then gave it a cleaning with Lysol and put a bandage on it.

'What happened?' Mother inquired.

'I was reading in the table mango tree,' I said, 'and could feel someone looking at me. I looked up and there, hanging by its tail, was a snake, its head on a level with mine. I was so frightened that I dropped out of the tree.'

Since this experience, I have never been keen to climb trees. Even long, steep steps make me giddy. Walking on a jetty with the sea at low level makes my head spin. I'm sure that blinking snake is the cause of it all.

Jessie had read *The Prisoner of Zenda* and was telling her friends how wonderful it was. I dashed to the bookcase and hid with the book in my room. No coaxing could make me go out and play.

All the others were at the botanic gardens romping and kicking balls when Mother discovered me in bed with Baroness Orczy.

'Oh dear,' she sighed. 'If you must read, go into the garden and get some fresh air as well.'

I sat on the garden bench reading and I knew something was disturbing my concentration, so cocked an ear.

Someone was sobbing. A tiny, shattering sob.

I looked around and could see no one.

Sob, sob, sob, sob. It was pathetic so I put the book on the seat and walked in the direction of the sound.

Near my feet, whose toes were now covered with the verbena vines, I could hear the sound rising. I looked down, I stooped down, I lay on the grass and gazed in wonder. There, on a petal of a dwarf marigold, was the tiniest creature in the entire world. She could barely be seen, as her dress was the same colour as the yellow flower, her wings a lighter shade and transparent.

I lay on the grass and gazed and gazed; the sobbing went on.

Afraid to touch her because she was so small and one wing drooped, I asked, 'What are you?'

A perfect little head raised and looked at me with light brown eyes. 'I am lost,' she said. 'Lost, lost, lost.'

'Where are you from?' I asked.

Sob, sob, sob. 'I am lost forever,' she continued. 'What shall I do?'

I thought very quickly that I could keep her in a matchbox for ever and ever. I answered, 'You could stay with me?'

Sob, sob, sob, sob. 'Oh, I'm lost for ever, what shall I do? What shall I do?'

'Where are you from?' I asked again.

'The buttercup bush,' she wailed. 'Oh, I *am* lost.'

'The buttercup bush is only on the other side of the garden,' I said. 'I can take you there.'

I put my hand out and the little creature stood in my palm. Careful to keep my hand steady with fingers outstretched, I walked across the lawn to the alamander vine, bringing myself as close as possible to an open flower.

There was a little flash of light and a lovely perfume filled the air. My dear tiny creature had disappeared.

For years, many years, I looked and searched but never again did I see the little person in the buttercup vine.

Another Saturday was here and Jessie was bored to tears. We had baked little cakes and alas, they'd already been consumed. She bathed the dolls and the teddies were soaking wet on the clothes line, supported by string. Jessie did not know what else to do. The sun was positively stinging, so a walk was out.

'Let's go and pick Mr Guthrie's mangoes,' Jessie suggested.

'You're crazy,' I said. 'They're not ours, so how can we?'

We looked out of the window and hundreds of rosy, Ceylon mangoes dangled, tempting us. We climbed through the window on to the bathroom roof, then on to Miss Slinger's wall and jumped into Mr Guthrie's yard.

Not a sound was to be heard. We shinned up the nearest tree and began eating.

All would have been well if Jessie hadn't suggested we pick about twelve and go home with them. She stretched to get a truly succulent-looking fruit and it fell with a thud. She swore. Mrs Guthrie put her head through the window and called to her husband, 'Harry, Harry, some little boys are picking the mangoes.'

Mr Guthrie came to the window and shouted, 'Get down, you horrible ragamuffins. Leave those mangoes alone!'

Jessie got into a temper. 'Who you calling ragamuffins?' she demanded. 'You're nothing but a stingy, old mango-bearing faggot,' and with that we jumped down the tree and raced home, hoping we had not been recognised.

We arrived just as the telephone was ringing. We had been recognised.

What a spanking we received. That hairbrush really hurt us. We were told to go at once – in all our tears too – to the Guthries and apologise for stealing and rudeness.

We stood in front of Mr and Mrs Guthrie with bowed heads and said, 'I'm sorry for stealing the mangoes and being so rude, Mr Guthrie. Please forgive me.'

How ashamed we felt when Mr Guthrie accepted our

apologies and gave us each two lovely mangoes to take home, adding that if ever we wanted any more, we were to come and ask.

We loved him very much and slunk home with our tails between our legs.

We washed our hair with Pears soap. No one had heard of shampoo until Mother came in one day with a packet of powder which she told us was shampoo and we were allowed to look at her washing her hair. We looked at everything she did, revelling in the delightful, sudsy smell.

Lunch over, servants having their hour, Mother resting, Selby and I thought it a good idea to have a shot at shampooing. We put on the kettle and when it boiled took it to the bathroom. There, I wet my hair and rubbed the powder to a lather.

'Ready?' Selby asked.

I said, 'Fine.'

He picked up the kettle and poured.

I screamed and screamed and, luckily, Selby stopped pouring.

Mother came running and what a plight I was in – hysterical and positive that the boiling water had bored a hole through my head to the centre of my forehead.

Poor Selby was inconsolable. Fancy not thinking that the water was too hot! Fancy nearly killing Nellie! Fancy! Fancy!

Mother rinsed the shampoo out of my hair and great clumps of hair came away and she was sure that a certain patch would never grow back. It did, but it grew straight up in the air and is always a puzzle to hairdressers.

Mother felt that we should be laughing and happy at mealtimes, expressing the day's happenings and having words buffetting back and forth in family give and take.

Daddy, 'The Impossible', as we nicknamed him, thought mealtimes the place for stimulating the brain. That is, learning new words, discussing world politics and solving sinister problems.

A battle raged and Mother won by saying, 'This is the chance to get to know your children. You'll be sorry.'

To compensate, Daddy set us a daily task.

Each morning at six o'clock, we had to go to his room, knock, be admitted, say, 'Good morning Daddy' and recite a quotation.

Poor little Daisy was still lisping her way about, and, my word, we asked ourselves, 'Couldn't he spare her?'

'No, no, never too young to learn,' was the slogan.

No two quotations were to be the same. There were to be six different ones each morning.

Vince got hold of an almanac with a daily quote of no more than six words, so he was well set up.

I got hold of a book of proverbs and I think Daddy thought many a morning that I was being sarcastic.

Jessie and the others got stuck with Nuttalls.

Six a.m. Knock, knock.

'Come in.'

'Good morning Daddy,' says child number one.

'Good morning, child,' says Daddy.

'The heights by great man . . . in the night.'

'Thank you,' says Daddy.

(Child number one had learnt this in school last year.)

Knock, knock. Same routine.

'*Honi soit qui mal y pense*,' says child number two.

'Thank you,' says Daddy.

Knock, knock. Same old routine.

'Law is powerful, necessity more so,' says I.

'Hurrump,' says Daddy.

Knock, knock. Routine followed.

'Laugh and be fat,' says child number four.

'Ah,' says Daddy. 'Tonight you will all learn my little poem.'

Knock, knock. (Great scrambling for the bathroom is heard.) Same, same routine.

'Wen a man is wong and won admitt he aways gets angwy,' lisps May.

'Very good,' says Daddy, waiting for the sixth knock.

94

Poor Daisy in her two years of life has discovered the meaning of worry. She is flying back and forth, from Vince to Jessie, Jessie to Nellie, to Selby, to May, for one of us to teach her a quotation.

Vince looks at the almanac and sees something about happiness being born a twin and he says, 'Go tell him: "Happy is the man who sings along." '

Knock, knock. Same, same, same, routine.

'Appy ith man tings ayon.'

Daddy is no fool. Someone is playing the ass. It is not he and it is not Daisy.

A terrific bellow, '*Come here!*'

He who is on the lavatory seat literally hauls on his pants and pitches to Daddy's room. He who is in the bath wraps his wet body in towel and runs. Oh, we know it, we know it, we are all going to be late for school.

Daddy has decided to laugh at it all and we sigh and laugh and get ready for school.

This is Daddy's poem which we thoroughly enjoyed learning:

'Laugh and grow fat'

There's a poor man who lives cross the way over there
A fellow well met and devil may care;
Tho' poverty stricken, he's happy, at that,
For he laughs like hell – just laughs and grows fat.

This guy I speak of has a family so big
When 'round mother you'd think of a pig.
Tho' they're all clad in rags and never wear hats,
They all laugh like hell – just laugh and grow fat.

Who could envy a living as dreadful as that?
Who would like always at meal time to squat?
Who'd like to spend nights on a dirty old mat?
Or to laugh like hell – just laugh and grow fat?

By old Holy Moses I swear that I'd better
Prefer to be clutched in serfdom's fetter
Than to eke out a life far worse than the cat
By laughing like hell – just laugh and grow fat.

Now, this luckless beggar is jolly as Mammon,
So long's to life he continues to hang on.
Reckless, impoverished, heart-broken? – O what
If he laughs like hell – just laughs and grows fat.

Well, I copied his method and worked on his plan –
Would you two weeks after have known me a man?
Not by a damned sigh, tho' I haw-hawed, tit-tat –
How I laughed like hell – but failed to grow fat.

Discontented and wretched, in decency be –
The meaning of life we never can see.
This happy beggar's a huge human rat
Who's laughing like hell – just laughs to grow fat.

(From Poems by W. O'Brien Donovan
Shakespeare Press, New York, 1914)

I have never, never liked cats since Minnie saw the ghost and ran up the wall. However, we always had a cat or two around the house and one was always called Minnie and the other Butterball.

Minnie and Butterball consumed gallons of milk and often woke us up with their caterwauling. This sound in the still of the night is most frightening.

Oh, horrible, horrible animals who always insisted they wanted to sit on my lap or rub against my legs! It was necessary to remember Mummy's quote, 'Be kind to dumb animals,' when these animals were around.

Minnie was a tabby and no lady. She was not even a snob. She was plain common, fighting with dogs and associating with anyone who had a handout.

One morning, Minnie stuck her head in a salmon tin and could not get it out. Mother tried but Minnie's head must have been in the tin for many hours and was no doubt swollen. Mother oiled the area but Minnie's head stuck fast.

The six of us stood and looked on in pity and I was sick.

Daddy said he'd send a man to get rid of the cat.

The man came and drowned the cat in the Roman bath and Mother was furious. We all wept and I was sick again.

Of course, another Minnie was brought home. She grew up and fell in love with Butterball. We noticed how fat Minnie was getting and how *jealous* Butterball was of her.

Mother had an antique French wardrobe, the top of which was open save for beautifully worked wooden curtains. We called this the 'hole-in-the-press' and Mother usually kept chocolates and almond rock in there.

Minnie began visiting the hole-in-the-press and Mother said that Minnie had chosen there for her babies. Butterball sat on the floor and gazed adoringly at Minnie.

For a whole week the other children awoke with pleasurable anticipation. Perhaps Minnie had had her kittens? Minnie kept disappointing them. One night I had a terrible nightmare. I dreamt that I was walking in a lonely forest and a tiger, a huge tiger began stalking me. I began running but found that try as I could, my feet remained in the same place and the tiger was advancing by leaps and bounds. I knew that if the tiger caught me I would die, so in the dream I lay on the ground and the tiger came and lay on my chest and cried and cried and produced amid the tears, four tiny tigers.

The dream was so vivid that I awoke and put my hand on my chest. I could feel a baby tiger there and yelled at the top of my lungs, '*Tigers! Tigers!*'

Mummy came with a lamp. She told me, 'Don't move, it's all right. Minnie has had four little kittens on you.'

Mummy put the kittens on my blanket on the floor and gave me a bath.

I was quite a heroine next morning and I must say had great pleasure in watching Minnie take each baby in her mouth to Mother's room. There, she jumped with a kitten in her mouth to the window, then into the hole-in-the-press where she nursed them for many days.

It seemed to us after a while that Minnie was having kittens every weekend and after Mother could find no one to whom she could give another kitten, the problem became serious.

One of Minnie's kittens from the first batch was still with us, as my sisters and brothers had fallen in love with her and called her Wee Ball. Wee Ball turned out to be female and she was now producing babies – if possible, faster than her mother.

There were thirteen cats in the house; gingers, tabbies, black cats, black and white cats, sandy coloured cats. Oh my, they were always underfoot and if one forgot one little pussy in the house at night, the place smelt like blazes.

Mummy made a great decision. A fisherman would take them out to sea in a bag and drown them.

A wail of wails rose from six throats. In the end, Daddy put all the cats except Minnie and Butterball in a number of baskets and took them for a drive. In the country, he let them loose and that we thought was the end of that.

About two weeks later there was a pitiful meowing at the front door. It woke everyone up. Daddy opened the door and there lay a bedraggled, tired and hungry Wee Ball. She had found her way back. She had travelled some sixteen miles of country roads all on her own, without food, to find us.

We kept her and in a few weeks she was up to her old tricks again, producing babies, at a rate which now seemed to us to be every other day.

Daddy always had dogs. He spent lots of money on dogs. Big dogs, little dogs, bad dogs, good dogs. He bought dogs that turned into killers, huge mastiffs that only he could attend to. He went off these animals when the last one, 'Savage' (pronounced in the French way) made him spend pounds and pounds on compensation and Mother said, 'I think I will get a little dog.'

Mother got Rover, a dear little black and tan. For seven years Rover was the most loved, most affectionate and most beautiful dog on this earth. Everybody loved Rover.

We had just celebrated his seventh birthday when Mother

went to Trinidad on a holiday. We all went to see her off, taking Rover with us. All six of us gave Mother wet, soppy kisses and told her to have a good time.

Every day, about two o'clock, the hour that Mother had left, Rover disappeared. Every day at two thirty we received a telephone call from the water police on the pier that our dog was there crying and howling and could we come and take it home. Every day, one of us, chiefly Selby, would go to the pier and walk home with Rover in his arms. We told Rover all sorts of lies that we thought would comfort him. 'Tomorrow,' we told him. 'Mother is coming tomorrow.' Rover would not eat. He would lap weakly at a little milk. No meat bone could tempt him.

One day, the telephone rang and the water police, a chum of Selby's, told him to come now.

Selby ran all the way to the pier and his friend told him, 'Mr Silvie, dat dawg cry too much today. He stretch out he neck an' he howl loud and long, then he mus' be die as he fall overboard and when we pick he up, he was dead, dead.'

We buried Rover in the garden and Mother never owned another dog.

Grandma kept pigeons. She told me that at the beginning she had only two, a male and a female. I found it hard to believe her as there were hundreds of these birds and the tiled roof of her home was white with their defecation. A boy named Claude would get on the roof once in a while and scrub it while Grandma gave him instructions from below, threatening him with hellfire should he damage one tile.

Those pigeons were kept because Grandpa liked squab for breakfast and if I overnighted there one was always on my plate in the morning. There was no refusing this delicacy and I would go around all day with the horrible feeling that the baby pigeon in my stomach was fluttering for release.

One morning at the table, Grandpa ever absorbed in reading, I got a very lonely feeling and brooded for a while, mentally having a two-sided conversation with two 'me's'. Unknowingly, I complained aloud, 'But I can't talk to him, he never hears.'

My other self replied, 'Perhaps he's deaf, dear, or you're so small he can't even see you're there.'

I: 'Then why do I have to sit and eat squab with him?'

Me: 'Slip away, dear. He won't even notice.'

I: 'I think I'll just do that and puke up the old squab.'

Me: 'Oh horror! The preciously baked baby pigeon!'

I: 'Drop dead! If I am forced to eat another . . . '

'Good God,' said Grandpa. He held my chin and looked me in the eye, 'You'll never have squab here, child. I'll tell your grandmother. Now get up and get rid of whatever's upsetting you.'

After this, it was a pleasure to look at the pigeons billing and cooing, laying and nesting in their cotes. Their restful ruckatacoo became background music. It was even exciting when the long ladder was placed against the kitchen wall and Claude climbed with a brush and hose to scrub the roof and the day following this, he scrubbed the outer walls with Jeyes Fluid so no pigeon lice could breed. The smell of this lingers. It is about one hundred and thirty years since Grandma first bred pigeons, and she did begin with one pair. There are still some around the home and other houses in the vicinity – white ones with red legs and hard eyes, and the soft grey and white ones that seemed so gentle. These pigeons I am positive are descendants of Grandma's original pair. I see them constantly picking in the dust and flying in frenzy at the approach of a vehicle. No one cares for them anymore.

We, that is, Majorie, Jessie and I began going to church very regularly as the parson's son was out from Scotland on a holiday and he was, as Majorie put it, 'Too tweet!'

But we were bored in church and to make up for this sang lustily and were asked if we would join the choir. We did, as this meant going to choir practice and meeting Arthur *after* six o'clock in the evening.

Tired of going over and over some silly anthem, we left the choir. On Sundays, to relieve our ennui, we brought food in our handbags to nibble during the sermon. Jessie and Majorie thought they could increase the food supply by taking change from their pennies from the collection plate.

This was done only once, because parents were notified and we were lectured and made to take our 'change' to the Manse with apologies.

However, the picnics in church continued and Arthur began sitting in the pew directly in front of us. Needless to say, we thought him to be imbued with sanctity and piety.

One Sunday, he astounded us by turning around and extending his hand for some of our goodies. We thought, 'If the parson's son can do it, oh boy, it's OK.'

To our amazement, the following Sunday in the middle of our picnic, the parson, already in the pulpit said, 'Arthur, Jessie, Majorie, Nellie – please leave the church.'

I cannot, simply cannot, relate the pandemonium that erupted from this. We were spanked, lectured, deprived of pocket change, not allowed to spend days with our friends. Holy Mackerel, it was abominable the way we were treated! One would have thought that we had beaten a baby or forged a cheque.

However, there are fond recollections of church-going, the best being the morning when the hymns chosen were 'O come, O come Emmanuel' and other Gregorian chants. Mr Jerome Fletcher slipped into our pew and the singing began. Hearing my voice, he switched and began to descant in his lovely baritone. Soon I could hear only our two voices blending and there was a feeling of oneness.

I looked forward to the next hymn, impatient that the Lesson was taking so long.

At last the organ played the opening bars. We stood and a great shyness overcame me. Mr Fletcher sang, looking at me, urging me on with his eyes, but not a note did I sing.

I raced home when the service was over. There I cried for the beauty and enjoyment that I had let slip away and for the disappointment I had read in Mr Fletcher's eyes.

During the holidays, we discovered something.

Mother was visited each morning by an epileptic. At nine a.m. he would come to the back door and Mother herself would give him a cup of cocoa, a loaf of bread with butter and cheese, sometimes an egg. After eating this, the epileptic would religiously get a fit and Cook would push an old spoon between his teeth.

Mother was always upset and Daddy told her to send the food to the boy's home in order to avoid this demonstration of gratitude. Whether Mother sent it or not, the boy appeared at nine a.m.

On our first morning of these particular holidays, Mother seemed pretty anxious to have us go out to play but she could not send us out each day. So on one occasion we saw her hand the boy his cup and bread. He sat on the back steps having his breakfast.

Cook began saying agitatedly, 'De spoon, de spoon,' and there was the poor boy, eyes all turned up, thrashing about.

We spent a very sober day thinking how lucky we were with only malaria fever and an odd cut or bruise to worry about.

We always became inventive in the holidays and Jessie got hold of a baking powder tin and a half-pound cocoa tin. After placing the smaller tin in the larger one, she packed the space between them with salt and ice. She mixed vanilla, milk and sugar, which was poured into the baking powder tin and through the lid she put a swizzle stick. Swizzling the stick, she soon had a miniature tub of ice-cream which she sold to us at a ha'penny a teaspoon.

Soon she was making larger quantities and our pocket change was pouring her way. She bought a one-quart ice-cream freezer for one pound one shilling and was soon in business.

We never knew how much she saved but I am sure she made hundreds of dollars over a period of time. Using only the best materials, she soon had orders from adults for the entire can for which she charged four shillings.

Jessie had a marvellous business head but she was also very generous. She was particularly generous to me with kindness and cash and I loved her best of all my family. Funnily enough, even though I was puny, soft, sickly and most unbusinesslike, I always felt I had to protect Jessie. From what, I have never found out, but the feeling persists.

Holidays came to an end and back at school we were looking forward to Guy Fawkes day. Daddy supplied bombs, sparklers, 'petax' and Catherine wheels. We made the guy. He was an ugly caricature made of straw with a stuffed cloth head and painted face. We tied him to a broomstick stuck in the earth and Selby produced a rubber hat. A beautiful doll-sized fireman's helmet that fitted the guy to perfection.

'Where did you get the hat?' we asked.

'I found it in the fort,' he replied.

'The *fort*,' we said, 'but we haven't been to the fort for ages.'

'I went,' he pouted.

'When?' we wanted to know.

It transpired that he, Clive and Gordon had run away from school and played in the fort for a whole morning.

'Gosh,' we said, 'you're in for it if Daddy finds out.'

The rubber hat was a mistake as when it burned it stank and had us all coughing. We filled a pail of water and dumped it in and were sorry that such a beautiful hat could be so disappointing.

Mother and Mrs Commissiong supplied us with a large can of ice-cream and delightful little chocolate cakes and the Commissiongs and Donovans had a lovely party in the yard which refused to stop smelling of burnt rubber.

I now have a colossal bump bang in the middle of my forehead. My eyes are black- and blue-encircled and I look like a calf trying to push up a horn. Blindness is my preoccupation. I go all over the house, down steps and up steps, counting the treads. From room to room I feel my way around, practising, practising, in case I ever get blind.

Mother told me I'd better look where I was going as I had nearly blinded myself, as indeed I nearly had – the maid had pulled out the dining room furniture for extra cleaning and I had walked, eyes shut, into the cabinet, hitting my forehead such a sharp blow on the protruding key that little red and blue stars had twinkled before my eyes.

I looked in the mirror and who could think that a little key could do so much damage! And, just at the time I had to go to Beryl's birthday party!

Beryl was living at Mount Hartman now, and the great excitement was that all the children invited to the party were taking the bus, which had been specially chartered for the occasion. None of us had ever been on a bus before.

I again sat in front of the mirror and groaned. Could I look different on Friday afternoon? Would I ever look different? I groaned and groaned.

Using Mother's powder, I made a paste and covered the bruises. I stared at myself. What a ghoul! I looked steadily into my reflected eyes and saw myself become blotched and distorted and thought a ghost was looking over my shoulder. Shaking my head, the picture returned to normal but I no longer liked the mirror so got up and washed off the caked powder.

I returned to the mirror and stared until my image changed, and I no longer recognised myself. Frightened, I shook my head and all was again normal.

'It's the eyes,' I told myself. A new and wonderful game began.

I called Jessie and Selby and they thought the whole thing fascinating, but this wasn't changing the black and blue and the swelling. But by Friday my face was miraculously healed except for a yellow-green mark where the bump had been.

Seventeen little girls in pretty dresses went to the corner of Scott and Montserrat and got excitedly on the bus. We sang and chatted, clutching the presents we were taking to Beryl; by 4.30 we had arrived.

We were immediately given a long, cool drink and off we went to roam on the farm. Auntie Marie told us to be back at five o'clock sharp.

Diana Berkley, a fairylike child with long golden hair, put her dainty shoe into a lump of fresh cow dung. She looked in misery at her foot. 'It's ruined,' she said.

Embarrassed, we stood around feeling that Diana was sure to burst into tears. To our amazement, she gave us a sly glance and deliberately put her other foot into the smelly mess. What a party! Thirty-six little shoes paced the pasture looking for fresh cow dung and thirty-six little feet found what they searched for!

We heard the tea bell balanging away and dashed over to the house where Auntie Marie was standing at the front door saying, 'Come along, come along to tea, children.'

Then, 'Oh my God, my good God, your *feet! Off with those shoes and socks.*'

We trooped to the bathroom to wash our hands and sat barefooted to a scrumptious tea of two kinds of sandwiches, chocolate cake, jam tarts, cornets filled with cream, meat pies, fudge. We gorged ourselves and were amazed that there were still plates of left-over goodies.

Auntie Marie kept us on the verandah after tea and taught us a delightful little song.

The bus arrived to take us back but we were too tired, over full and sleepy to get much spirit into our singing.

I arrived home as our supper bell was ringing, sat down to table and there fell fast asleep. I remember being taken upstairs to bed but the person leading me seemed to be going in the wrong direction, even though I tried to point out that my bedroom was on the opposite side. The entire house seemed to have spun around and the clock had left the top of the passage and was now nailed at the bottom.

I have always longed to have a party with heaps of cow dung laid on so that the children could all be barefooted at table, after which, still barefooted, they could romp through rooms in exciting games of hide-and-seek or follow-my-leader.

Selby suddenly became very eager to be dressed for school. First man up, first to the bath, first dressed, first at the breakfast table. Ockie predicted a brilliant future for him.

Little did Ockie know what was happening!

Selby was going to Jakie's school and we would drop him

in the school yard on the way to our school. He'd say 'bye' and run down the wide school steps leading to the back yard where the boys collected to play 'kick the pan' or some such game.

This yard had a long flight of steps connecting with Scott Street, so Selby never stopped to play; he kept on running until he was in Scott Street, where Clive Commissiong, his pal and buddy, was waiting for him. Clive was a Methodist and attended Nursie's school.

Together, these two little boys would sneak around the wharf, crawl up to 'Fort Cottage' where the Roy Taylors lived and creep through Mrs Taylor's drawing room to the rocks at the back of the house. There, they took out their hooks, lines and bait. After casting into the beautiful blue sea, crushed cigarettes and matches were brought forth.

At twelve sharp, with a couple 'shitties', rock hind, a crapaud fish and perhaps two or three mariannes, they would go home for lunch. Selby explained that a wharf boy had given him the fish, and Ockie would fry the edible ones for him.

Mother remarked that Selby was getting amazingly sunburnt and suggested she get a cap with a wider peak. Surprisingly, Selby agreed to a cap that would offer more protection; Vince, Jessie and I looked at our plates with interest.

For two weeks, Selby and Clive had a wonderful holiday. Pearl Taylor never saw them go through her drawing room except on Saturdays when she gave them a glass of fruit juice. For two weeks Selby had a steady supply of fish 'from the wharf boy who seemed to like him very much.' For two weeks, Selby got steadily browner and browner. For two weeks, Daddy never met Mr Jacobs who ran the school Selby attended.

On Thursday evening at supper, Daddy remarked to the air, 'All good things come to an end.'

May and Daisy did not have supper with us and they were already in bed, so four children on hearing this remark reacted differently.

Vince immediately thought, 'Oh God, he's going to cane

me for stealing regularly – daily, twice daily – the tamarinds he has soaking in the "sling".' He clasped his hands in anticipation of the stinging lashes.

Jessie reflected in vexation, 'Damn, damn and blinking damn! He knows I've been writing love letters to Charles Farrel (film actor). Hell, hell and double hell!' She wanted to run away. (The letters had never been posted as she had used the money to buy sweets from Miss Murray.)

Nellie squirmed and squirmed and wondered vaguely how on earth he had found out that she was pouring her daily dose of whale oil through the window. 'Oh God, oh God,' I thought, 'I just can't swallow it, I just *can't*.'

Selby spilled his cup of cocoa and it ran across the white tablecloth in a dark stream which commanded all eyes.

The cloth was mopped, another cup of cocoa was brought and still no one spoke.

Mother said, 'Eat your supper, children.' But it was no longer tasty.

The maid cleared the table and Selby, pushing back his chair, said, 'Excuse me, please.'

'*Sit down*,' from Daddy.

Vince, Jessie and I sighed with relief. It was Selby. What had he been up to?

'Today,' said Daddy, 'I met Mr Jacobs. He was very sorry, Selby, that you had been sick for two weeks and so missed much schooling.'

Selby was positively yellow under his sun tan. He cleared his throat.

Vince, Jessie and I gawped. '*Two weeks!*' our minds screamed.

Daddy's eyes were like gleaming beads. 'Have you anything to say for yourself?' he asked Selby.

'I went fishing, Daddy.'

There was a terrible, terrible silence. Jessie and I began to giggle with fright and nerves.

'*To your room!*' said Daddy, through clenched teeth.

Selby got six with the cane and cried himself to sleep. He cried because Daddy had lectured him and he had felt this so deeply that he swore he never, never would run away from school again.

Being blind seemed so sad, and so many hazards had to be avoided, that we thought being dumb might be more exciting. Mother preferred this 'game' as she had a little peace and quiet; but how difficult it was for us to be able to communicate that the dove's nest had two eggs or that Ockie was making a batch of cookies!

I broke our silence to say that in the *Books of Knowledge* I had seen the deaf and dumb language which meant that we would have to spell each word with the letters formed by our hands.

We lay on the carpet with Vince teaching us and in one morning we had conquered the world of silence.

Mother was most annoyed, not that we'd learnt something, but that the rapid flutter of our hands was beyond her understanding. She too got hold of the book and soon it was a great game.

Mother, while getting ready to bake, would snap out on her fingers 'b-u-t-t-e-r', 's-u-g-a-r', and Jessie and I would dash to get them. And, sometimes in the middle of mixing scones she would spell 'm-i-l-k', the floured fingers raising a fine cloud.

Ockie was at a loss. No one speaking! Fingers curving, crossing and resting on each other! Surely, this was the maddest set of children, and madam was just as bad.

We had been quiet for over a week. Daddy, engrossed in a butterfly and sea-horse collection, was happy. The game was, however, palling and we were more than glad when Daddy at lunch one day said, 'This nonsense has to stop; you'll lose your voices at this rate.'

The gabble of conversation that broke out at this announcement was enough for our father to retract his statement, but he was laughing and it was a happy family around the table that day.

Oh dear, we had been actors, actresses, blind, deaf! What were we to be now? We could think of nothing honourable.

Thieves, gangsters, cut-throats we could not be. Life was getting dull.

We waded through the dictionary, to find a word that would conjure up something.

Terry, Clive and Gordon joined in the search and Terry said, 'Why not make up our own language?'

It was easy. We could say things in front of the servants and they would not understand. Many was the bad word we used and got away with it.

'How are you?' would sound like: 'Heeyoubee eeyoubee, yeeyoube?' 'Go to hell': 'Geeyoubee teeyoubee heeyoubee.'

So many words were alike that one had to get the gist of the conversation to really understand, but we had a ball.

The boys all got nicknames. Vince was called Dr Vum Vum. I don't know why. The name did not stick. Selby: Tats, as he was the best scooter rider and could go around corners like a Whizz. Derivation? Tattenham Corner. The name stuck. Clive: Chickie. The name stuck. Terry: Tub. The name did not stick. Gordon: Hag. The name stuck.

Jessie and I were still Big Noo-noo and Little Noo-noo.

Mother went mad with all the teeyoubees, heeyoubees and cheeyoubeekeeyoubees. Vince's name – Deeyoubeeteeyoubee Veeyoubee Veeyoubee – literally drove her up the wall. She remarked that we could have invented something more musical and simple.

Invented! My heavens, that was the word we should have found in the dictionary! It was lunchtime, so Clive, Terry and Gordon said that they would be back at one o'clock to discuss an invention.

We had a hill at the back of our home and many hours had been spent sliding down its slope while sitting in the wide, slippery handle of a palm branch. All of our pants had reinforced patches from this occupation. It was decided to invent a non-capsizable sled.

Hard, hard work kept us busy for two weeks. Pitt lent us a plane and a saw. There was always a pail of nails and planks in the storeroom. We bought sandpaper – sheets and sheets of it. We got cuts, blisters and hammered out thumbs but we never quarrelled. It was a master-invention and seven little minds belonging to Vince, Jessie, Nellie, Selby, Terry, Clive and Gordon worked as one.

Jessie and I did most of the fetching and carrying and we put the sandpaper to good use.

At last the base was finished and now we wanted a pole so that one could have a grip. Jessie found an old broom handle (stick) and fixing this was the hardest part of the job. We had no tool with which to bore a hole. Vince thought it should be easy to burn a hole with a hot poker. We had no poker.

Mother was asked. 'Necessity is the mother of invention,' she remarked, handing us a bolt and a pair of pliers. We heated the bolt, holding it with the pliers over the flame of the stove. Patiently we stood until it was red hot. Energy wasted! By the time we took the bolt across the yard to the room our invention was in, the bolt was no longer hot enough.

We called a break and it was decided that when Mother and the servants were resting we would take our invention into the kitchen and bore our hole.

It took us the entire afternoon to get the handle to fit properly. We eventually had to use a wedge to keep it steady.

Mother had promised us a bumper tea as today was to be the christening of our sled. We filled a vinegar bottle with soap suds and launched 'The Original' on the lawn. The original what we did not know but many years later I saw a strong resemblance between it and the catamaran.

On the first ride the grip broke and the rider fell off, but 'The Original' did not capsize.

We sawed the grip down to about six inches and found our sled such a good thing that we ventured over to the Spout Hill. There the land was hard and the grass dry and slippery.

The boys were terribly eager, and between them they lifted the sled to the top (the crater of an extinct volcano) and shot off at terrific speed to the bottom where the yacht club is now standing.

Oh, it was well worth it to haul our heavy contraption to the top, just to be able to sit, stand or lie on it and like a bomb, shoot off, feeling a wild freshness until it slowed to a halt at the bottom.

What glorious August holidays they were! My malaria seemed to have disappeared; no doubt the pills Daddy had ordered from Italy had done a good job. They were nasty little pills called 'Esonaphili' or something very much like that. Never did my stomach feel so good. No vomiting, no ague, no fever, no delirium. My weight was up to sixty-five pounds. I had never been able to get past forty-two and someone made the remark 'What a beautiful child.' I was stunned. I looked and looked in the mirror but never could I find beauty in my face or figure. In fact, I could not care less; so long as I was happy and loved, nothing else mattered.

Dismay reigned on Sunday before school re-opening. Daddy made us all keep quiet with books, and Jessie demonstrated her rebellion by going into corners to talk to herself and by letting out muted screams.

Daddy and Mother went off to tea with the Ferguson's in Sauteurs and left home at two o'clock. Ockie was in charge.

We all trooped into Daddy's room as soon as they left as he had all sorts of strange things from the land and sea in bottles of formaldehyde and it was fun reading the labels with the local names in brackets and their Latin equivalents. The animals from the sea were exotic: sea horses, baby octopi, sea anemones, centipede-like creatures which resembled the land varieties, only more weird looking, etcetera, etcetera.

Daisy remarked, 'I got a balloon,' and began blowing. What a strange-looking balloon! It was cream in colour, long and had a nipple on the end. She blew and blew but it couldn't blow up like an ordinary balloon. Vince thought it would be better if we filled it with water, tied it and played catch. We had just finished tying it when Ockie rang the bell for tea.

Sunday teas were always magnificent and served as tea and supper combined.

We fled to the groaning table. After having our fill we bathed, dressed and took off to hear the band concert at the botanic gardens.

The balloon, filled with water and looking like a nippled sausage, lay on Daddy's bed.

At the gardens there were natural swings made from vines from two large trees and we had a lovely afternoon flying through the air, marching in time to the music of the Police Band, or standing behind the conductor and imitating his every move.

We had forgotten about the balloon and were never told what had happened to it.

A couple of weeks later, we went to spend the day with the Winslows and their son Peter at Mon Plaisir. Peter asked us if we'd like to blow balloons as he'd found some. There, behind the dressing-table, on a ledge, was a tin that looked like a Brooklax tin, with a number of these balloons, so we each helped ourselves to one.

Like the first one we had found, it did not blow well, so we filled them with water and went into the yard to play.

A half-hour later, when Mother and Mrs Winslow came out, no doubt to see what we were up to, their faces were a puzzle. Both had a strange seriousness mixed with embarrassment and hidden smiles. They took away our toys and told us to go and wash our hands as lunch was almost ready.

Maybe it was the cold, damp air but both Jessie and I began feeling sick and soon we had ague and were vomiting. Malaria fever had struck and we were put to bed with quinine and heavy woollen blankets.

Peter sat at the bottom of the bed and stared at us with interest. He had taken off one sandal and was swinging it by the strap.

After a while he said, 'I hope you don't itch, the dogs love to sleep on this bed.'

Jessie and I were too ill to care and when it was time to go home Mrs W. insisted we stay until we were better, but

Mother thought it better for us to go home and could she wrap us up in the blankets?

These strange objects that would not blow up and could only be filled with water were cropping up in all our friends' homes. We only had to go with a friend to her parent's drawer to look for a needle, a piece of ribbon or some oddment, and there in a little tin, would be these mysterious things.

Vince told us they were grown-up things, and when we asked Sidney Munro he gave us a crooked smile and told us to run away, he was studying.

At school, during French I mentioned to our teacher, Miss Bertrand, that I had got a French letter from my pen-pal in Montreal. I was corrected and told to say that I had received a letter in French as, a 'French letter' referred to something disgusting. This was mentioned at home and Vince said that that was the name given to the 'balloons' and they were used for grown-ups not to have babies.

We were awed and lost interest.

Mrs Peter de la Mothe was an old lady and another good friend of Mother's. They never addressed each other without saying 'Mrs' even though they repeatedly told each other not to be so formal.

Mrs 'la Mothe was a delight. Handicapped by TB, she did not let this impair her happy nature; she and her faithful factotum Gertrude made the most delectable cakes and buns, which other ladies bought each Saturday. The buns were in loaf form or in little round balls, as light as a sponge cake.

Mother went to see the old lady once a week and each Saturday she sent one of us to collect our bun and also pay a visit.

We loved these visits. We would sit in a beautiful little rocking-chair near the windows and during our half-hour stay she would tell us a little story and give us a round, hot bun. Sometimes she would laugh with us so much that she'd cough and Gertrude would come in from the kitchen with an anxious look.

113

Sometimes, again, but so seldom, on a bright afternoon Gertrude would take Mrs 'la Mothe for a walk and they would come to our home. How beautiful the old lady looked! How transparent was her skin! One could see the veins, even in her face. How wonderful was her hat with the widow's veil, and her black silk dress which reached to the ground! She always took off her gloves and placed them in her hand-bag, each movement so delicate.

We would crowd around her – Mother telling us to leave Mrs 'la Mothe alone – and she'd tell us a little story about a hen or a robin.

Each year the old lady got smaller and smaller and one day she died. She left Mother a Royal Worcester flower vase in the shape of a basket. It was very ornate with bunches of fleur-de-lis and green china leaves. I have it now and keep it filled with roses on my dining table.

Lucille Richards introduced me to the *Winnie the Pooh* series and I fell desperately in love with Christopher Robin. I wanted him for my very own, to play, to care, to feed, to collect stamps with. I longed also for him to want me in England to show me the guards at Buckingham Palace and keep me for his constant companion.

These books I should have read at least three years ago instead of being lost in *Thelma*, *The Prisoner of Zenda*, *Hard Times* and *The Frozen Deep* (how I wept reading this) also, *A Maddening Blow* and *Mr and Mrs*. I was even reading O. Henry at that time and believing deeply in fate.

I got very restless and bad-tempered and could not under-stand what was wrong with me. Somehow, I either loved something very much or hated it violently. Mother thought I needed a dose of castor oil but it only made my mind more alert and I became critical as well. In short, I was very unhappy.

My whole life seemed a long stream of quinine, Esonaphili, castor oil, Scott's Emulsion, whale oil, senna, worm powders hidden in strawberry jam, chemical food; I was not even the first born or the baby, I was stuck bang in the middle, wearing Jessie's outgrown dresses and shoes and, distressingly, my pocket change never lasted for more than three days.

I would sit and think myself dead. Yes, yes, there they all were, weeping and breaking their hearts, sobbing and tearing their hair as poor Nellie was dead. Soon, with so much sorrow around me, I would be crying hard and Mother said, 'She couldn't be at nine!'

I did at nine! I became what Mother called a 'young lady' and she bought huge napkins, an elastic belt and two colossal safety pins with which I was to protect myself.

But it didn't all happen as easily as this!

We, the girls of our group had by this time heard that we all possessed something called a virgin. This virgin which we understood resembled a sliver of bamboo, lay across the mouth of our wombs. If this virgin got broken, we would immediately have a baby.

A virgin could be broken by a serious fall or by a vicious *man* who did horrible and unspeakable things to one. And one bled gallons of blood.

If this happened before marriage, you could *never, never* get a husband.

After many conversations between us about the best way to protect ourselves from men, our 'virgins' became very important.

The day I 'became a young lady' I had been swinging from limb to limb in a mango tree and felt I wanted to go to the bathroom. I went, sat on the seat, did my numbers and wiped. Splashed across the toilet paper was a red, terrifying smear. Panic gripped me and I ran from the seat to the door, to the window, to the seat again and back to the door in absolute terror.

My *virgin* had been broken. Oh God, Oh God, how? No man would marry me now! How did this tragedy happen?

Forcing myself to be calm and to try and think it all out, I decided that while swinging in the tree, the 'sliver of bamboo' must have been rotten and snapped.

How I lived through that Sunday with my secret, I do not

know. I felt that anyone looking at me could tell what had happened. After our high tea, we sat down to play bridge – at least we were trying – and at seven o'clock Mother called to say it was time to revise our homework.

I left the table to go to my room and Vince said, 'B-boy, oh b-boy! You'd b-better s-show M-mother the b-back of your d-dress!'

Trying hard to be brave and avoiding the eyes fixed on me I went to Mother and said, 'I'm sorry Mother, but I think I've broken my virgin.'

Poor Mother was putting away bath towels in the bottom drawer of a press. She was stooping and after my announcement she went plop into a sitting position on the floor, a pile of towels clasped to her bosom.

She got up and after a few questions she told me what was what and the over-sized napkins, etcetera, were brought to light. She showed me how to fold and wear one and sent me to my room for privacy.

That blasted napkin was so big and I so small that the front had to be pinned to the top of my slip and I had a heavy-looking fold which must have puzzled many people as it was visible through my dress.

Jessie told me that this monthly visitation was called 'Suzie'.

I was absolutely furious with the damned huge napkins and colossal safety pins. I loathed the bulge they made under my clothes. I detested the discomfort and felt like a bundle of old clothes, and confided this to Majorie.

Majorie came and examined the huge napkins. She did not say anything but let out a long whistle. Fetching the scissors from my work basket she cut each napkin in four and we both had a lovely morning stitching hems on the sewing machine.

A reign of terror existed. A cock the size of a sloop roamed the streets. A donkey of magnificent proportions, wearing goggles and watchikongs (sneakers), was also on the prowl.

Their popular habitat was under the silk cotton tree in Top Road, the extension of Tyrrell Street.

To get to our home from town, one either took the Wharf Road or the Top Road.

As the evenings were a little longer, that is, the sun did not set until six thirty, one could stay out until then without encountering any of the Devil's representatives, who only presented themselves when it was dark. But, with the cock and donkey in mind, each little girl and boy on an afternoon jaunt made for home long before sunset.

At this time, Selby was getting in extra studies for the scholarship examinations and asked if after supper he could study with Terry and the gang. They would meet at Terry's home.

'The cock?' we asked.

'The donkey?' we asked again.

'Oh,' replied Selby, 'the boys will walk home with me and as it's a bunch of them, they won't be afraid to go back.'

Selby was accompanied on his way to study by Ockie, her day's work done.

We nervously telephoned him to find out if he had arrived safely. His reply was boastfully brave.

Ten o'clock came. No Selby. Ten thirty and still no Selby.

Daddy was getting worried and we could hear him muttering about young boys being led astray at a tender age. He was also working himself into a rage, as he would not use the telephone and thus disturb Miss Glean, the operator in charge. It was an understood thing that one never used the telephone after ten p.m. as the exchange was 'closed down' and Miss Glean would have retired for the night. In an *emergency*, however, she would get out of bed and help.

Poor innocent Selby. Poor, poor, little Selby, hardly out of rompers and wearing as a special treat a pair of Vince's long white drill trousers which had shrunk. Poor, poor, poor Selby, with no thought in his head except getting Terry to help him with his arithmetic.

The boys had completed their studies by nine thirty and had hung around chatting for a further fifteen minutes.

Unfortunately, they chose 'the cock' and 'the donkey' as their subjects.

At nine forty-five they began their walk home with Selby; before reaching the silk cotton tree, they stopped and would go no further. The thought of meeting the enormous, super-natural beasts had their hearts beating double time and arm-pits wet with fright.

They discussed the situation and promised to wait until Selby had passed the tree by at least thirty strides, but the second Selby reached the tree the boys deserted and scam-pered back into town. The lone little boy faced the dark, dismal road with no street lamps to light his way. The night was black and deathly quiet and not a breeze blew.

Selby said an 'Our Father' and was remembering fast all the things one did to guard against the Devil.

The first stride he made, a swishing step followed him. He walked faster and, in time with his pace, the swishing followed.

'I shall turn my clothes "wrong-side",' he thought, and did so in a hurry. Off again he set and with every step, the swish, swish, swish followed.

'I shall play drunk,' he told himself and he staggered and reeled, hoping the Devil would disappear.

The steady cry of 'Oh God, Oh God, Oh God, *Oh God*,' was a background to his thoughts. The two words joined and then those two words joined the other two words and on and on until in one unending plea his mind roared, 'Uhguduguduhgud.'

But the swishing footsteps followed him still.

'I shall curse,' he said and Selby used his full vocabulary of bad words. He damned as he reeled and blasted as he rolled but the footsteps still followed.

'The devil can't touch a naked person,' he thought and put the thought into action. With his clothes on his arm, Selby fled through the street stark naked; at the bottom of our driveway he noticed that he was no longer pursued.

Slowing his pace, he reached the verandah, where a livid

father sat awaiting a son whom he was sure had 'strayed from the straight and narrow' on his first night out.

Daddy expected to see a boy slinking home, tip-toeing and praying that he could make it up the stairs and slip into bed without anyone knowing. Daddy was struck dumb to see a boy, pale and naked with sweat streaming down his body.

Selby received a shattering blow on his shoulder and an ominous, 'Where have you been?'

'At Terry's, Daddy.'

'*Naked?*' lifting his hand to strike again.

'Daddy, Daddy, listen to me,' gasped Selby.

Story told, both males laughing with relief, Selby was made to put on his clothes and as soon as he walked across the verandah, the swishing began. The trousers he had borrowed from Vince were too long and were scraping on the floor.

We were all awake and roaring with laughter. Mother made hot cocoa and we went to bed thinking what an exciting life we lived.

Harold Lloyd was playing at the Gaiety cinema and the film would be over after sunset. The cock and the donkey were still on the rampage. So Clive and Selby would go with Jessie and me and we would all return home together. Selby was given one shilling and fourpence which would pay for four tickets in House.

On our way we noticed that the boys were lagging behind, so we waited until they caught up with us. A minute later they were ahead and try as we could we never seemed to be walking together.

'Don't you want to walk with us?' asked Jessie.

No reply.

'What's the matter?' Jessie demanded.

It transpired that the boys were afraid to be seen with girls, as their friends would rib them no end the next day. Besides, they would not know that we were Selby's sisters.

At the cinema, Selby paid for House tickets for Jessie and me and bought Pit tickets for Clive and himself; these cost tuppence each. With the remaining fourpence change they

119

bought scores of bananas and stoned us with them during the picture. I did not enjoy this film as it seemed that Harold Lloyd was continually having his head squeezed flat in an old-time press; besides, ducking whizzing bananas was no experience of delight.

I suppose this was the first time Jessie and I were officially escorted. What bores boys were! As far as we were concerned, the boys we were going to marry hadn't yet been born!

The following week I was ten years old. I did not want a party so Mother asked what I would like. I chose a silver-backed mirror and we were all happy at tea with a huge birthday cake.

I was elated, knowing that despite all forecasts of an early death, I was still alive. I secretly hoped to live until I was at least seventeen.

Another seven years seemed centuries away.

Jump-Up-and-Kiss-Me

Jean Buffong

Jump-Up-and-Kiss-Me

The house stood like a lost child in the midst of the rambling unkept garden. Here and there the murky green paintwork was chipped and cracked. The flowers around the gravelled front yard were very neglected, a jungle-like patchwork of blooms and green shrubbery that no planning can produce.

I fell in love with it – house, neglected garden – the lot. I wanted to get in there and start cleaning up. We stood in the gap leading from the main road to the house, and looked right around. My mother said the people had only moved out a couple of days ago, but it looked like the place had not seen broom nor cutlass for months. I felt all itchy and jumpy inside. I wanted to go in and start work. In my mind I saw where all my flower pots would be, that is if Mammy allow me to bring them.

The house itself was so different from where we lived before. It was built on wall pillars instead of wood like most of the houses in the village. The verandah ran almost all around, even the step leading to the verandah was wall. There was space between the house, so no one would get wet when passing in front of the door. I noticed that the windows in the front were of glass instead of the usual board. Everything was so different; I was so wrapped up in the view around that I forgot Mammy was with me until I felt her hand on my shoulder. I leant against her and she hugged me tightly. I didn't know why, but I started to cry. Could've been the thought that Mister Oscar would not be living with us ever.

I know that was wicked of me because he is dead, but it was true. I was glad he would not be living in this house. Mammy said his money was paying for the house, but I didn't care. Anyway I didn't see how a dead man could buy a house.

When we went to live in Concord she said it was his money. Now he is dead and we have to move she still says it's his money. I don't understand any of the things she says sometimes. All I know is that I am not afraid anymore. He would never be here and that's that. From the day I first laid my eyes on him I didn't like him. The way he used to turn the cokey-eyes and stare at me. To make matters worse, one day he came up behind and put his hand on my chest and laughed; I hated him even more.

I didn't tell Mammy because she always on about how the little girls in the village womanish, before they could wash their panty they talking about big people thing. She would say things about how since my father left her with her belly big, she see trouble until Mister Oscar came.

I never understood some of the things she said. All I know is it's always been me and her living in our house. I remember when I had about six the man who lived in the big house facing the Seventh Day Adventist church used to come to our house late at night. After a while he stopped.

I didn't understand why he always came in the night, or why he came at all, because these people was too stuck-up; they thought they were better than us. They didn't even want their children to play with children like me and my friend Merica. They said we didn't know our fathers, and then Merica always had 'uncle' living at their house. I didn't think that was any of the man's business. Miss Berty made Merica call the men who came to their house 'uncle' and that was that.

As for me it was only me and Mammy, and then Uncle Ben started to come to our house now and again. I called him Uncle because I liked him. He was really nice to me and Mammy. He lived in the little house behind Mr Magnus' shop down by the bay road. Mammy used to cook and wash for him. He would come to our house, eat, and pick up his bundle of wash clothes. Sometimes he would ask Mammy if he could stay for the night; she used to curse him, or just give him one bad eye. All he did was laugh.

Everything was all right until the day that that cokey-eye man came. I had finished eight going on nine then. I remembered I was on the top step planting a piece of jump-up-and-kiss-me in the old milk pan when I heard the gravel in the yard shuffle. I didn't bother to look up, because I thought it was James passing. I kept on planting the flower. Merica gave it to me so I wanted to plant it before it dried up.

Merica and I were best friends because for one thing we loved flowers, we planted all different ones all around our house, but she was better off than me, because she had a bigger front yard, and nobody made short cut in front their house to mash down her plants. Miss Seeta and her children took in front our house for main road. The yard so narrow already and that made it worse, so instead I planted most of my flowers in empty tins, and lined them up on the four steps leading to the door. I had one or two on each side of the step depending on the size of the pan, and in each pan was a different flower. Even though I didn't have a lot of space to plant the flowers I looked after them well because I liked to see them when all the blooms were out.

Anyway, that day I was planting the piece of jump-up-and-kiss-me when I heard the shuffling behind me. I didn't pay notice because I thought was James and I already warned him about my flowers. In front his house looked like where people planting provision. He always teased me about how he would dig up all my flowers. I warned him, the day I catch him he dead as a dead fish. I knew he was only jealous, but I still cautioned him.

One day he took to his farseness and kicked down one

flower pot. He was surprised when the stone landed on his forehead; from that day he never tried it again.

Anyway, I heard the gravel shuffle again, and someone cleared his throat. I turned around and almost screamed when I saw this tall, skinny, meagre-looking man standing in the yard. He stood grinning, his mouth packed with gold teeth, you'd think he owned a gold mine in Guyana. Not only his mouth packed with gold but he had gold rings on all his fingers – just fancy a man with gold rings on all his fingers. And you know something, he stood there sort of karwaying the hands and looking at his fingers, as if he think he nice. What made matters worse he had on one of those wide-rimmed felt hats slanting on his head, half way covering one eye. Tanty Muriel used to say, is only damn scamp that covered his eyes. Nothing usually frightened me, but for a minute he did. I stared at him and he stared back.

'Hello Glory,' he said.

I poked out my eyes and stared at him even more. I didn't like anybody calling me Glory, and certainly not Mister Goldy. I'm sure whoever told him my name didn't tell him it was 'Glory'.

'Glory, isn't it?' he asked, coming towards me.

'My name is Gloria, not Glory.' I don't know why, but I didn't like the look of that man one bit. He saw the way I looked at him and then at the flowers; he backed away a little.

'Eh-em, Gloria, I'm looking for Miss Beryl, Beryl Johnson. Somebody by the road said she lives here. Is she home?'

I looked at the man. My mouth dropped open. What he want with Mammy? I thought. She always talked about her friends, I never heard her say anything about Mister Goldy.

'Is she here?' he asked again.

'She lives here, but she ain't home, mister.' I eyed him.

'When she comes tell her Oscar was looking for her. Don't forget. Tell her it's Oscar Parker, and I was looking for her,' he repeated as if I was deaf. Then he gave me a long funny look before he strolled back down the road.

When you little you don't say to your mother or anyone

older than you things you like and things you don't like, especially not about another person. I remember the last time I play womanish and asked Mammy why the man from the big house came to our house in the night; she gave me one beating. She hauled me from in front the door, grabbed a piece of peas bush and beat me until I almost turned stupidy. The lashes fell everywhere. The more I bawled, the more she beat me, all the while shouting me to shut up. I didn't understand why she was beating me. She said I must see things and keep my mouth shut.

Sometimes she was real nice. There were times when we would sit on the step in front the door and she would tell me stories about when she was a little girl, especially about her school days. She always said she wanted me to grow up to be a lady. Sometimes she hugged me and rocked me like I was still a baby. She would rock me until the tears poured down her face. I loved Mammy very much and when she cried it made me very sad. I promised her I would always be a good girl.

Times like those we were very close, but other times she would beat me for nothing. Like the time she said she saw me and Malcolm talking for a long time, said I was up to no good. I didn't know what she meant, but I made sure I never talked to Malcolm again. The problem now is, should I tell her about Mister Goldy or whatever his name is. I didn't want to, but I had no choice. Well you should've seen her face when I told her. It was like a Christmas picture.

'You sure he said Oscar, Oscar Parker?'

'Yes Mammy, that's what he said.'

'Did he say if he would be coming back or where he is staying?'

'No Mammy. All he said is to tell you he looking for you.'

'Why didn't ask him, eh girl? You telling me Oscar came here and you didn't find out where he staying?'

'But Mammy you always telling me not to ask big people any question.'

I did not understand why my mother acted the way she did. It was like she had news of the king or something. She moved about the house like she was searching for something, all the while mumbling and laughing to herself. Then I noticed that she tied up a bundle of clothes and put them in a corner of the house, by the front door.

That night when Uncle Ben came for his dinner, I thought Mammy had gone completely crazy. For months, maybe a whole year Uncle Ben was coming to the house and everything fine. Tonight all of a sudden things were different. As soon as he came Mammy started to look vex as if somebody interfered with her. Uncle Ben asked her what was wrong.

'Nothing wrong,' she snapped. 'What you see wrong?'

He was so surprised he stood with his mouth wide opened. Then just like that she chucked the bundle of clothes at him, like it was old rags. She picked up a bowl of food she had wrapped up on the table, pushed it into his hand and told him to leave her house and don't come back – just like that. I don't know what Uncle Ben thought, but I was trembling. I thought Mammy was completely mad.

'But, but Beryl, what's the matter? What's wrong? Who start telling you things about me?'

'I tell you Ben, nothing wrong, just take your things and go. You hear. Go, and don't come back in front my door.'

Well! That got under Uncle Ben's skin. He moved towards her as if he wanted to fight. Mammy put her hands up and started to bawl. Uncle Ben called her all kinds of names. Words I never heard him use before, he called Mammy. I didn't know what was happening – Mammy bawling Uncle Ben cursing – it was one Bacchanal in the house that night. I got hold of Uncle Ben's jersey sleeve, pulled it and shouted at him to stop calling my mother those names. One minute he was cursing, the next he was looking at me as if he hadn't remembered I was there.

'Sorry Gloria, sorry. I don't know what's wrong with your mother. I think she gone damn mad.'

Uncle Ben was looking at me, yet not at me. If I didn't know him, I would think he was drunk or something. He looked so dazed. The people in the other yard came outside, pretending they were cleaning around their house, but I knew they had been listening to Uncle Ben cursing Mammy. Old Mr Jacob in the broken-down house behind Miss Melda's latrine, he could hardly walk, even him I saw crawling behind the house listening. I wanted to stone him, but I knew Mammy would only give me a beating later.

That night was the last time I saw Uncle Ben for a long, long time.

My friends Merica and Pamsue stopped coming to my house to play with me after that night. I didn't mind about Pamsue but Merica was my best friend.

Anyway, after that evening Mammy was really nice to me. She bought me nice new clothes. For my birthday she asked Miss Wilma to make a special birthday dress for me – nice light pink, with plenty frills, white ribbons trimmed the skirt, and there was a thick layer of can-can below. To go with the dress, I had new shoes and socks – white. When I tried them on I looked like a black princess.

Mammy said I mustn't worry too much about Merica and Pamsue. The Friday before my birthday she dressed me up and we went to town. She took me to a photographer; she said she wanted my picture to send to someone special. When I asked her who, she laughed and said, 'Someone special.'

I was too happy that day to keep on asking her questions. Then she said the picture was for my father. That almost spoilt the day for me.

I didn't even ask her where he was. She always said he left her to fend for herself, now she talking about sending my picture for him; I was a bit sad about that. But anyway Mammy treated me really nice.

After we took the pictures we went to the roti shop where I had chicken roti and pop. I was very happy because in a way Mammy was happy too. For one thing, I noticed that that cokey-eye Mister coming to our house very regular. I don't know what happened to Uncle Ben. I heard he closed up his house and moved clean away. One day I asked Mammy for him. She gave me one bad eye, I shut my mouth quick, quick.

As I said, Mister Oscar started coming to our house, but

he never stayed the night. I was glad about that because I never liked him, especially as he had a habit of skinning those old eyes and looking at me. I never really sure if was looking at me or behind me. After a little while Merica started coming to play with me again. Then Jane moved into the house next to Merica with her mother and little sister.

She was a little older than me and Merica, but she said she wanted to be our friend. We didn't mind, we liked her. She made us laugh with her funny jokes. Sometimes I didn't understand the things she said, especially when she talked about boys, but still she was all right. She used to tease the boys about all kind of things.

Then one day Mammy told me she didn't want me to talk to Jane anymore.

'And don't let her come to our house either,' she said.

I asked her why, but she threatened to beat me. According to Merica, Miss Eva came home one day and found Jane and Henry inside the bedroom and nobody else was in the house. I didn't see anything wrong with that, but Merica sounded shocked, so I didn't say anything. Anyway, to me Jane was the same person; I saw nothing different with her.

I missed Uncle Ben very much, but things were all right with me and Mammy. Mister Oscar came and went as if he owned the house. Mammy was like a complete new woman. Now she was always jolly and happy. Not that she was unhappy before, but she seemed happier since Mister Oscar came.

One evening she came home early from work. She was all happy and singing like a choir girl. Her face was fresher and younger than ever. I couldn't think what made her so happy. I was sitting on the step in front the door; she ran up the steps, dropped the bag and hugged me tight, tight.

'Gloria, Gloria,' she said, 'child, we're leaving this old house. Leaving this place. We moving out.'

I twisted myself out of her embrace to face her. The last few weeks every evening Mammy and Mister Oscar been going out; then I heard her talking to James' father about putting some new doors and fixing a window; but I thought she wanted him to repair the house we were living in.

'We moving out of this place,' she carried on. 'This place is too corrupt. No place to bring up a young girl. Before the little girls can wash their panty they coming home with big belly. Look at Jane; she came here all nice and innocent, look what happen to her. Before she had six months her poor mother had to move away in shame.'

'What happen to Jane, Mammy?'

'What you think happen? More than she belly!' Mammy stopped abruptly, then said, 'Stop asking questions, you too damn farse. Little girls today have too much damn thing in their skin. The whole village is nothing but corruption, that's why I'm making sure I get you away before it's too late.'

'Where we going, Mammy?'

She looked at me so soft and loving, you would not think she was the same person a few minutes ago. She reminded me of when I was much smaller, the way she used to pick me up and hug me, and things like that.

'Gloria,' she said, 'child, at last you and your mammy could settle down in our own house. No more landlord coming every week asking for rent for this old leaky place. He won't even repair the place, the door only want a little push to fall off the hinges. Well child, we putting all that behind us once and for all.'

'Mammy, where we going?' I asked again.

'You would have your own room where you can do what you want,' she went on.

Funny, I thought. Here me and Mammy shared the one bedroom. I have a little bed in one corner, and she always on at me how I'm too damn nasty, because I don't make my bed, how I keeping the place like a pig pen, now she telling me I'll be getting my own room and I could do what I like. The way she kept on and on about the new house I became frightened. I don't know why, just frightened. I kept on asking where we moving to, but she wouldn't tell me. I didn't want to leave my friends behind. Although Merica left a long time ago, I still had other friends.

We lived in that house a long time, since I had about four. Everybody knew us. Stand in the fore-road outside the police station or by the Seventh Day Adventist church and ask for Miss Beryl and Gloria, and you don't have to ask twice, now Mammy talking about moving.

Merica moved quite some time ago. No one knew where she and Miss Berty went. One morning we woke up and there was no Miss Berty, no Merica. A few weeks later somebody said they had seen them way up round Grand Etang. Miss Berty walking up and down the road preaching like a mad woman. Everyone knew she was not right in the head. The strange things she did, only someone that's not right in the head would do them. In the middle of the night she would get up and start bawling blue murder, how some man or the other crawled into her house and hid under her bed. Sometimes she would dress she and Merica in black – black dress, black shoes, black hat, black everything – then tie a big red piece of cloth around her waist; real funny she was. Still, Merica was my best friend. I missed her a lot when she first moved away. It's not her fault that her mother is sick in her head.

Anyway, was not only Miss Berty who was funny. That man in the big house; that Mr Grant. He and his wife thought they were better than everybody. They said they didn't want their children to play with those 'wayward' children, meaning children like me and Merica, because our fathers were not living in the same house as us and Mammy and Miss Berty had to scrape a living as best they could.

One day Merica told me about the man not wanting his children to play with us. I said, 'If he don't want his children to play with us, how come he always in our house in the night?' Merica burst out one laugh. She grabbed me with one hand and put the other one over my mouth to shut me up. It was not long after that Uncle Ben started coming home.

He was different; I really liked him. He'd come in the evening, eat his dinner, leaving his dirty clothes, then he and Mammy would sit on the step or sometimes inside and talk and talk until time for him to go to his house to sleep. When he got paid he used to treat me and Mammy to all kind of nice things. One day he took us on a bus party around the island. I really enjoyed myself.

Uncle Ben was all right, but that man in the house – I was not sure about him, especially when I heard things about he and his mother. People said he deal with the Devil. I heard when his mother died – that was a long time before we came to live in Grand Roy so I don't know how true the story is – but I heard when the woman died he started crying. Not crying like everybody else when you have someone that died. He was not bawling, 'Lawd Gawd have mercy, me mother dead'; or 'bonjay oye Lawd have mercy' or anything like that. He was crying and at the same time mumbling some old jibberish nobody could understand. I heard he sat on the bed next to the dead woman and kept on mumbling and mumbling and wiping his eyes. When he opened the kerchief he used to wipe his eyes it was red, as if his eye-water was blood.

The story was the old woman used to work obeah and she passed on her nastiness to her son. You ever hear a thing like that, eh? You ever hear that? One day Merica told me that Miss Berty said the old woman hand was never clean.

'Why don't she wash her hand, then? Devil must be afraid of water,' I said.

'Gloria you really stupid, you know.' Merica started to laugh at me. 'You does never understand anything.' As time went by I heard so much bad things about this man and his family, I was glad he and his children stop coming to our house.

Since the day Mammy run behind Uncle Ben and then Mister Oscar started to come home, Mammy's friends hardly visited us. Friends like Miss Irene and her sister Miss Polly always used to come home and beat mouth with Mammy. Now they don't come anymore. I think they must be afraid of Mister Oscar, like me. He wanted me to call him uncle! Not me. He is not my uncle. I call him Mister Oscar and that's that; as far as I know that is his name.

Mammy was very happy now and I was glad for her because that made me happy too. Only thing is I don't like the way Mister Oscar does look at me funny, funny all the time. Sometimes I'm not sure whether he was looking at me or not. The other thing was I couldn't stand those gold teeth he always grinning. Mammy wanted me to call him uncle. When I said he is not my uncle she said I'm too womanish, she had to keep eye on me. I wanted to ask her what she meant, but was afraid she would give me a beating. Things were all right and I didn't want to make her vex. Everything went on nice, nice for a long time, must be for about a year, because I have nine and some months and the first time Mister came, I had eight about two months before.

That was the time Mammy and Uncle Ben promised to make a party for me. Uncle Ben had said he would pay for the things as I was such a good girl. Then one night he came home crying; must be about two weeks before my birthday. Anyway, this big man came in the house crying – not pretend cry, you know, but real eye-water. I wanted to laugh but I felt sorry for him. It was funny and not funny. Mammy and me didn't know what happened. He was crying and holding his left hand in an awkward way. When we looked closer, I jumped back and Mammy started bawling, because it looked as if somebody chop out the poor man's fingers.

'Lawd have mercy, tonight,' Mammy cried out. 'Lawd, Ben what happen to you? Who chop you up so?' She started running from the hall to the bedroom and around and around Uncle Ben where he was standing just inside the house.

'Come, come let's go to the police station,' she ordered. 'Stop crying like a stupidy. You should go to the station before you come here.'

'Beryl, Beryl listen. Nobody chop me,' Uncle Ben shouted at her. Mammy kept on prancing and eyeing Uncle Ben's blood-up hand.

'Listen Beryl, if you stand quiet for a minute I'll tell you what happen. Nobody cut my hand.' He was then standing in the middle of the room, with one hand in the air tied up with a bloody piece of cloth and the other trying to hold on to Mammy.

'What you mean nobody chop you? You come with your fingers hanging out and telling me nobody chop you? Your clothes wet as if they duck you in the river and you still telling me nobody trouble you? Lawd Jesus, look at my trouble tonight.' She started lamenting and stamping again, not giving Uncle Ben a chance to explain.

I thought Mammy had gone clean out of her mind like Miss Berty. Uncle Ben's eyes were popping out of his head like two round saucers. When I think about it afterwards the whole thing was kind of funny, with Mammy stamping up and down and bawling, whilst Uncle Ben stand there like a helpless zombie, his hand wrapped in the old piece of cloth, his clothes soaking wet. Afterwards it was funny, yes, but at the time I was just afraid. Long, long beads of perspiration were running down Mammy's face, making all sorts of patterns, like fancy work on a smooth piece of black silk cloth.

Mammy's face so jolly all the time, like she never get vex, but when she did, God help the person who annoyed her. She always said I don't resemble her. I resembled my father, with my light skin and straight hair. When I asked her about my father she would get vex like I say something bad. She'd shout at me and tell me to shut up.

One day we were sitting in front the door, when she started to comb my hair. She brushed and brushed it, sort of playing with it. She said she liked playing with my locks because they so long and pretty. All of a sudden she started talking. At first I was not sure what she was on about until she said, 'Your hair just like your daddy.' I was so surprised. 'Just like your daddy, long and black,' she repeated. This time I turned around so quickly the comb almost pricked out my eyes.

'What you say, Mammy? I look like my daddy?' I asked, wanting to hear more, yet afraid she hit me, for it was the first time for a long time I remembered her mentioning anything about my father.

'Yeh, you look like your daddy all right. He was fair-skinned and his hair was like half Indian. Good thing you take his hair as well, because with your light complexion, if your hair was natty like mine, I don't know. That Ulric was something. He had class, a real smoothy. He belonged to Mon Jalou where most of these mixed race people belong. Nose as straight as a pin and those eyes not more than two slits across his forehead, but when he looked at you it was like he was dreaming. We used to call him "sheepy" because of those eyes. A real saga boy he was, real saga boy. When he first came to Palmiste those girls went crazy over him, always dollsing up themselves and shaking their tails when he passing. I didn't have time for all that stupidness. I had to work to help your grandmother fix up the house for when your uncle and his wife come from Trinidad. Years your uncle went overseas, never bothered with Grenada, then all of a sudden he write to say he coming home with his wife, so we had to fix up the house for when they come. When those girls were running after Ulric I had to make sure I worked in case I lose my job. It wasn't a lot of money, but every little helped.'

Mammy was talking as if things had been bottled up inside her and now she had a chance to let them out. I was glad at last to hear something more about my father, so I wouldn't feel different when my friends talking about their fathers. I stayed quiet, quiet, so that she would continue.

'Anyway,' Mammy went on, 'when all the girls ran after him I kept out of his way.' Then she gave a little laugh. 'While they chased him, in his way he chased me. In the end we end some good times together. When my friend Myrna found out he was seeing me, she stopped speaking to me. We tried to be secretive, but some old farse woman saw us talking and went and tell your grandmother. When she asked me if it was true, I told her he said he loved me and I really liked him. Child, your grandmother acted like she was going mad. She pulled me in the back yard, grabbed a broom handle and hammered me. Hammered blows on me like as if she was purging my soul. She said I didn't know anything about love and make it the first and last time she ever hear me talk about love. That didn't stop us from hiding to meet up.'

It was as if Mammy wasn't really talking to me but to herself, and all the while she was brushing my hair harder and harder.

'Mammy, you hurting. Mammy!'

'What you say girl?' Her voice sounded like I startled her. When I looked at her, tears were streaming down her face.

She did not mention my father again for a long time. A few days after that I met Uncle Ben for the first time. He's such a nice person. He looked old but I'm sure he is a younger person really, perhaps about same age as Mammy.

Anyway, there he was now with his cut hand and Mammy stamping about not giving him a chance to say a word.

'Beryl, listen,' he pleaded, 'listen, is nobody cut my hand. It's my cutlass that cut me. My own cutlass.'

'What you say?' Mammy stopped and stood facing him.

'Yes . . . the . . . cutlass. I was . . . ' he stammered.

'What stupidness you saying Ben? What cutlass? How your cutlass could cut you up so?' She peered into his eyes. 'You sure you not drunk?'

'Drunk? You know I don't drink to drunk. If you hush up for a minute, I'll tell you what happened,' he tried to explain.

I moved a little closer. I wanted to hear how his own cutlass cut up his fingers like that.

'I was crossing the river holding the cutlass under my arm. I was bringing it for Mr George to sharpen for me. With all the rain yesterday and last night, I didn't realise the river stones was so shaky. I thought it was safe to cross in the middle by the big pool. As I jumped on the big stone, it rolled over and the paper fell out of my pocket.'

'Paper? What paper? Ben you sure you all right in your head? What paper you talking about now?' Mammy's eyes popped out of her head.

'I'm trying to tell you. If you hush up for a minute I'll tell you everything.' Poor Uncle Ben. 'The paper had all the money for Gloria's birthday party, every penny.' He was having trouble saying whatever he wanted to say.

'What!' Mammy jumped so high I thought she had knocked out the roof. 'Ben, you either mad or somebody give you bad food to eat.'

I don't know what happened after that. All I remember is Uncle Ben shouting murder, police, while Mammy licking him with the broom in his head.

I ran and hid under the mango tree in the back yard until things cooled down.

The story I heard afterwards was that when he tried to cross the river the paper bag with the money fell in the water; he forgot he couldn't swim and still holding the cutlass under his arm, he jumped in the water after the money. That's how the cutlass cut his fingers. He was lucky; some of the boys who were sitting on the church step saw when he fell in the water, and went and rescued him. I didn't get the birthday party after all. A few months after that Mister 'Goldy' Oscar came and Mammy told Uncle Ben don't come back.

Mister Oscar must have a good job, because he always well dressed and he have a nice car. It was a few months after he started coming to our house that Mammy got all excited and said I don't have to go to school. It was a Friday. I remember because it was the first time she ever kept me from school. She said it didn't matter if I missed school for one day, and she already told the teacher. I was shocked. I never missed school; not a single day. One Friday I took my farseness and because my friend Merica was not going to school, I didn't want to go. I got up early and started crying for belly pain. I expected Mammy to say stay in bed; instead she said if my belly hurting it's because I wanted a wash out, and out came the castor oil bottle. When I saw it, I said I felt better, but she said I must drink the oil to make sure the pain don't come back. I had no choice, either I drink it without any fuss or I'll get the whip to help it down my throat. From that day I learnt my lesson.

But before I tell you about that Friday when Mammy said I wasn't going to school, let me tell you about the school, because it have something to do with what happened that day.

When I was nine I moved to the big school on the hill. We had to wear nice smart uniform – navy-blue skirt, white bodice, black shoes and white socks. The first day I stepped out in my uniform I felt like a princess. Mammy thought I was a princess as well; she said I looked smarter than all the other children. Only some of my friends went to that school; the others went to different schools. Jeannette and Marcelle came but Pamsue went to a school in town. We didn't miss her, because she only played with us at school. Her parents told her not to play with us, because they think they better than us.

I really missed Merica. She and Miss Berty gone without a word to anybody. When she was here we shared each other's secrets. I liked Jeannette and Marcelle, but they weren't the same. Sometimes I thought they laughed at me behind my back. I don't tell them any of my secrets. Anyway, my new teacher was very nice. The first week I went to that school she told me she came from Mount Granby. I told Mammy about it and she looked sort of strange. I wasn't sure if she was vex or not. She looked at me and all she said was 'really'. The following Tuesday she gave me a letter to give to the teacher. I was afraid. I kept on thinking it was something bad about me, but when Miss Oliver read the letter she started to laugh. She was real pretty when she laughed. She was not as dark as Mammy but had the same short tough hair and stubby face; they could even pass as family. I was surprised when Mammy said that Miss Oliver knew my grandparents.

It was the first time I ever remember her saying anyone knew anything about her background. The only other time was once she said that when she was pregnant some of her family wanted to take the baby as soon as it was born. They said she could not look after herself let alone a baby, but she told them that no one was having her child. Because she was determined to keep me her father and mother threw her out of their house, saying she disgraced them. She lived with a friend until I was born then she moved to Happy Hill. When I had about four someone found the little house in Grand Roy for us. We lived there for a long time. All that time she never mentioned about her parents in Mount Granby, but now Miss Oliver teaching in my school, it seem as if things will change. A few days after she sent the letter to Miss, she came to the school. She didn't tell me she was coming, when I saw her in the corridor, I almost wet myself. Anyway it was Miss she wanted, not me. They talked and laughed for a long time like old friends. When Mammy was ready to leave, I heard her tell Miss that she'll see her when she get back. I didn't understand what was happening and I didn't want to ask questions.

Since Mister Oscar started coming to see Mammy she was a lot happier, well now she was even happier. Always singing and joking even when she was washing and ironing. The other thing was Mister bought a new car; brand new it was. He would come home in the evening and take us for long drives to different parts of the island. He treated us real nice, but I still didn't like him. I didn't trust him. The way he would turn those eyes and look at me and grin those gold teeth as if he knew something nobody else knew. Apart from him I was very happy. He was taking care of Mammy, and now Miss and Mammy became friends, things were good for me. Me and Mammy were good friends as well, but still I was surprised when she told me I wasn't going to school.

'Why Mammy? Where we going?' I knew I shouldn't ask but I was so surprised I wanted to know.

'You ask too much question,' she teased. 'You'll soon find out when we get there.'

'Is Mister Oscar coming?'

'*Uncle* Oscar!' she snapped. 'Why you treat him so bad, eh girl? Why? Everything you want he give you. He brought all those fresh flowers and even new tins for you to plant them in, because he knows how much you like flowers. He always talk about the first time you two met. The bad eye you gave him when he almost knock down your flower plant. He knows you don't like him and he feels bad about it, and . . . '

'Mammy where we going?'

She sighed, then gave a little laugh. 'Somewhere very, very special. You don't think I'll take you out of school for nothing, do you? Hurry up and get dressed.'

About nine o'clock we were ready to go to wherever that 'special' place was. We were dressed in our best clothes. Mammy looked so young and nice. I kept looking at her, wondering if something was wrong with her. I remembered once, Merica said that sometimes when people started changing, when things like their hair got longer and prettier and their faces get all bright and things like that, is because they'll soon be dead. She said sometimes they do strange things like going to places they never been before; all the while it's death playing with them. Now Mammy started acting strange and her face is much prettier and younger looking, and though I was all dressed up in my nice pretty clothes I was frightened; afraid that it was death playing with my mother.

By the time we were ready to leave I was so afraid my clothes were wringing wet from sweat; suppose Mammy dropped dead when we went out, what'll happen to me? I don't want to stay with Mister Oscar, that's for sure. I told Mammy let's make short cut down by the church. I said it like I wanted to see somebody there. The Pentecostal church was always open. I thought if we passed there I would go in for a few minutes and pray. And maybe I would get the spirit like the Pentecostal people do when they prayed. Sometimes when they prayed and beat the tambourine, they would start to dance and sing and shake and all sorts of things would happen to them, strange things. Merica said it's the power that fall on them. She said when they have the power they can do all sorts of things. That God answered their prayer better than the other church people.

I remember once there was a big service in that church, people came from all over the island and even from Trinidad and St Vincent, they said it was the celebration of the first time the power ever fall on anyone. I didn't know; I didn't understand. Anyway, that night me, Mammy and a lot of people from the other churches – the Anglican, the Catholic, Seventh Day Adventist – all of us stand up outside to listen to the service.

I would never forget that night. The people made one amount of noise in the place – bawling and shouting, screaming and chanting – all at the same time. I heard Mr Bayne calling for help for his sore foot, Miss Melda begging to heal her jigger hand. Old Jacob, who lived up in the bush in Boawden, he asking God to send his daughter back to him; I never knew he had a daughter. All the while they shouting and chanting their eyes closed tight tight. Merica say is to shut out the world. Some of them danced up and down the aisle, up and down the aisle, all the while we heard the preacher's voice above the rest calling down the Holy Fire.

They went on and on like that for a long time. One minute things quieten down, only the moaning you could hear, then all of a sudden someone shouted and things started again, worse than before. Some groaned as if people was beating them with old stick. Some looking wet, wet as if they fall in the river. Water was running down their legs and faces as if they walked in a shower of rain. The next day Merica told me it wasn't ordinary water running down their legs but is pee they pee themselves. That Merica always! I don't know if is true. But they say when they have the power in their soul they have no control over what they do. Next day they don't remember a single thing.

I don't believe everything, but I wanted to give it a try. I thought if I went there for a few minutes things would be all right. Mammy was a bit worried when I said that we should pass down by the church, because she never send me to that church and she said she did not know that I had any friends living around there. She said it was getting late and we don't have time to waste. I decided to keep a close watch on her all the time.

When we reached the fore-road outside the police station, instead of catching the bus going down town side, we catch one going the other way. I was sure something was wrong.

I remembered we only went up the western side once, and that was to Miss Ellie's funeral. Anyway, we stayed on the bus until we reached Douglastone Bridge, then Mammy said we would wait for another bus. She asked the driver how long he think we would have to wait before we get a bus to Mount Granby.

My brain almost exploded. Mount Granby! How stupid I was! Mount Granby! That's what the meeting and letter between Mammy and Miss Oliver was all about. Merica always saying I stupid; now I agree with her. Miss Oliver came from Mount Granby. Mammy parents belong to the same place! Well, how strange.

Soon another bus came and we were on our way. Mammy settled me down at a window seat where I could look at the view, while she chatted to the conductor like they were old friends. She made friends with any stranger. One of her sayings was a stranger is a friend you do not know. If she said howdy to someone and they don't answer, then they could go to hell. I did not listen to their conversation; I was watching the road. I never seen so many holes in a main road. Deep, deep holes in the middle of the road. The driver kept swinging the bus from side to side to prevent it from going down in the holes. The best piece of road was like a track between a steep white rock and a deep precipice. It seemed as if we travelled miles and miles before we came to the first house – a big white house. I don't understand why all these big houses had to be painted white, as if that's the only colour paint.

Mammy and the conductor chatted and chatted; every few minutes she'd smile at me and say we would soon be there. At last the bus stopped at this place. It was like a little town in the middle of nowhere. Everything was so clean – the road, the houses around – everything clean, clean. It was about eleven o'clock when we reached Mount Granby but there was a lot of children around when they should be at school. Everything was strange to me. I held on to Mammy's hand.

I heard someone shouting Mammy's name. I looked across

the road and saw this big man running towards us. He was shouting and waving his hands to us like a lunatic. I held on to Mammy tighter.

When he reached up to us, his voice became very quiet as if he was not sure.

'Miss Beryl; it is Miss Beryl,' he whispered, sort of half asking and half saying.

Mammy looked at the man, squinted her eyes, and looked into his face. 'Marco; Marco, is that you?' she said.

The man grinned, showing his teeth threaded with mango strings, then he nodded. He tried to speak again, but no words could come out. He stood in front of us nodding like a lunatic.

Mammy grabbed his hand, 'Marco; Marco is that really you?'

'Yes, yes, is me Miss Beryl; is me Marco.'

Mammy took the man by the shoulders and turned him around examining him and looking him up and down.

'Marco! You turn big man. Lawd! Just look at you. If I meet you in town I might of pass you. Gloria, this is Marco, say howdy.' She introduced us.

I don't know why but I was looking at Marco's eyes. In my mind I was praying they were not like Mister Oscar's. Funny how stupidness come into your mind.

Marco took the basket from Mammy and lead us across the road. I grabbed hold of Mammy's hand again, this time no Marco will make me let go. We started going up a little hill. Then Mammy stopped and stood gazing at a house a few yards away. It was a nice big house, painted green and light brown, with a lovely flower garden in the front. She stood there staring at the house like a statue. I looked at her and saw her eyes full of water.

'Come on, Miss Beryl, come on, we almost there,' Marco nudged her softly.

I was still worried. I couldn't forget that I hadn't passed by the church this morning. Shouldn't have let anything stop me. As we approached the house I saw a man and a woman waving from the verandah. Then the woman started coming down the steps. When Mammy saw her she started running towards them and I started running too. I don't know why really, but I think is just that Mammy running and I was not letting her get away from me. When the woman reached close to us I felt as if I knew her. There was something about her that made me feel nice inside. I don't understand it; I just knew I was glad to see this stranger. She and Mammy stood looking at each other, not a single word, just staring at each other; then as if somebody gave them a great push, they were in each other's arms. They were hugging, shaking and crying all at the same time. I held on to Mammy's dress, but for a few minutes she forgot me. She clung on to this strange woman.

I did not notice the man had come into the yard until I heard him call my name. I turned around and he was standing behind us. He lifted me up and started kissing me. He was crying too. Although he was a stranger, I was not afraid. I felt safe; felt as if I knew him too.

'Gloria,' he whispered in my ear. 'Gloria; at last, at last.' He pressed my face tightly against his as he spoke. 'Gloria, I is your grandpa.'

I almost jumped out of his arms. I tried to look at his face but was unable to turn from the way he held me. He lifted me into the house. I wanted to get off and walk, thinking he would strain himself lifting up a big girl like me. If he was my grandpa then I supposed the lady was my grandma. We went inside. Everyone hugged, kissed and cried all at the same time. I was so happy. Now Jeannette would not be able to show off on me anymore. She on about her grandmother this and her grandpa that; everyday she come to school she bluffing about her grandparents. Wait until I go to school on Monday; just wait. As soon as she open her mouth I'll make her shut up. I saw a different Mammy. She was sort of peaceful, like a child herself – the way she spoke to her parents, the way she answered them.

It was a new world to me and I loved it. I was happy; Mammy was happy, but still I had that nagging feeling to visit the church, if only to make sure the Devil was not playing tricks. A lot of people came to see Mammy. They said they were glad we came home and they hoped we wouldn't stay away so long again. Miss Oliver's mother came to see us too. I remembered her from the time I saw her at the school. I wish Merica was still living near us, then we would have a lot to talk about when I got home. The strange thing is how she and Miss Berty went away without saying a word to anyone. No one knows where they ended up. I can't talk to Merica, so I will have to talk to Miss when I go to school on Monday. Since I went to that school I liked her; now I like her even more. If it wasn't for her, Mammy would not have had the courage to get in touch with her parents.

Grandma had breakfast ready for us. She cooked all kinds of food, but my favourite was the chicken roti. Then she had a big basket of fruit on the kitchen table – all kinds of fruits – some you only see in town, because they don't grow all over the island. I thought she must spend plenty of money on them. I did not want it to look as if I was greedy, I only took one little sugar apple.

'It's for you, Gloria,' Grandma laughed, 'eat as much as you want.' She said there were all sort of fruits growing in their yard at the back of the house. I was very excited. Fancy not having to buy skin-up and damson, I thought. I loved it at Grandma's; not only for the fruits but there was plenty of flowers growing in front and around the house. Some I'd never seen before. I decided to ask for some plants, at the same time I thought I would have to get some more empty tins. I remember thinking, that follow-fashion Jeannette would do the same. If I plant two or three different flowers in one tin, she would do the same. She used to copy everything she see and then she say she had it first. I decided that one of these days I would set a trap for her.

While Mammy and Grandpa chatted, I was in the kitchen with Grandma, but I could not help what I overheard. Mammy always told me not to listen to big people conversation, but I can't help what I hear. I don't know what they were talking about but I heard Mister Oscar's name mentioned. That really upset me. And I thought, I hope he don't intend to come here and spoil things for me.

We spend the whole day in Mount Granby. Marco and his sister Rosa lived in the little house behind Grandpa's. They were like Grandpa's children. They helped my grandparents around the house, gardening, cleaning and things like that. Grandma said that their mother died when they were very young and since then they treated them like their own children. Grandpa cleared his throat, and Grandma gave him one bad eye. Then Mammy started laughing. I didn't find anything funny in that, but big people are very funny sometimes. I don't always understand them.

I liked Rosa. During the day she asked Mammy if it was all right to take me to the shop with her. It was the first time I saw such a place. One big house with a lot of little stalls. It was just like harvest time in the big school. I asked Rosa why it was like that. She said Mount Granby is the only place in the whole island with an indoor market. It was like one long house taking up one side of the road. Rosa asked if I wanted an ice cone. We went over to where a lady had her ice-cream can on top of a box, and other things like sugar cake and fudge next to it.

'Choose anything you want,' Rosa said. 'If you want it mix, Miss . . . '

At that moment the stall woman turned to face us. Merica always telling me about spirits and I heard other people talked about them. They say things like when someone dies the spirit comes back and walk about. That never frightened me because I always thought that when you dead, you dead, and that's that. I remember once Merica said you turn spirit even if you are not dead. I told her she talking stupidness. Now I wasn't sure. She told me about this woman called Miss Mary, who used to live in the Bay Road – how she went away for a long long time, yet people used to hear her shouting in the back garden every morning. I still was not afraid, until now. I don't understand why, but I look at the woman in front us and I'm sure she is a spirit.

'You all right Gloria?' Rosa was asking. 'What's the matter?'

I did not realise that I stood there staring at the woman and shaking like I had ague fever. I just couldn't believe my eyes. Months ago she vanished. The last time anyone saw her, she was preaching up and down Paradise New Road, dressed in black, with red ribbons tied around her head and waist. No one knew what happened to Merica, now Miss Berty turn up in Mount Granby selling ice-cream. The way she was staring at me, she didn't believe her eyes either.

'Gloria!' she screeched, holding her head and squinting her eyes. 'Gloria! my goodness. Gawd bless my eyes.'

She left from behind the can and came to hug me. This is not a spirit at all, I thought. This is really Miss Berty. My eyes were fixed on her face.

'Good-day Miss Berty,' I said.

'You know that lady, Gloria?' Rosa asked, even more surprised than me.

'Aye, aye how you mean if she know me. We used to be neighbour,' Miss Berty answered Rosa.

'Where is Merica?' I asked. 'Is she here?' I got really excited.

'Glory, Glory,' she hugged me. 'I know you never liked anyone call you Glory, but I'm so glad to see you, I can't help it. Child, you get so big. How is Miss Beryl?' She prattled on.

'Mammy well. Where is Merica? Can I go and see her?'

All the while we talking, Rosa stood by the ice-cream drum laughing. I'm sure she thought it funny someone saying they knew Miss Berty.

'Glory; what you doing in Mount Granby? You have people here?' Miss Berty went on.

'Where is Merica?' I asked again, this time a little louder, because it looked as if Miss Berty gone deaf.

Before she had a chance to say anything Rosa told her that Mr Johnson across the fore-road is my grandfather and we up here to spend the day.

'Mr Johnson!' Miss Berty screech. 'You mean that old

bugger is Gloria's grandpa and all this time I didn't know. Lawd what a life; this world is really small in truth. Wait a minute! If he is Gloria's grandfather, you don't mean to say he is Beryl's father, eh?'

'Yes,' I piped in. 'And the lady is my grandma. Miss Berty where is Merica?' I asked over and over for Merica, but it seemed as if Miss Berty wasn't hearing me at all. She just wasn't answering me, not saying a word about my friend. I felt strange. I thought perhaps she still mad. Maybe she done something funny to Merica.

'Is Miss Beryl up here?' she turned to Rosa.

'Yes, she over at Mr Johnson.'

'Lawd Gawd,' she started to laugh. 'I never come across anything like that in all my life. He always talking about his one daughter who went somewhere or the other and he never hear from her, all the time he mean my friend. Just fancy that; aye aye just fancy that.' Miss Berty prattled.

'Miss Berty,' I shouted, 'where is Merica? Can I see her?'

All of a sudden she became vex, vex. I didn't want to make her vex, but I wanted to know about my friend. She handed me a big ice-cream, twitched her mouth and said that Merica gone to stay with her father in Calivigny. I was confused and frightened. All the time we lived near each other Merica never knew her father. Now Miss Berty saying she gone to live with him. I wanted to ask her more, but she was really vex now. She started quarrelling. I told Rosa let's go.

'Tell Miss Beryl howdy,' Miss Berty shouted after us.

I was sorry I didn't see Merica. One good thing, if what Miss Berty said was true, now Merica might have a grandma as well. All the time the man in the big house back home didn't want his children to play with us because he thought we were nobodies, me and Merica had our grandparents. I had the mind to go and tell him all about it when I got back, but Mammy might have given me a beating. One day when I get big I sure will tell that man what I think of him and his family.

'I didn't know that you know Miss Berty!' Rosa said.

'Yes, they used to live by us. Merica was my best friend, then one morning we woke up and she and Miss Berty wasn't there; they just disappeared. Not a word to anybody, they just went. You don't know where Merica really is, do you Rosa?'

'Merica in Calivigny with her father's mother.'

'Her father's mother! Good . . . oh good. Is true what Miss Berty said then. That mean Merica really has a grandma.' I was so glad I wanted to run home to tell Mammy.

'Yes,' Rosa said. 'Somebody told Mr Cato how Miss Berty had the child preaching up and down the road every day, with her head tie up with big red cloth. The woman is crazy like a cricket. She had the poor child dragging behind her.'

'So Mr Cato, that is Merica father, just come and take her away?'

'Well, he came a couple of times before to see Merica. Then one day, I think was the day after the motor bike almost knock down Merica, he came up here, told Miss Berty either she stop her stupidness or he taking his child. They had one Bacchanal in the middle of the road, right in the junction. She threatened to chop him up if he touch her child. He threatened her with the police. Was one thing in the place that day.'

'Where was Merica all that time?'

'The girl went and hid behind the shops, crying. She didn't know what to do. She didn't even know she had a father until a few months before. Apparently her mother told her that her father died a long time ago. Then when Mr Cato traced Miss Berty and asked about his child, she told him that the child died a few months after it was born. That woman crazy a long, long time. I don't know why she not in the crazy house, you know!'

I don't understand all these things. Why Miss Berty told Merica her father died and then told the man that the child died? I don't understand at all. Perhaps she have a reason. Or perhaps is what these people say. This woman has the Devil in her head for sure.

'How Mr Cato find Miss Berty and Merica then?' I was really confused now. All the time me and Merica playing together we never thought about our fathers; not a lot anyway. We always had our mothers.

Rosa shook her head, looking as if she was confused too.

'Well, it's a long time before the man knew his child was alive. Somehow, someone they both knew years ago met him in Trinidad and told him about Miss Berty and a little girl. One thing led to another, so he decided to try to find the woman when he came back to Grenada. Apparently every time he heard she was somewhere, by the time he get there she disappear. Eventually he catch up with her, up here. The first time he came she was preaching. He threatened her then, but that didn't make any difference. The strange thing is sometimes Miss Berty is as normal as anybody else. Like now, she would sell in her shop, go to church and things like that, then she'd change.'

'I know. She used to do some funny things when they lived by us as well.'

'Is a strange woman, Gloria, strange woman. They say she change with the moon. Anyway Mr Cato kept on coming to see Merica, then one day he came with his sister and took her away. Since then we never saw her again, but I heard she going to school at the Girls' High School in Tanteen and she looking real nice.'

While Rosa talked I was thinking about my father. Suppose he is looking for me. I know is nothing like Merica and Miss Berty, because the woman real crazy to say people dead when they're not dead. With Mammy it's different, she said he went away. Since that time long ago when she was combing my hair and said how flashy he was and things like that, she only mentioned him once. That was when Mister said something stupid like I could pass for his daughter. I don't know how he could say a stupid thing like that. The gold teeth must make him blind or something. Even a blind man could see that I don't look anything like that man. He only want to show off. Well, when he said that, Mammy got so mad.

151

'Don't be stupid, Oscar,' she said. 'You want people to laugh at you? Look at Gloria's hair. People would make fun of you, and say you had an upside-down nine.'

He looked at her, rolling those eyes even worse than they are, 'Chupes, at least she'll have a daddy.'

'Don't, don't start on Gloria about her daddy, you hear, don't start. He gone but one day he might come back.' Mammy was vex. I don't understand why Mister Oscar got more vex than Mammy, because he started to curse. He said all sort of nasty things. I didn't worry about him hurting Mammy, because I know she can quarrel more than him. He said something about how Mammy sent my picture to my father because she wanted him to come back. She only pretending she love him, when all the time is Ulric she wanted. Well that sent Mammy sky high.

'Hush your mouth, Oscar,' she shouted. 'Just hush your mouth. You start on Gloria and her picture and I'll swallow you up this morning. Just start; just start and you'll have a real mad woman on your hand. If you want me to open my mouth this morning, just start; heem just start.' Mister Oscar didn't say anything else, he stamped out of the house like a maniac.

Strange how you remember things. All that came to my mind while Rosa was talking about Merica and her father. I remember the picture we took. I wore the nice pink dress Miss Wilma made for me. I only saw the picture once. I forgot all about it until Mister mentioned it. Things started drifting through my mind. I must definitely find a way to go to the church to pray for the power. I didn't want to leave Mammy, but I would like to know my father and perhaps see Merica again. I wanted to stay with Grandpa and Grandma, but I wanted to go back home. I told Mammy about Miss Berty and what Rosa said about her and Merica. Mammy shook her head. Grandma said the woman is as crazy as a bat. She said Miss Berty changed with the moon. She said lately she's been good, but they don't know how long it would last. I knew I definitely had to go to the church. I had to pray for Miss Berty too.

It was getting late. I thought we should leave soon or we'd miss the last bus home. When I told Mammy it was time to go she said don't worry, we'll get transportation. Every minute Grandpa was hugging and kissing me. He and Grandma pretended to fight for me. I was real happy. All the time that stupid girl at school boasting about her grandparents as if she alone in the whole world had grandparents, all that time mine were not far away. Wait until I go to school on Monday, then she would know who she showing off on.

It was already dark when Mammy said it's time to get ready to go. I was a bit disappointed as I thought she had changed her mind and we were staying the night, then again I would have the chance to go to the church. Anyway, Grandma said we must come back soon and during the school holiday I could come to spend time with her. I had asked for a plant off the big rubber plant at the side of the house. Grandpa said he would set a piece for me.

It was just like Christmas when we were ready to leave. Grandma packed up a big basket of all sort of things for us, then Marco and Rosa brought some more things. Grandma gave me a dollar and Grandpa gave me two. I was worried about how we were going to carry all that load, when I heard Grandpa asked Mammy if she sure 'he' would remember to come to meet us, and Mammy saying, 'Yes, Oscar is a good man.' Although I was worried, now hearing his name made me real vex. Fancy he had to come up here to spoil things for me. I don't see why he had to come right up here. I was there thinking that I hope he just wait for us on Douglastone Bridge.

After that first visit, we went to Mount Granby regularly. Marco and Rosa were like my big sister and brother although they were as old as Mammy. One day Mister Oscar drove us up there. He took a different route from the bus. He said he don't like driving under the big rock, if big stone break away it would throw people right down the precipice. He spent the whole day with us. I was really vex. Fancy having the cokey-eye watching you all day at your grandparents'.

Somehow he and Grandpa seemed to get on well; they were mostly together. I spent most of the time with Rosa, but one time when I went in the kitchen for something everybody was serious; serious as though they were discussing death.

I didn't know what they were talking about, but one time I heard Grandpa shouting and Grandma trying to shut him up. Anyway, whatever it was, was sorted out by the time we were ready to go home. When we got home Mister Oscar told Mammy it was too late for him to go to his house, can he sleep in our house. She gave him one bad eye and said no man sleeping in her house, the same thing she used to say to Uncle Ben. Anyway, we only had the one bedroom. When it was Uncle Ben, I didn't see why she didn't give him some bedding and a pillow and let him sleep in the hall. I used to feel sorry for him, because I really liked him, and sometimes I thought he must be lonely on his own. With Mister Oscar it was different, I didn't like him. There was something about him that frightened me. I still had the feeling to go to the church to pray for the power to make him go away and don't come back, but that would have made Mammy unhappy, because she liked him and it looked as if Grandpa like him too.

It was about two months after Mister Oscar first went to see Grandma that Mammy came home happy and singing. That's when she told me that we moving away from the village. We lived in that little place for a long time; everyone knew us, even the police in the station were always friendly. I hoped we were not moving too far away. Everyone was nice around here. It was only that man in the big house that used to play big shot. Since I found my grandparents and heard about Merica, I didn't pay him any mind. He couldn't show off on me and Mammy anymore. People said that with all he think he was so high and mighty he couldn't control his own children. His big daughter ran away with the Syrian who used to pass every Sunday selling clothes and things. Since Merica gone, was Isabel who told me what was going on. She told me that the girl ran away to live with the Syrian in Ducane. Every Sunday he used to come with his bundle of cloth and things in a bag, he talking nice, nice to the parents all the while was the daughter he was after. When the father found out what was going on he kicked up one hell. The daughter didn't pay him any mind; she packed her bags and moved to Ducane with the Syrian. Her father was so 'shame he hide himself in the house playing sick.

That's what Isabel told me and one day I heard Mammy and Miss Silla talking about the same thing. Miss Silla said the man was like an imbecile. He stopped hiding and wanted to talk to everybody he didn't use to say howdy to before. I was surprised to see Mr Joe and Pamsue going to the house to drink rum. Before, that man didn't even used to drink a malt with nobody, now he knocking back white rum like water. He didn't want his daughter Pamsue to play with children like me and Merica, now she following me everywhere I go. One day she started to cry. I felt sorry for her. I asked her what was wrong, is then she told me that her mother was not home. Apparently the woman had enough of the man, the way he was carrying on, so she left him with the two younger children and went to stay with her daughter in Ducane. I didn't say anything, but I did notice how dirty their yard was. Rubbish piled up high, high in the front yard. Pamsue said that every night her father drunk, he didn't care what happened to she and Derek. In a way, I was glad if we did move away.

'Where we going to, Mammy?' I kept on asking.

She didn't say anything. All she on about was how I would like the house and it wasn't far away. She said I would still see my friends because I would not change school. The day after she told me about the move I heard she and Miss Mabel talking under Mr Maurice's mango tree. I say Mr Maurice mango tree, but he don't even sure where his boundary was. The old lady who was living near the gap said it was not his, because she knew where the line is suppose to pass. Everybody picked up the mangoes when they fall. We don't care who they for. We pay rent, so no reason why we shouldn't pick up the mango.

Mr Maurice so mean, one day he came to collect the rent,

he saw Stephen and his little brother picking sugar apple from the tree behind the mango tree, he started quarrelling with those boys. Threatened to lock them up. Just then Miss Mabel was coming up to her house and heard him. She gave him one piece of cussing down. She told him, he renting those old houses so dear, won't even repair them, she don't see anything wrong with the children picking the sugar apple; he too damn mean, he should be ashamed of himself.

From that day, whenever he came to pick up his money he didn't hang around. What made matters worse was the day Mammy cornered him about fixing the old rotten board at the back of our house. She told him if the wind blow too hard the board would fall out and beast would easily come inside. She said she would not pay him one cent until he repair the house. He knew she meant what she said. The next week he sent a man with two pieces of re-dressed board to patch up the house. He didn't even do it properly, only patch, patch. Anyway Mr Maurice never came around when he know Mammy was home, not even for his rent. He always sent his boy for it.

Well, as I was saying, Mammy and Miss Mabel was talking under the mango tree. Mammy told her about the new house and when we moving and thing. Miss Mabel was so glad, she laughed and laughed and clapped her hands. She was so glad to hear we were having our own house. I heard Mammy say how she is going to 'cut style on the old devil in the big house'. How he look like la diablesse' son. Then Miss Mabel said something that made me jump. I didn't understand these things; I shouldn't even be listening to big people talk, but I couldn't help hearing.

'So you and Oscar make up your minds at last. You decide to do it now!' Miss Mabel said.

I started to shake. I didn't wait to hear what Mammy said. I went inside and started to cry. All the time Mammy said about we moving; on about me having my own own room, I never thought about him. I was not sure what Miss Mabel meant, but I was sure I am not going to live in any house with him. Mammy came in a little while after and found me crying. When she asked me what was wrong, I said nothing, nothing is wrong. Then she said if nothing wrong with me and I'm crying she'd take me to the doctor the next day because perhaps I want a wash out. I didn't want to go to the doctor because I knew he would end up giving me some old bitter medicine or a dose of stinking castor oil.

I decided to ask Mammy about Mister Oscar; if he was coming to the new house. Is then she told me it was him buying the house for us and it was only right for him to live with us. I started to cry even more. I couldn't help it. Mammy was so happy for us to move to that new place, all the time she knew he was coming too. She went on to say all he wanted was for us to be happy; how she know I don't like him, she wish I would tell her what he ever done to hurt me. The more she talked, the more I cried. She got so vex, she said if I don't shut up she going to give me something to cry for. It's a long time since she gave me a beating and I didn't want her to start again, so I shut up. I asked her if it was all right for me to go to live in Mount Granby with Grandma. She didn't say a word, just gave me one long look and turned away.

All the next day she was still vex, because she said nothing to me except, Glory do this and Glory do that. I knew she still vex because that is the only times she called me Glory.

I spent most of the day with my flowers, talking to them. I changed some of the tins around, made sort of different patterns. Swapped the ones with heavy flowers around the yard and along the steps and even under the window. When I was finished, everything looked new. I trimmed the branches off the hibiscus and the tall sunflower because they were climbing the side of the house and beast could jump from them straight on to the house. When Mammy said we were moving I said to myself, I'll take all my flowers with me. The big trees, I'll take cuttings from them to plant around the new house – but now I hear that that man would be coming, I decided that I would take all my things up to Grandma.

That evening I sat on the step thinking; then Mammy came

and sat down beside me. She said nothing. Just sat there
watching me under the skin of her eyes. I wanted to go and
sit in her lap, but I was not sure if she was still vex. Anyway
after a few minutes she put her arms around my shoulder. I
felt real good.

'What the matter Gloria?'

'Nothing!'

'Why you don't like Oscar? Tell Mammy; he ever do you
anything? You know anything bad? Tell Mammy!'

'No.'

'Then tell me why you don't like him.'

'I don't know Mammy; I just don't like him.'

'He buying a nice house for us, it's only fair for him to
live there too. He don't have any children. He likes to think
of you as his daughter.'

'Sorry Mammy, he is not my father.'

'I wish I knew what he's done to you. He is coming to
the new house, instead of going somewhere else every night,
it's the best way. He would look after us better; you'll see.'

'When I have my own room, where would Mister Oscar
sleep? Is there three bedrooms in the house?'

Mammy took a deep breath. I was shaking inside. I had a
feeling I had asked a big person question. She shook her
head, rubbed her hands in my hair and went back inside. I
don't know what made me say about the bedroom. I remember one day, before Jane went away, we were talking, and she
told me and Merica, all sort of things about what happened
between a man and woman in the bedroom, but I didn't
understand. It sounded like Jane was too womanish for us.
I didn't know where she got these things from. I wanted to
tell Mammy at the time, but I thought she might get vex
and beat me for listening to Jane.

Anyway, after about ten minutes Mammy came back and
sat beside me on the step.

'Gloria,' she said, 'you getting a big girl now, and there
things you must know in this world. I don't want you to
listen to your friends because what they say is not always
true.' My mind ran back to Jane.

158

'Mister Oscar, as you choose to call him,' Mammy went on, 'will be living with us, just like if he was your daddy.' She then went on to tell me about husband and wife. She said she didn't want to fill my head too much yet, but she hoped I understand enough not to think bad of her. The way she talked it didn't sound bad at all. Not the way Jane made it sound, especially when she said about seeing blood every month. *She* made it out like only bad girls these things happened to. I didn't understand everything Mammy said, but I felt a bit better in my mind.

After Mammy told me things, I accepted that it was better for Mister Oscar to come to live with us. I did not like him, but because Mammy seemed so happy when she talked about him, I decided to accept him. Me and Mammy sat on the steps for a long, long time, until it started to get very dark. The next day being Saturday, I didn't have to go to school. Friday was a special holiday, so it made the time feel different, like it was a long time since I been to school. Anyway, I stayed in bed a bit later.

'Mammy Beryl!' someone called from the main road.

It was about nine o'clock; we were not expecting anybody. At first I didn't take any notice. I thought it was one of the girls from the bay selling jacks or something.

'Mammy Beryl!' the person called again, this time right in the front yard. I got up and went in the hall to see who it was. Well! I almost dropped down. I thought I was seeing spirit. Fancy! Just fancy after all that time.

Mammy looked out of the kitchen window at the same time. She gave one screech. 'Good Lawd; Gawd bless my eyes this morning. Gloria, Gloria look outside, look in the yard.'

Well, quick, quick I catch my breath, and jumped outside so fast I almost knock down the tin of jump-up-and-kiss-me. I couldn't believe my eyes. Fancy Merica standing in the yard this morning! She just standing there laughing. She looked so nice. Well dressed up in blue and white pleated dress and nice black shove-on on her foot. The girl looked so nice; she even looked taller than when she lived here. I stood in front of her and just stared. I couldn't take it in. My best friend come back to see me. Now I can tell her all my secrets. Everything I couldn't tell anybody else. I would tell her about my grandma, about we moving to another house, even how Mister Oscar coming to live with us. I was so glad to see her, I didn't know what to say, so I stood looking at her like a zombie, all the while my mind turning over and over.

'How you looking at me so?' was the first thing she said, her eyes shining like a new moon.

I laughed. Then she started laughing. Then we hugged each other and laughed and laughed like two idiots. I looked at Mammy and saw she was laughing too; laughing at us. I was so glad to see Merica, I didn't even ask her what she doing in Grand Roy. We spent the whole day together. Talked, laughed and roamed all over the place, just like old times. She said she asked her father a long time ago to take her up to see us; all he said was one day he would, but he never did, perhaps he was afraid she was going to run away to Miss Berty. Anyway they heard that Miss Berty was in Trinidad, so he decided she could come to see me. She said she missed her mother but she loved her father and grand-mother very much. When I told her about my grandparents she was so happy for me, she started to cry. She said she hoped one day my father would come and find me. I told her about how I didn't want Mister Oscar to come to the new house, because I didn't like him, and I didn't see why he had to sleep in Mammy's bedroom.

'What you vex for?' she laughed. 'Where you want him to sleep?'

'I told you all the time; I don't like him. I'll never like him as long as I live. I don't know why he don't stop where he is.'

Merica thought that was very funny. She laughed louder still, all the while looking at me as if she was a big woman.

Then she started telling me how it would be better for Mister Oscar to live with us because he and Mammy like each other and things like that. Another thing is the money he was spending living somewhere else he could spend on me and Mammy. Hearing Merica saying that made me feel a bit better and Mammy already told me about these things. I thought it strange how Merica knew all these big people things.

'Eh, eh, how come you know all these big people talk, Merica? Who tell you all these things?'

'I older than you, remember,' was all she said, still looking at me like a big woman.

'You older than me. Just wait. I soon have ten years. In December, December ninth I'll have ten. Only two months to go.'

'So you think that will make you a big woman, then?' she teased.

Mammy had cooked our favourite food. After we had eaten she gave us some money and told us to go and enjoy ourselves.

'Remember Merica has to go home tonight,' she shouted as we ran out of the yard.

Merica told me that her father would be coming to pick her up about six o'clock that evening. I was real glad because I wanted to see what he looked like. The way she talked about him, she really liked him. We knock about all over the place. We went by the old school because Merica wanted to see the new things that were there. Although it was Saturday, Mr Mac the caretaker was there. He remembered Merica and felt proud to show us the things. The day was hot. We went over to Miss Peter's parlour for ice cone. Just as we were leaving, Pamsue came into the shop. Merica looked at her in a stuck up kind of way, cock up her bottom in the air and passed the girl without saying howdy. Pamsue's face looked as if someone had beaten her. I felt sorry for her. I then told Merica how the girl's father took to drinking white rum and calling all kinds of people in the house to drink with him. I told her how all that started after the big daughter ran away with the Syrian and then his wife went to live with the daughter in Ducane. Merica was shocked, but that didn't stop her from bursting out laughing.

'What so funny?' I asked. 'You wouldn't like people to start laughing at you, would you?'

'Serve her right. Serve all of them right. Remember, Gloria. Remember how they used to play big shot? Used to cut style on us? We were not good enough to play with her. Her father thought because they had a big house and a little money that they were better than us. Serve them right. If I see him, I'll make sure I laugh in his face.'

'You wouldn't do that, really Merica? Would you?'

'Naw, you know me. I couldn't laugh at a big person in the face; I feel a bit sorry for them, especially Pamsue. I going be well tempted to show off on the father though. Perhaps one day when I turn big.'

'Well you can't. Because he dead.'

'Dead! What you mean dead?'

'Yes, Merica, dead . . . dead.'

'Dead! Oh my Gawd! You didn't say he is dead.'

'You didn't give me a chance. Girl it was one hell of a thing in this place that time. I never see anything like that in my life.'

'What happened? Lawd, Gloria, he didn't kill himself? Did he?'

'I don't know. I don't think so. Some people said he drank the old white rum for days without eating and the rum cut his liver. But Miss Mabel said Uncle Baba told her that the man did not touch a drop of rum the day he died.'

Merica stood in front of me, her mouth wide open.

'You remember Miss Mabel and Uncle Baba that used to live behind Uncle Ben dasheen piece? Well according to Miss Mabel he told her that the man wasn't drunk, but was acting strange.'

'Strange? How you mean strange? Girl, I wish I was here. I don't understand how he could be stranger that he was already.'

'I don't know. He was just funny; strange; making all sort of macaque. Uncle Baba said the man went a funny, funny

162

colour. Like all his blood in his face and hands settle in his foot. Then he started calling on all people who died years ago. You know; all the people who bury in the burial ground under Kakaul.'

'Lawd, you mean he remembered all these people name. He must've been working with the Devil.'

'I tell you was one thing in this place that day. One time they say he started shouting for his mother, telling her to meet him under the boli tree.'

'Boli tree? Which boli tree? You don't mean the one in front his door?'

'I don't know; could be the one by the busherie. You remember he used to go and sit down under the tree late, late in the evening? This man was always funny. Well Uncle Baba told Miss Mabel that the man called him in the house early, early that morning and started telling him things about his family. He was just running, running his mouth. He was drunk but not from any liquor. It was the evil coming out of him. That's what the people said. He had so much badness in him, his heart string couldn't take anymore and it just burst.'

'Lawd!' Merica poked out her eyes at me.

'Yes, they said the load was too heavy for him to carry, so he dropped down dead, just like that. He said he was tired and wanted to lie down. He reached the bottom of the stairs, put one foot on the step, missed and dropped – dead.'

'I would've liked to see that. Just fancy, he used to think he and his family was so nice and look what happen. Remember, Gloria, remember he won't let Pamsue play with us?'

'I know, but I sorry for her though. It's not her fault her father worked with the Devil. Well that is what the people say. They say he work with the Devil and the Devil wanted payment, so it take possession of his soul. That's what they say. Me; I don't know.'

'Poor girl,' Merica muttered. 'I know what I said, but I feel sorry for her. I feel bad now. Let's go and find her.'

We went after her, but when we met Albert crossing the road, he said Pamsue had caught a bus going up to Ducane.

Since her father died, her mother came down for a couple of days and went back. The woman said she will never live in that house again. Pamsue, her brother and Aunty Rita live there now. Anyway we didn't let that spoil our day. We had a very good time. When we got back home, Merica stood in the gap looking at my flowers, her face kind of sad.

'When you move I hope you take all your plants with you,' she said.

'Yeh, she could take all she wants to take,' Mammy said. She was standing in front the door watching us, but we so busy with each other we didn't notice her.

'She really like her flowers, eh Mammy Beryl?'

'I know, I know. Did she tell you all about the other house? The front yard is bigger than here. I could just see her planting this, that and the other. You used to like flowers, Merica, don't you plant anymore?'

'Yes, I have a lovely garden at my grandma's.'

'How would I bring all these flowers with me?' I turned to Mammy. 'I don't even know where the house is.'

'What time your father coming for you?' Mammy asked Merica.

'He said about six. Knowing him it will be after seven,' she smiled.

'Good; if we leave now, we could see the new house before he comes,' Mammy said.

'Yes please, Mammy. We could do that. Please.' I jumped for joy. I was so glad my best friend was coming to see the new house with me. Since me and Merica talked about Mister Oscar moving in with us I don't feel so bad. Mammy was surprised to see how glad I was. I think she was waiting for me to say something else. We looked at each other and laughed.

The house was something else. There was space in the front for me to make a real flower garden. Merica showed me where to plant the flowers when I bring them over. The place was really nice and it was not far from where we live now, so I could walk down the road to see my friends. I liked how it was painted as well, although Mammy said that

Mister Oscar will paint it over when we move in. Merica made one loud noise when she saw my bedroom. She said she will ask her grandmother for her to come and spend time with me during the school holidays. That's the best day I had for a long time. We didn't stay long at the house because Merica's father was coming for her. He came a little after six. He was really as nice as Merica said.

Even long after Merica left I was happy. Mammy said is God that send Merica that morning. I not sure what she meant, but she said it after I say that I don't mind living in the same house with Mister Oscar, so she must feel Merica make me change my mind. That evening when he came home Mammy told him what I said about the house, he said he was glad. Then he take his forwardness and try to hug me and the same pinch my bottom. Well, that made me vex. I just made up my mind to stay in the house with him and he had to spoil things. I told Mammy what he did, all she said was, he only playing with me and how I too stupid and womanish.

Mammy was always busy getting things ready for the new house. She said she wanted us to move before Christmas. Mammy didn't have a lot of time to spend with me as we used to, but I didn't mind because Merica started writing to me every week, telling me all her stories, and secrets and things. That kept me very happy.

The week before she had twelve, in her letter Merica send me an invitation card to her birthday party. I was really glad, not so much for all the new clothes and things Mammy bought for me, but I wanted to see Merica's grandma. Mammy made sure I went down to Calivigny early to have time to see the shops and things where Merica lived. I was so glad; but when I got there I find Merica sort of funny. She was acting like she was bigger than me. As if she didn't even want to talk to me. I thought perhaps Miss Berty came back or something because Merica looked kind of sad. Her grandma was nice though, as nice as mine. My grandma was tall and thin with a head of thick greying hair, but this lady was short and stubby, her hair short and natty and black like charcoal – real nice. She was always smiling.

She was nice, but Merica made me feel funny, she didn't even want to hold my hand. I didn't want to stay there, so I said I wanted to go back. Is then Merica told me. I was shocked. I didn't have ten yet but I remember Jane telling me and Merica about this thing a long time ago. Jane made it sound so funny we laughed at her. She made it sound funny and not funny at the same time. Jane said one day it would happen to us, because it happened to all girls, that's what turn them into woman. Me and Merica asked her how she knew all those big people things, and she said she bigger and older than us. We asked her more questions but she didn't answer. She said we asked too much questions. Me and Merica did not really believe her. We decided to keep what she said a secret and it could be why everybody say she is not a nice girl because she too farse in big people business.

One day Mammy told me about this thing; I said I understand, but seeing Merica now and hearing what she was telling me, I'm not sure. When Jane told us, we said we will make sure it never happens to us. We thought it must be something different from what she said that's why it happen. Now Merica was saying it happen to her; I was afraid. The way she said it was not as when we shared our secrets. It was like she is a big woman and I still a little girl, so we not friends anymore.

I asked her how it happened; she shouted at me that I ask too much questions. I started to cry and said I was going home. *I'm* not waiting for her stupid party. Then she hugged me, and held my hands just as before and said she was sorry. She didn't mean to make me cry and I still her best friend. Then she told me the most secret secret.

She said sometimes it happen to girls as little as ten, so it could happen to me. She made me promise when it happens to me I would tell Mammy and not try to hide it, then I must send and tell her. I promised, but I kept watching

Merica to see if she different, but she was still the same Merica.

I enjoyed myself at the party but was glad when Mammy and Mister Oscar came to take me home. As soon as we reached home I dashed to the latrine to see if anything happened to me, in case I catch it from Merica. Mammy kept watching me and asking if I was all right. I wanted to tell her but Mister Oscar was there; he was always there. As soon as he went out I started to cry, then I told Mammy what happened to Merica. I thought she would get vex, but she started to laugh. She told me the same thing Merica said her grandma told her. She also reminded me of what she told me about Mister Oscar coming to live with us. I know all that but I don't understand everything. Jane made it sound different; that's why I was afraid.

When my birthday came Mammy bought me a big card and some new clothes. She said she didn't have a lot of money, but she also bought me a nice little book. She hide it between the clothes. It was all about how a girl's body change, and about monthly period although they called it some other long word.

One day I forgot the book on the table and Mister Oscar saw it. He laughed a funny, funny laugh, then said, 'Eh, eh, Gloria turn woman.' He said it as if he was glad because he had some old secret. I didn't like it at all. Mammy heard him, she gave him one bad eye as if she wanted to strike him dead. Sometimes I feel like going to the church to pray for the power so that I could do something to him, but then I know that would upset Mammy because she still like him.

We moved into our new house just before Christmas. I was still going to the same school, but Mammy said next year she would send me to the new girls' school in town. I would have to change school anyway, because after you have ten you go to a bigger school. The girls' school in town is better than the big school near home. For one thing you have to pass exam and things before they take you in. Mammy said she didn't worry about that because she know I was bright enough to pass the exam.

167

One night I heard she and Mister Oscar quarrelling because he wanted me to go to the school nearer home. He said town school too expensive. With bus fares and all kind of books I would have to get, he don't think I should go. Mammy gave him one cursing down. I stayed in my room and laughed.

That Christmas was the best I had for a long time. I had so much presents, I didn't know what to do with myself. The best thing was when Grandma and Grandpa came. They brought two big baskets of things: cakes, ginger beer, sorrel, all sorts of things – even a Christmas ham. They stayed for three days. Grandpa even brought new flower plants for me: a glory vine and some yellow buttercups that I always wanted. Mister Oscar kept his promise and brought cuttings of all my favourites from the old house. When I finished planting them where I wanted them, and they start to flower I sure could win competitions. My new front yard was beginning to look like one of those picture postcards.

While Grandma and Grandpa was with us, one time I noticed Mammy crying. When I asked her what was wrong, she said she was so happy to find her parents again and to know that they are in her home she can't do anything but cry.

Christmas time everything in the house and around was so new and clean I was hoping it wouldn't finish. We had more different things to eat and drink than I had ever seen. I even thought the cards were prettier. There were lots from my friends at the old place, but the best one was from Merica and her grandmother, wishing me and Mammy Beryl Happy Christmas and a Prosperous New Year in our new house. Christmas morning me and Mammy dressed in our new clothes, looking like Christmas stars and went to church. Mammy asked Mister Oscar if he not coming; he said he don't have time for that, and we should pray for him. I believe he fraid the Bible. He looked like the Devil anyway, with his gold teeth shining as if he scrubbed them with ashes and dry bush.

I was glad he didn't come with us, because when people see him with me and Mammy, they keep calling me his daughter. Anyway, me and Mammy left him and went to our old church in Grand Roy. Although when I want to pray for the power I always want to go to the Pentecostal church, we really belong to the Anglican church. As usual, Christmas morning everybody was in church. We met up with all the old friends: Miss Mabel, old Miss Maline and George with his wooden leg. Everybody looking so nice and spruced up in their new white clothes, as if they ready to meet Jesus. Not so long since we left the old place but people hugged and kissed us as if they hadn't seen us for a long, long time.

I met someone that made me happier than ever. Since he left Grand Roy almost two years before nobody heard a single thing about him, was as if he vanished into the air, now Christmas morning who should be in church but Uncle Ben. It was the best Christmas present for me. He looked so nice and spruced up. I heard that deep straggle voice behind me, 'Happy Christmas, Glora.' I knew was him before I turned around. I couldn't forget that voice ever, and anyway he was the only person who call me Glora. I didn't mind, because I like him. Well, even Mammy was glad to see him. She asked him where he was living now, because we know that an Indian man and his wife living in Uncle Ben's old house. He didn't answer her.

'Where you living, Ben?' Mammy asked again.

He gave a big grin. You could see half of his bottom row of teeth still missing. He always said he would go to the dentist for false teeth, but he never did.

He looked at Mammy in the middle of her eyes, still grinning, said, 'Where you think I'm living, eh Beryl? Where you think?'

Mammy stood looking at him waiting for him to tell her.

'Well,' he laughed, 'you didn't want me to sleep in your house when you were there, nothing to stop me now.'

'You mean you come back and living in my old house?' Mammy was very surprised.

'Don't look so surprised. When you chucked me out, I knocked about a bit. Then I heard you moved out of the village. Me and my wife moved in when old Maurice agreed to rent the place to me.'

Well you should have seen Mammy's face. I don't know if she was vex because he was living in our old house or because he said about his wife.

'Wife!' she panted.

'Yes, I married last month.'

Mammy stood in front the man as if she lost her tongue for a minute, then shook her head. 'Fancy that!' she said. 'Fancy that. After all that time now Ben gone and married. Where is your wife now?'

'She gone to her own church. She wanted me to go with her, but I don't like these people and them. Always shouting like they crazy, saying the power falling on them. I don't have time for that stupidness.'

'I don't trust them either,' Mammy laughed.

Uncle Ben gave me a big squeeze. 'You getting a big girl now, Glora.'

I was so glad to see him. I wished he would come home with us. Now that he living near by, perhaps Mammy would let me go by him sometimes. When I asked her if I could, she got so vex. Sometimes I don't understand her at all.

The first year in the new house was very happy. We were like a happy family. The new school was all right. The teachers were nice but none like Miss Oliver. I missed her very much. In that school everyone had something special to do – handicraft, housecraft and things like that. Me and a girl call Denise asked if we could look after the school flower garden. The teacher said yes. Denise was a nice girl and we became good friends, but I would not tell her all my secrets as I used to tell Merica. She loved flowers and together we decided to make the school garden the best around.

In that school we were always very busy. Sometimes we would go on a bus party to other schools and then invite them to ours. We would plan all sort of fun and games for that day. The first year the headmaster made me and Denise enter the schools' flower garden competition. We won first prize. The last day before the August holiday started, was

170

prize-giving day. Schools from all over the island came to us. It was a real big day. Parents were invited as well. When the headmaster called me up on the stage for my prize and certificate, you should have seen Mammy's face. She was so proud, you could see she didn't know what to do with herself. Only smiling and looking around. Afterwards she said she wanted to shout and tell everybody that it was her daughter on the stage. Mister Oscar said he was coming, then afterwards he changed his mind. I was glad because he might have spoil things for me. I still didn't like him; in fact it got worse now he was living with us.

At first it was all right, then he started acting funny. One day he came straight in my room without even knocking. I was changing my clothes. He looked at my chest and then went out without saying anything. I wanted to tell Mammy but I thought she might get vex. I didn't say anything, but I kept an eye on him, and made sure I was out of his way. I was glad when the school holidays started because I would be spending the whole five weeks with my grandparents. Mammy said she would come up when she get her holiday.

One Saturday me and Mammy went back to the old place to see Miss Mabel. The place looked dirty and mash up, as if nobody bother to clean up anymore. We got there early in the morning and boys and girls were liming along the roadside as if they didn't have anything to do. Mammy got vex, vex, saying is a good thing she took me away. She was muttering how these young people not trying to find something worthwhile to do for themselves, just standing by the roadside playing the damn fool. We went by Miss Mabel but she was not home; someone said she gone to the market. As we crossed the road who we meet up again but Uncle Ben and his wife. People really funny; Mammy hardly said a word to the man, but started chatting to the woman like they were old friends. When I asked her why she didn't speak to Uncle Ben she let go one long chupes.

Anyway, August holiday I went to Mount Granby as Mammy promised. Marco and Rosa was always there. Rosa took me everywhere. I asked her if Miss Berty came back.

She said the woman does be mad with the moon, so it's better if she stayed where she was in Trinidad. She could get better treatment there. Rosa said that before Miss Berty went to Trinidad, one day Merica's father brought her up to see her mother. And was as if Miss Berty see some kind of evil spirit in front her. She fly into one rage, cursing and shouting. So Merica's father just put her back in the car and drive away. Little afterwards Miss Berty went to Trinidad.

After about three weeks at Grandma's, one morning I woke up feeling sick, not sick with pain like headache, but funny sick in my belly, and my tits hurting me as well; nippy, nippy hurt. I told Grandma I wasn't feeling well. Told her about the funny pain. She looked at my eyes and then my chest as if she was a doctor, then asked me again what sort of pain I was feeling. I didn't understand. Then the funny thing is she asked me how many years I have. I stared at her. I didn't know what my age had to do with me feeling sick.

'I soon have eleven,' I answered, very puzzled.

'Em, em,' she cleared her throat. 'Em.' For a few minutes she didn't say anything else. I expected her to give some medicine or something, but she just looked at me in a kind of way, that kind of way that only big people understand. Then she give a little laugh and said, 'You all right child, you all right, don't worry. You starting young like your mother.' She gave me a little hug and walked away. I became frightened. I didn't know what Grandma meant. Mammy was coming up that day so I thought I'd wait until she come, but my belly was hurting worse. I told Grandma and she made some bush tea for me. She said it should pass the belly pain. The tea tasted bad; I never tasted anything like that in my life, not even when I had the bad fever.

That was the worse fever I ever had. Mammy thought I was dying. We were living in Grand Roy at the time. Me and my friend Isabel was going up to see Tanty Germain in Boawden. Instead of going the long way, we decided to jump the river stone. As I put my foot on the middle stone, it rolled over and splish, splash, I fell in the water. I was soaked from head to foot but decided to let the clothes dry on me. That night I began feeling hot and cold at the same time. One minute I hot hot, the next I freezing cold. Mammy boiled some sugar-dish and things for me, but that didn't help. I got worse. She got frightened because she said afterwards that I started saying all sort of funny things, chatting loads of stupidness. She went to old Miss Maline for some medicine. Anybody that sick bad, instead of going to the doctor first would go to old Miss Maline. She had her own kind of medicine.

Anyway, Mammy went to her and she came home and gave me a bath with a load of funny smelling bush. I didn't get better. I got worse, so Mammy called the doctor. He said I had pneumonia. He gave me one injection and came back in the night and gave me another one. The bush tea Miss Maline gave me at first tasted so bad, I thought all disease would 'fraid it. Anyway, after the doctor injections, Mammy said for three days and nights I didn't know anybody, not even her. She went to the church and asked the priest to pray for me. She really thought I was dying. After the third day, I began to feel better. Miss Maline still came with her ointment. Mammy said it couldn't do me any harm.

Well, the bush Grandma gave me to drink for this belly pain worse than Miss Maline's. I didn't want to drink all of it but she promised me some sweets. I drank it quick, quick and prayed I wouldn't have to drink any more. I was glad when Mammy came. When I told her about the pain, and how my tits hurt as well, she did the same thing Grandma did, then rubbed my face the way she used to do when I was smaller. The way she looked at me, I knew something was up. I was frightened. She went to the kitchen to Grandma and I noticed them giving each other funny looks, like only big people understand. It frightened me more.

During the day I felt a little better. Me and Rosa went shopping. Although the pain was not so bad, yet I had that niggle, niggle feeling under my belly, right down to between my legs. That evening when I went to clean up I saw strange colour spots in my panty. I forgot what Merica and Mammy told me. I panicked. I was sure Mammy would give me a beating, although I didn't do anything wrong. I thought about everything, trying to figure out what happened to put blood in my panty. I wrapped it up small, small and put it in the trash bin. I stayed in bed all evening. Every minute Mammy came in asking me if I was all right. I said my belly still hurting. I wanted to go to bed. I so stupid, I never imagined that Mammy had more sense than me. About eight o'clock Grandma came in to say goodnight. Then Mammy came in with a cup of cocoa and some biscuits. She sat on the bed while I drank the drink. All the while she was watching me and saying nothing. I tried to eat the biscuit but had trouble chewing because I was 'fraid. I was thinking Mammy was out to give me a beating.

'Gloria, you clean up tonight?' she asked. Just like that.

I didn't answer.

'Don't worry,' she went on. 'Did you change your panty?'

Well fancy asking me a question like that. I didn't know what to say. Mammy knows I always clean up in the evening and put on my sleeping panty. Why she come asking me that question?

'Well, did you change your panty?'

'Yes Mammy,' I grumbled.

'Did you wash the dirty one?'

This time I couldn't answer. I was shaking like a leaf. I was afraid and vex at the same time. Imagine asking me all these strange questions now! She must find the dirty panty in the trash bin. She sat there looking at me as if she had something on her mind and didn't know how to say it, but that's not like Mammy at all. She had a tongue sharpen like cutlass, Uncle Ben used to say. Then she lift up the sheet I had over me, she lift up the nightdress too and look first at my belly, then my tits, then pull down my panty and looked inside it. I almost died. I never felt so ashamed. I always changed my clothes and bathe in front Mammy. She had to scrub me down when I was bathing anyway, but somehow this was different. I felt dirty and I wanted to hide. I didn't understand it at all. I lie there stiff as wood. Then she said the same thing Grandma said; I start early like her. She pulled the sheet back over me and started speaking. She told me about the things she talked to me about before. The time she bought me that book for my birthday. Oh Lord! How I could be so stupid. I remembered then.

I remembered what Jane and Merica said, but now it happen to me it was different and I was frightened. I didn't even want Mammy to know. I remember Merica was twelve but I only have ten going on eleven; something bad must be wrong with me. Mammy showed me what to do and told me more about babies and things like that. That really scared me. I made up my mind there and then that I would never talk to any boy as long as I live, not even Marco. With all the talk Mammy talked, one thing I asked her, please don't tell Mister Oscar. She laughed. She said it's woman's secret, nothing to do with men, and it's definitely none of Oscar's business.

I was glad that I was at Grandma when I started 'menstruating', as Mammy said is the proper word, not the 'ting' or 'Devil blood'. I still call it the Devil blood though; it's like that. For the next four days I passed the blood. I wondered if it would ever stop. Mammy was there, always talking to me. She said not to worry; it happens to all girls and women until they get old. Fancy bleeding every month until you get old like old Miss Maline in Grand Roy! When I asked Mammy if men and boys see things like that, she laughed.

One day I heard Mammy and Grandpa talking. He asked her when she and Oscar getting married. I almost fainted. I never thought about Mammy and that man ever getting married. That will make him my father for good. Mammy said something that made me feel a little better, but had me thinking as well. I was remembering about the day Mister Oscar came home early. Mammy was still at work. He came home vex, vex, and cursing some woman or the other. He said how the woman damn wicked and if he ever catch up with her he will break her neck. He didn't know I was home. I was in my room and I could hear him pulling things about like a mad man. Tumbling, tumbling down things. I kept quiet, quiet, because I thought he was looking for a cutlass or something to go and cut that woman's neck and if he see me he might cut me up first, because all he was saying is if he catch her she dead like a dead herring. The next thing I heard was the door slam, one big loud bodow, and he bolted out like the Devil was behind him. What made me vex was he kicked down the tin with the evergreen in his rage. I was so vex, perhaps if I went outside I would want to cut him up.

As soon as Mammy came home I told her. She didn't say much, only 'funny'. When he came home that night I noticed the way she was quiet with him. She always laughed and made all kind of joke when he was home, but that evening she was quiet, quiet. He made a joke and all she said was, 'Hhhmmmmmmm . . . is that so,' in a sort of don't-care way. He didn't tell her about any woman.

For the whole week, he came home late. Every night Mammy ask him where he was, he say he working. I was glad when he came late because by then it's time for me to go to bed. I don't see him or say anything about him, but I noticed Mammy getting quieter and quieter, not vex-quiet; was like she was planning something. I always knew when she was planning in head. I had the feeling she was waiting for him to say something or maybe do something.

One morning the postman brought a letter in one of those long brown envelopes. The address was typed out nice and neat to Mister Oscar Parker. It looked very official because Mammy had to sign for it. She turned it up and down as though she might be able to read what was inside without opening it. I don't know why, but she put the letter in her handbag instead of on the table.

Mister Oscar was expecting the letter because for a change he came home early and the first thing he asked was if the postman brought anything. He asked the question and the same time looking where letters would be. Mammy asked if he was expecting a letter. He didn't answer, but you could see he had something on his mind. I just wanted to have my dinner and go to my room. I didn't like the way he kept on rolling those eyes all the time. As soon as I had my food, Mammy told me to go to my room. I was glad for that, because something funny was going on. I left my room door open a little. A few minutes later I heard him say he going out, he soon be back. Well, it looked as if he stepped on Mammy's sore foot.

'Oscar where you going?' she asked, kind of soft, soft. 'Where you think you going, eh?'

'I tell you I soon come back. Why you on my back so?'

'If you thinking of going to the Post Office, don't bother,' she shouted.

I couldn't see his face, but from my room I could feel how his jawbone twitch and twitch from the way I heard him grinding his teeth.

'Post Office! What you on about, eh woman? What Post Office?'

'Don't "woman" me. You think I stupid, don't you. You think I stupid. You better have the right answers tonight. I tell you here and now; have the right answers.'

Well, Mister Oscar gone mad now. 'What the hell you on about now, eh? What you on about? I tell you I soon come. You carrying on as if you mad or something. What's the matter with you, eh woman? What's the matter with you?'

'I tell you don't woman me. I want to know what is going on. Here is the letter. The so-important letter you almost have cardiac arrest for when you hear the postman didn't come.' Knowing Mammy I'm sure she flung the letter at him, because the next thing I heard was the envelope ripping.

'Well, what is all that secret about?' Mammy started again. 'You coming home early, early some days, cursing your head off like a mad man. Other times you staying out all hour in the night telling me you working. You think I stupid or something, eh Oscar, you think I stupid? Come on, I'm waiting to hear what you have to say, and you better make it good.'

'What!' he exploded, 'those damn people around here too damn farse in people business. They don't have anything to do. If I come in my own house for something they have to run and tell you, like I don't have any freedom in this place. You think I'm some kind of prisoner or something? Eh, you think I some kind of prisoner?'

Mammy was ready for him. 'If you feel you is a prisoner, you know what to do. I sure I'm no turn-key. You know just where the door is.'

The two of them started one Bacchanal in the house that night. I don't understand half of what they said. Mammy shouting at him to pack his things and get out of her house; he shouting back it's not her house. Then he said something about God must be sorry he ever made woman. I don't know what God have to do with their quarrel. Mammy asked if the all-important letter was from a woman. Then just like that everything went quiet, quiet, like the wind finished blowing.

And you wouldn't believe me, but the next thing I heard was Mister Oscar crying. At first I thought was Mammy. I peeped to see, because if it was her, I was going out there after him. I would pelt something at his head and run. Well! The man was sitting on the edge of the sofa, the letter in his hand, his hand holding his head and eye-water running down his face like his mother dead. Perhaps his mother was dead, because nobody knew what was in the letter. I don't think he even had the chance to read it yet. His eye-water must have shocked Mammy, because she just stood by the table watching him with her mouth wide open. Then she walked over to the sofa and put her hand on his shoulder as if she ready to pet him.

'Oscar, what's the matter? You in some kind of trouble?' He didn't answer, just handed her the letter. I crept outside just as she took the envelope.

'What you want, Gloria? I thought I told you to go to bed.'

'I want a drink of water. I'm thirsty,' I lied.

'Look girl, go back to your bed, you hear. Farse you farse. You just eat, had a glass of juice, you come telling me you thirsty. Go back in your room, you too damn farse.'

I was back in my room as fast as lightning. I still left the door open a little. A few minutes later Mammy brought me a glass of orange juice. She looked at me, shook her head and smiled, and went back to Mister Oscar. At first the two of them were quiet, quiet. Then I heard Mammy ask in her normal voice, but just as how she says things when she planning in her head, 'What you go do now?'

'I don't know,' he mumbled, 'I just don't know.' He sounded as if ready to give up. Whatever it was they must've sorted it out because next morning Mammy got up as usual, made the tea and things before she went to work. I think he went to work too, because he took his working things. I thought, is nothing bad otherwise the police would come and lock him up.

About the next Wednesday morning Mammy got up and said she was not going to work. I was glad about that, because she usually have time to cook something special for dinner. Although she said she was not going to work, yet she was up her usual time and dressed. I asked her where she was going, all she said was, 'Out.' Since they quarrelled about the letter, Mister Oscar was keeping very quiet about everything. He would come home from work early in the evening and don't go back outside until the next morning. Like he was sick or something, but I couldn't see anything wrong with him, just his face start looking like a spirit. He would sit in the chair and stare straight, straight in front of him, at nothing. I kept out of his way.

One night, his friend Mr Nedd passed by the house. He said he hadn't seen Mister Oscar lately and his friends at the rum shop were wondering if he was sick or something. I thought that was nice of Mr Nedd, but when Mammy heard what he said, she gave the poor man such a bad eye, he just got up and went away. Maybe because she always on about how these men and them spent all their time and money in the rum shop. I know Mister Oscar didn't drink a lot of the old white rum, but he liked to sit and talk stupidness with his friends.

Anyway, he got up and walked to the gap with Mr Nedd. I heard him tell the other man, he not feeling too good. He always so tired that when he finish work he come home, have his dinner and go to sleep. Mr Nedd looked back over his shoulder at Mammy, shook his head and left. I believed Mister Oscar when he say he was sick, but I'm not sure what sickness he was suffering from.

Two days after that a tall, skinny old man came to the house to see him. He had one of those doctor bags, but I didn't think he was a doctor, not a proper doctor. Me and Isabel was going down the road to buy provision, when he came into the yard. Mister Oscar was home as if he was waiting for somebody or something important. Anyway, by the time I got back the doctorman already left and Mister Oscar looking a bit better. Funny man! I'm sure he doing things behind Mammy back. I didn't worry about that, though. Because I knew was a case of God help him when she finds out.

Strange how you remember things. Only when I heard Grandpa and Mammy talking about Mister Oscar and Mammy getting married, I remembered all these things. I'm sure that brown envelope had a lot to do with whatever was going on. The Wednesday Mammy didn't go to work, she left the house about the same time as when she going to work and came back late in the evening. I heard she and Mister Oscar talking about some woman called Dolly something or the other. Mammy always tell me I'm too forward in big people business, but I can't help hearing things. They were talking about this woman, then Mister Oscar got vex, vex.

'I tell you this woman is the Devil,' he said. 'She is the wickedest person Gawd ever made.'

Mammy took a deep breath. 'I don't know Oscar, I don't know. I wanted to see her, perhaps talk to her, you know reason with her.'

'Reason with her? Beryl you don't know what you saying. I tell you that woman curse, she don't have any reasoning.'

'I know what you say Oscar, but I thought I'll talk to her, you know, woman to woman. But, when she stretched her long backside and those elastic lips and had the nerve to tell me she is Mistress Parker, well . . . '

'Mistress Parker!' Mister Oscar screeched, you'd think he was trying to wake up the dead in the burial ground. 'Mistress Parker! I'll break she blasted neck. I'm telling you. I'll finish her for good.'

'What good is that, eh what good is that? Break she neck and they only goin' jail you.' Mammy tried her best to calm him down. They talked and talked about that woman for a long time. I don't know what happened in the end, it didn't bother me because that is big people business and Mammy didn't look too worried.

After that, everything was going on all right, until the evening I came home from school and saw that strange woman standing by our gap. She was sort of waiting between our gap and Mr Jacob's. I knew Mammy wouldn't be home yet and there wouldn't be anybody at home, so I crossed the road quick, quick to see what the person wanted. I always hear Mammy saying about how some people's spirit don't mix. Well my spirit and this woman spirit didn't mix at all. The way she stand there karway, karway, as if she own the place. The nearer I got to her the more I disliked her. Something about her made my blood boil. She stand up there, her bottom on top her back like when black ants climbing sour sop tree, and those high heel shoes, I don't know how she don't break her foot. On top of it she had on a hobble skirt; skirt tight, tight on her. I don't know; the woman was a right sight.

'Evening!' I said.

She turned and look at me, skin up her face as if she see mess. Afterwards she moved up in the gap a little bit, following me. I was so vex, I nearly burst.

'Evening,' I said again.

'Oscar Parker living here?' she asked. Just like that. No evening or anything. The woman don't even have manners. I just opened my mouth and looked at her in the poke of her eyes.

'Oscar Parker,' she repeated, 'is he living here?'

'Yes!' I snapped. 'He live here, but he ain't home. He gone to work.' I turned my back on her and started walking in the yard.

'You just come, how you know he not home.'

I was about to answer her, when Mister Oscar pulled up in his car. I looked at him, then at her and walked straight inside the house. I hoped he wouldn't bring that woman in Mammy's house. I didn't know who she was, but she looked like trouble and I didn't want any trouble in Mammy's place. When I looked outside they were talking by the roadside. I don't know if he called her out of the yard or what, but the way they were shaking their heads and waving their hands about, it looked like they were quarrelling. I say to myself, I hope she gone before Mammy come. I went to change my clothes and then I heard him slam the door and come inside cursing to himself. I thought he would be vex because I left the woman outside, but he didn't say anything. I thought that I would tell Mammy as soon as she came home, but I didn't get the chance because he went and picked her up at her work place.

When they came inside I heard him saying, 'She come quite here, you know, Beryl, quite here.'

'Oscar, listen to me and listen good,' Mammy sounded just as when the headmistress telling us something serious. 'Tell that woman she is one hell of a lucky woman. She damn lucky I wasn't here. She damn farse to come across my yard. Tell her for me, make it the first and last time she put she cocobay backside in my yard. You hear? Tell her.'

'She wanted to know if I answered the lawyer letter,' Mister Oscar went on as if he didn't hear what Mammy said. 'The stupid woman telling me if I give her two thousand dollars she wouldn't bother with anything.'

'What!' Mammy was shouting as if now she wanted to wake up the dead in the burial ground. I hadn't heard her shout that kind of shout for a long time. 'She must be eating too much of Dillon nastiness and it gone to her head. What you tell her when she ask you for that kind of money?'

182

He let out one long chupes, I thought his gold teeth stick together.

'What you think I tell her. I ask her if is my money she want to go and work obeah. My money she want to take to Dillon to work his nastiness!'

'Oscar, tell that woman don't ever put her foot in front my door; you hear me? Tell her. Anyway, you have a choice. You free to go back to her. I'm not holding you back. Just don't expect me to help you pay her one cent. She blackmailing you for divorce and it's your problem. If what you tell me is true you could tell her to go to hell, but again I don't really know, do I? Just tell her, she was lucky this time, don't try it again.'

I didn't understand a lot of things, but when they talk about word like 'blackmail' and I remember how my blood run when I saw that woman, I knew is trouble. Mister Oscar went over and hugged Mammy. Is a long time since I see him do that.

So now when Grandpa ask Mammy about she and Mister Oscar getting married and she answer in the way she answer, I was sure it had to do with that woman. Grandpa gave Mammy a little squeeze on her shoulder and said it would soon clear up.

'Yes Daddy,' was all she said. She sat on the verandah by herself for a long time.

The second Christmas was coming up that we were going to spend in that house. I was happy because I settled down real nice. The house was pretty as ever. My flowers as pretty as the government botanic garden. I was happy at school. Holiday was coming and I was looking forward to going to see Grandma, but I don't think Mammy was happy. She wasn't working any harder but she looked very tired. She didn't laugh as she used to. I have twelve now and though we still like big sister and little sister, things were not the same. Then we got a letter saying Grandma was sick. We went to Mount Granby the same day. Grandma was sick bad. The doctor sent her to the hospital; they sent her back saying they couldn't find anything wrong with her. We stayed with them for about a week. Grandpa said if she didn't get better in the New Year he would take her to Barbados. A week before Christmas we went back to help sort their Christmas things. Grandma was much better but Grandpa began to look sick. He kept on and on about if Grandma die he didn't know what he'll do. He can never live without her. That frightened me, because although Grandma was feeling better I remembered Merica once said that people does look better before they die. Perhaps Grandpa knew that too. Before we went home, Mammy made all the Christmas preparations as best she could and left the rest to Rosa and Marco.

Our house was real nice for Christmas. Mammy bought new curtains, nice white lacy ones for the hall windows. She let me choose new ones for my bedroom. She tried to make everyone happy but she was not happy. You could see it in her face. One day I asked her what was wrong. All she said was, 'Nothing.'

'Mammy,' I said, 'I know you will tell me to shut my mouth, but you look so tired and you don't laugh anymore. Since the time that ugly woman came to see Mister Oscar you not the same; you always vex, vex. What's wrong? Tell me!'

I half expected her to shout at me, but she only turned and looked at me. Her eyes looked so sad, I started to cry. Didn't know why I cried, but I held on to her and wouldn't let go with eye-water bathing my face. She hugged me and said I was silly; she was all right. But I was frighten, frighten for her. Mister Oscar started looking meagre and poorly as well. Sometimes he would cough and cough as if he had TB. I was even more afraid for Mammy. Suppose he give Mammy TB. I felt sorry for him too, though I still didn't like him. After all the time we living in the same house, he still do things to make me vex. Like the day I was cleaning the flowers on the step. I was busy, busy scrubbing the bottom of the pan. I didn't even hear the gate open. The next thing I know was a hand rubbing the back of my leg. I picked up the pan to pelt after him.

'Aye, aye, I only touch you, you get yourself so vex.' He skinned his eyes and grinned at me.

I ran inside to tell Mammy but he called her first and tell her how I turn big woman, he only make a joke with me, I get vex, vex and want to hit him. Mammy didn't say anything, just looked at me, then at him. Sometimes it's hard to know what she thinking. She knew that I never like him and it was worse because I was sure it was him making her so tired. I thought he must be trying to kill her or something. I was so frightened that the week before, when I went to Grand Roy to see old Miss Maline I went in the church and prayed for the power. Nothing happened, but I felt sure if I went regularly and said the right prayers I would get the power, then I would make sure nothing happens to Mammy.

Was in February, I don't remember the date, but I was in the class doing reading when Miss McQueen called me out. She said somebody was asking for me. When I went to her office Marco was leaning against the window. I had to look good, good to make sure it was him.

'Marco!' I shouted.

'Gloria!'

Miss stopped me. 'Where is your manners?'

'Sorry, Miss. Marco?'

'I see you know this gentleman,' Miss said, 'he has come to take you home.'

I rushed up to Marco while Miss was talking. His eyes looked puffy, puffy and red like loupgarou. I was trembling. I never seen Marco like that before.

'Marco; what's the matter?' He didn't answer.

Miss told me to collect my books and go home; she wanted to make sure that I knew the man. Still Marco said nothing, but I knew something bad had happened. I kept staring in his face. Still he said nothing. He held my hand tight, tight as if he was afraid I would run away. Even on the bus he held on to my hand, and still he said nothing. His eyes so sad, and around his mouth trembling. He looked as if water would pour out of his eyes if he only opened his mouth. When we reached home I ran up the step shouting for Mammy. She flew outside, grabbed me and started to bawl. I started bawling too, still not knowing what was happening.

'You tell her, Marco?' she turned to Marco.

'No Miss Beryl. I didn't say anything,' he whispered, tears choking him.

I stared from Mammy to Marco, from Marco to Mammy. Tears washing my face like a burst pipe. Nothing is wrong with Mammy. Marco is here all upset, so it must be Grandma. My grandma is dead.

'Grandma . . . what . . . happen. What happen Mammy? My grandma dead?' I stammered.

'We have to go to Mount Granby now,' Mammy said as she hugged me tight, tight. Is then Marco said is not Grandma, is Grandpa.

My head started spinning. Spinning and spinning, around and around. My grandpa is dead. No no no. Not my grandpa . . . he can't be dead, he mustn't be dead . . . no, no, no, not my grandpa. I pulled away from Mammy and bolted down the steps through the gate. I kept on running, just running, running. There is a church up here. I don't have to go all the way to Grand Roy. I had to get to the church. I had to go and pray, pray for the power. Papa God had to hear me . . . He must hear my prayer . . . I must get the power. My grandpa and grandma must not die. I kept on running. I turned the corner at the end of the main road. I didn't see the car, didn't see anything, didn't hear anything. Next thing I know I was in Mister Oscar's car on the way back to the house. They said when I ran out, Marco ran after me. He saw me dash in front of a car, and fall on the other side of the road. He say is a miracle the car didn't kill me. Then Mister Oscar pulled up the same time. I didn't know what was happening. All I could think about was my grandpa and grandma. Not a long time since I found them, and now . . .

All of us went in Mister Oscar's car. I thought we were going to Mount Granby but instead he turned the car towards town. He drove fast, fast, every minute asking me and Mammy if we all right.

'I thought we going to Grandpa,' I managed to ask between sobs. Me and Marco was sitting in the back, and Mammy in the front with Mister Oscar. She sat stiff, stiff wringing her handkerchief. Her face didn't even look like Mammy.

'Mr Johnson in hospital,' Marco spoke for the first time since we left the house. 'He is in hospital, Gloria. He went in the garden this morning and a coconut branch fall and hit him across his back.'

'You mean Grandpa not dead?' I squealed. 'You mean he not at all? He only in hospital? If coconut branch hit him, he will be all right, won't he?'

But Grandpa was never all right again. Grandma was sitting on his bed when we got to the hospital. Her face looked like she powdered with ashes. I looked at the person on the bed they told me was my grandpa. I never see anybody look so bad; not even when Mammy is tired. Not even when Mister Oscar look as if suffering from TB. He was all bandaged up; only his face was left out. It didn't look like my grandpa at all. They told me he was sleeping; I don't know . . . he looked . . . well, I don't know.

Mammy spoke to Grandma, then Grandma took my hand and started to walk down the corridor. Her hand was wet and sticky. Sort of cold. She didn't speak to me, just kissed me on the forehead and walked on. We had gone about two wards when we heard the scream.

'Oh Gawd, oh Gawd, papa Bunjay, papa Bunjay. Me father dead, me father dead . . . he dead . . . he dead.'

I let go of Grandma and dashed back to Mammy. She was lying across Grandpa bawling. A nurse tried to stop me but I dashed past her to meet Mammy. Marco was crunched upon a chair like an old piece of rag. Mister Oscar standing stiff stiff, staring out of the window. I don't know, don't remember anything much after that. All I knew was that my grandpa was dead. I only knew him for a little while and now he was dead. We stayed with Grandma a long time after the funeral. When we were leaving Mammy promised she would be up to see Grandma as regularly as she could.

With Grandpa's death, everything looked bad that year. Mister Oscar started acting funnier. He'd leave for work and then run back home saying he forget this, that and the other. All sort of stupid excuse to be in the house. I knew he was boxing brains, but I didn't say anything to Mammy. She took Grandpa's death really hard. She kept on saying it was her fault. All those years she left them, if she had tried to go back, Grandpa might've had an easier life, as if was she that made the coconut branch hit him. The doctor said the way he was hit his main backbone was broken and something or the other else happened. He said Grandpa didn't have a chance to live after that. Mammy took it hard, and Mister Oscar acting like somebody that have evil spirit on him. I knew he boxing brains, he was up to his old tricks.

One day I was in the kitchen drinking some juice, he came up behind me and the next thing I know his hand was inside my bodice.

'You getting a big girl now,' he grinned.

As soon as Mammy came home I told her before he make up some old lies. She went mad. She told him to make it the first and last time he ever forget himself, 'cause she sure like hell going to chop out his hand, clean, clean from his shoulder. He started on about how he mind me since I little and he can't even touch me. How because he sick everybody against him. I don't know what sick he was sick. The only sickness I could see is evil spirit on him. Mammy told him if he sick he must go to doctor, or else she sure doctor him if he try any nastiness in her house. I'm sure he was working with the Devil, because he started getting up in the middle of the night, walking up and down the house mumbling gibberish. I never liked that man, now I was afraid of him. He wasn't only acting funny, he started rubbing himself with stinking things and wearing a little black bag hanging from a piece of string around his neck. One night I heard Mammy cursing him. She told him to stop going to 'these people', they only eating his money and filling his head with nastiness.

He said somebody told him was a woman who worked obeah on him and he would have to do things to get rid of it. Mammy wasn't having any of that in her house. She told him so. She told him either he try to straighten out his mind the right way, or if he prefer to go downhill with this nastiness, he better leave her house. He started on about it's his house, was his money paying for it, he only put it in her name because he thought she loved him and all sort of stupidness. They quarrelled and quarrelled.

The whole thing burst out that Mister Oscar started going to an obeah man up in the 'hills' since that Dolly woman came to see him. I always hear them talking about Dillon who living in Maran, but apparently the person in the hills better than Dillon. Mammy wasn't having any of that. She said anybody who 'don't wash their hand' is not staying in her house. It's her house and he could bring the law there, if he want, is nothing they could do. Well, next morning Mister Oscar just packed his suitcases and moved out. Mammy didn't say anything. She didn't seem bothered about it. When he gone she gave the whole place a good cleaning down with bush and Dettol to get rid of the smell. All she said to him when he was leaving was 'good luck'. I don't know what luck had to do with anything.

One evening I came home from school and Mammy gave me a letter. The postmark said 'La Filette'. I didn't know anybody in La Filette. When I opened it, it was from Merica. Her grandma died, so she went back to live with Miss Berty. It seemed as if the treatment in Trinidad worked because she said Miss Berty was better now. That was good news, but I was shocked when Merica tell me that she had a boyfriend. Fancy Merica and a boy! I was glad and vex at the same time. If she had a boyfriend, she wouldn't want me for her best friend anymore. Grandpa gone, Merica had Dennis; things was different now. Still, I had Mammy, Grandma and Rosa. Mammy always said Marco is Rosa's brother, but when we went to Mount Granby the other day, I see Rosa belly big. I was still little but I knew what happened. I asked Mammy if Rosa had a husband. I thought she was going to hit me but all she said was that Marco would look after Rosa. If he is her brother how come . . . ? Only thing I could think was that he not really her brother. Rosa was still my friend. She showed me all the things she bought for the baby, and Marco was making a crib. I was glad for Rosa and Marco, then I started to think what will happen if Merica started to have a baby.

One day Marco came to Grandma's real vex and quarrelling to himself. It was the first time I ever see him vex. Grandma asked if anything was wrong with Rosa. He took a long time before he said anything. Then he told Grandma how this person call Andrew come back annoying Rosa. He said she didn't want the man hanging around her but he wouldn't go away.

'It's his baby as well you know. Perhaps he want to settle down with Rosa,' Grandma put her hand around Marco's shoulder to try to calm him down. I understood then that he and Rosa is really brother and sister, but I didn't know why he so vex.

When we came from Grandma that evening, as I opened the door is Mister Oscar who was sitting on the sofa. The man looked so bad I thought was a spirit. I jumped and called to Mammy to hurry up.

'Aye, aye, Lawd! Oscar what happen to you?' Mammy asked, staring at him as if she too thought was his spirit sitting there. She dropped the bag on the floor, went and stood in front him. Mammy's mouth stayed opened as if she seeing zombie. He sat there just staring at us. His eyes sink down in two holes, his face whitey, whitey, and those jawbones; Gawd: they so deep it could hold bucket of water. Even his gold teeth didn't shine any more. I never saw anything like that in my whole life. The man looked dead, just dead. Even when Grandpa died, he didn't look so bad.

'Oscar, what do you?' Mammy asked again, still looking at him as if she couldn't believe it was him. 'Two months you leave the house, you gone, not a word to anybody, now you come back, you look like something loupgaroux suck. What wrong with you?'

190

'Beryl, please. Not now, please, not now,' he pleaded with Mammy like a child. When I looked at him closer, I wanted to laugh. He looked sort of funny. He reminded me of the man in the big house in Grand Roy.

'I know you just come, but you have anything to eat? I'm hungry.' He begged Mammy for food. He looked hungry anyway, like he hadn't eaten for weeks. And his clothes! So dirty like he needed a bath as well. When he asked for the food Mammy gave out one long chupes and went to the kitchen. I heard the pots and things bashing about. She was cooking for him. She heated up some of the fish we came down with and cut up bread and a big glass of juice and gave to him. You should see how he gufflay up the food, as if had never seen food in his life. I didn't say anything, but I was hoping he was only passing, but it looked as if he came back to Mammy for good. I don't know what happened. All I knew was two months passed and he come back looking dead. Things were not right at all. Mammy started getting vex, vex all the time. Another thing, he was not working, so he always in the house. He said he was on sick leave but didn't know how long the company would pay him. Mammy starting chupsing, chupsing, and talking to herself, always vex, vex. The man getting more sick and he wouldn't go to the doctor. All he doing was rubbing himself with the same old stinking nastiness, making the whole house smell like obeah shop. All how Mammy tell him to go to doctor, he saying doctor medicine wouldn't help him.

He went on like that for almost two weeks, then one day he fell down in the hall. Mammy was in the kitchen. I was coming in the front door when I saw him trying to get up off the sofa. He manage to stand up, staggered and fell flat on his face. It's a good thing Mammy had taken out the centre table from the middle of the room and put in the corner, otherwise Mister Oscar would have gone through the glass top. By the time I called to Mammy, he was lying on the floor spluttering like a half-dead fowl.

Mammy ran next door to Mr Jacob. I was frightened, because I thought if he died, people would say is me and

Mammy that killed him, seeing as he wasn't home that long. Mammy and Mr Jacob put him in a car and took him to the hospital. When Mammy came back, she said he'd be staying there because doctors want to run some tests on him. She said he was talking a load of nonsense that nobody understand. I remembered when the man in the big house in Grand Roy died, they said he talked all sort of rubbish as well, perhaps both of them worked for the Devil. The way he smelt and the rubbish he drank I wasn't surprised. He stayed in the hospital a long time. They said everything the doctor tried wasn't helping; instead of better he got worse.

One day me and Mammy went to see him. I almost dropped when I see the man. Not only how he looked but that ugly woman, the same one who came to the house that day – I suppose is the one they call Dolly – well she was sitting on the chair beside his bed. Mammy went mad. She marched up to the woman, right there in the hospital and told her to get her backside out of there right now, now, right now. Mammy told her to move and don't ever put her ugly long backside near him again. She was blazing mad. She was perspiring and blowing as if she had been running. The woman just got up, looked at Mammy, then at the sick man, gave out a chupes, and said, 'Eh, eh, you don't see he dead already,' and walked out of the hospital. I held on to Mammy's hand, because it looked as if she was ready to strip down the woman. Anyway, I don't know how she knew about him being dead already, but the next week he was dead.

They said all his hands and fingernails got black, black, and everything they gave him to eat came up green, green. The day he died, he asked the nurse for some fish soup. That was strange, because for one thing he wasn't eating anything before, and the other he never liked fish soup. Mammy always had to steam his fish or fry it dry, dry. So it was strange for him to ask the nurse for fish soup. Anyway, they gave him some and he had the lot. The nurse said when he finished she wiped his mouth, then he lie back on the pillow and gave a deep breath. When she looked around at him, he was smiling – smiling in a strange way. Then he closed his eyes. He started breathing heavy, heavy, and by the time she called the doctor, he was dead. The nurse said the night before he blabbered on and on about a woman called Dolly. As if he and the woman was always fighting. One time they had to hold him down because he kept saying he going for his cutlass to cut off the woman's neck. When Mammy heard all that, she shook her head, 'Death was playing with him,' was all she said.

After the funeral and the eight days' prayers, the whole business started coming out. Dolly and Mister was supposed to be married, but he told Mammy that it was trick they tricked him to marry her, because he didn't even like the woman. He told Mammy that the person who married them wasn't even a proper priest. It's afterwards he heard the man was an old obeah man who go about pretending to be priest. When Mister Oscar realised what happened he picked up his things and ran away from the woman. That's when he first met Mammy, but they were only friends like. He said wherever he went the woman found him, so he went overseas. He went to St Vincent and Dominica and then spent some time in Guyana, just after their independence. It was in Guyana he got the gold teeth and things. In 1973 he came back to Grenada. He thought Dolly had forgotten him, until one day he bounced her up in town. Then he received the letter from her lawyer. Anyway, he said was she worked obeah on him.

Now Mister Oscar dead and buried, I didn't feel comfortable in the house at all. I always had funny feelings when I'm home alone. Mammy was talking about moving as well. She say the things he used to rub with still smell in the place. People tell her it was only in her mind. She say sometimes she sure he is there looking at her. She liked him at first, but afterwards she didn't trust him. Fancy getting mixed up in that nastiness! Eh, fancy! I heard Mammy tell somebody that when he left us for those two months, he went all the way up to Carriacou. When he reached Kick-em-Jenny, the boat almost turn over. When she asked him what he went to Carriacou for he said he went to somebody to take out the obeah on him. He said, people told him about someone up there who was better than anybody on Grenada, even better than Dillon. Mammy told him to go to church and pray, instead of filling up his head with stupidness. He never paid any mind to her, now he still dead. Mammy painted the house all over, inside and outside, but she still said she didn't feel comfortable. About six months after he died, Mammy got a letter from a lawyer telling her that Mrs Dolly Parker wants her out of the house within the next month. I thought Mammy was going to collapse. Her face change to all different colours like the people on pageant morning.

'Let her come; just let she and she lawyer come. She killed Oscar now she starting on me. Just let them come. They think Oscar left money. They coming for it, let them come,' Mammy stamped up and down the house, as if she ready for a fight.

She took the letter to a lawyer in town and they arranged some sort of business. The lawyer told her it's best to sell the house, because even though it was in her name, Mister Oscar had borrowed money from a lot of people, and they could try to make trouble for her. I always knew that man was trouble, even when he dead he was still trouble. When he lost his job he borrowed money to take to the obeah man. Sometimes I think it's a good thing he dead. Anyway, Mammy put the house up for sale and went about looking for somewhere for us to live.

One day I was inside when I heard somebody moving in the front yard as though in my flowers. When I looked out, who standing under the rose tree, but Uncle Ben. I was never so glad to see anyone for a long time. Just fancy Uncle Ben coming now. Mammy didn't look surprise to see him, as if she knew he was coming. I don't know. I don't understand. I was just glad to see him.

After Mammy made up her mind to sell the house and pay off all Mister Oscar's debt and things, one day that Dolly woman still take her farseness and come to the house. Well, she was lucky it was me and Uncle Ben home and not Mammy, because it would've been something else. Anyway,

Mammy did all her business with the help of the lawyer. Then one day she came and said we're moving. She said somebody bought the house, and that she found a nice place for us. She seemed happy, very happy, even running around doing her business. She did not look tired and vex anymore.

The first time I saw the house I fell in love with it. It was like when people talk about love at first sight. It looked like the houses you see in books. The steps leading to the verandah were made of concrete and the front yard so big I'm sure you could build another house. At the back there are lots of fruit trees and a big piece of ground where Mammy could make her kitchen garden. The verandah ran around three sides of the house, then there was a gallery at the back. Even the bathroom and toilet were inside. It seemed funny messing inside the house, but when you pull the toilet chain everything wash away. There was so much space in the front, I asked Mammy if I could bring some of my plants; she said to bring anything I wanted. Then I remember Mister Oscar brought some from Grand Roy, so I decided to leave all of them behind. I didn't want to bring his spirit with us. Mammy said we making a clean sweep when we move to Paradise. She say she didn't want people running their mouth when they see us; people too damn farse.

As I said from the start, I like the new house very much. I wanted to go and start cleaning up straight away, especially the front yard. Fancy no Mister Oscar for me to be afraid of, not even his spirit! Mammy kept on saying he buy this house for us, but I'm not worrying with her. Dead man can't buy house. It's her house, hers and mine and nothing to do with him. Uncle Ben turned up in time to help us move our things. He stayed with us all that day lifting things here and there. It was so nice having him with us. I was very, very glad to see him; very, very happy. I don't know why, but he looked much younger and happier than when we lived in Grand Roy the first time, even when we met him in the church that Christmas morning.

About two weeks after we moved, he came with a big bundle of flower plants. He said he cut them from the old house where he is living now, the ones I planted when we lived there. He spend the whole day with us. He helped Mammy fix up things and he made proper flower beds for me. That night when he said he was going home, I couldn't believe my ears. When I thought of when he used to come to our house before, and what happened that last night he was there! I just couldn't believe my ears now.

Mammy turned her head in a funny sort of way, said, 'Where you going Ben, where you going this time of the night?'

He didn't answer. I think he was pretending he didn't hear her.

'Well, Ben? Where you going this time of the night?'

'What you mean where I'm going? I'm going to my house.' He was mocking her. The way he said it I knew he was mocking her.

'Aye, aye, what so sweet in Grand Roy, eh? What so sweet down there? I don't see why you can't stay up here for one night. I'm sure the house could hold the three of us.'

That was Mammy talking; telling Uncle Ben to stay with us! I couldn't believe it. I looked at her to make sure she was all right. The last time he wanted to stay the night – well not even the night, all the man wanted was to eat his food and go home – Mammy wasn't having that. That night she gave him all his clothes, clean and dirty, and chucked him out. Now she telling him to stay. I don't understand; I wish he would stay though. Since I first knew him I liked him, now I like him even more.

'Heh, hee, hee, girl you sure? You sure you want me to stay?' He grinned.

'How you mean if I'm sure? What you say Gloria, you want him to stay, don't you?' Fancy Mammy asking me big people question. We only have two bedroom but I don't see why he can't sleep where he want to sleep, even if it's in Mammy's room. I don't understand a lot of things, but I think I know what Mammy mean, because since we saw Uncle Ben the last time, I hear the woman he was living with is not really his wife. She on and on at him to get married, but he didn't want to, so she got vex and went back to Venezuela where she came from.

I didn't answer Mammy. I turned to Uncle Ben and reminded him that he owes me a birthday party, and I soon have thirteen.

Glossary

boli tree   calabash gourd tree

chupes   sucking of teeth (usually negative response)

cocobay   disease similar to leprosy, so cursed, to be shunned (from Twi, a Ghanaian language)

coupee   children's call in a game to tell the searcher all is ready

farseness   inquisitiveness, impudence

gru-gru   fruit of a palm similar to coconut

guava   fruit used for making jam

gufflay   eat greedily

jumbies   evil spirits

karway   body language, to cut style

Kewpie   trade name of small doll with topknot of hair

macaque   stupidness, monkeying about (lit. monkey)

mal yeux   the evil eye

mas'   masquerade

nancy   folk tales (based on Ananse, spider hero of the Asante people of Ghana)

obeah   witchcraft, superstition surrounding herbalism

peak-skirted   uneven hemline, with six or eight points

peas bush   pigeon pea bush

petax   firework

pissannies   name for old-time mas' – the first to appear on Carnival Monday, carrying a chamber pot as part of the costume

quashie mango   very sweet, black-spotted mango. Also a surname and used to represent the 'man in the street', sometimes derogatorily

Saltfish Hall   once a dancehall of ill repute located close to the fish market

sankies   hymns named after a Methodist missionary who visited Grenada

senna   dried pods or leaves of cassia used as a laxative

shaddock   citrus fruit used for making preserves and drinks

shower   hen party for girl getting married